PLAGUE OF THE DIGITAL HEART

ENGEN
BOOKS

Published in Canada by Engen Books, St. John's, NL.

Library and Archives Canada Cataloguing in Publication is available on the CIP website.

Distributed by:
Engen Books
www.engenbooks.com
submissions@engenbooks.com

First mass market paperback printing: April 2021
Cover Design: Ariel Marsh
Slipstreamers Committee:
Amanda Labonté
Ali House
AJ Ryan
Ellen Curtis
Erin Vance
Lauralana Dunne
Matthew LeDrew

THE LOTUS FOUNTAIN

NICOLE LITTLE & JD RYOT

CHAPTER ONE

"Have they been located?"
"Yes, ma'am."
"I expected as much. Thank you."
"And, what of the visitor?"
"It's been… taken care of."

Boom.

***

The first sentence is always the most difficult one to write, she assured herself, *just give yourself a few minutes, you'll figure it out.* And yet there she sat (it had been inevitable of course) for endless moments, irrevocably stumped, tapping a pen against her lips, staring at that blank white piece of paper. She needed something clever but it also had to be heartfelt and sweet; something eloquent but not too formal.

She sighed.

Words. What were those again?

Congratulations! Cassidy finally wrote in desperation as the hands on the clock ticked by at an alarming rate. She chewed thoughtfully on the top of her pen for a moment and then, when nothing else came to her, she scrawled *Best wishes, Cassidy* at the bottom. There. Perfect. Or, at least, as good as it was going to get. She tossed the pen onto the desk where it disappeared amongst papers and folders, half full coffee cups, and general office flotsam. She crammed the card into its envelope and placed it inside the gift bag, atop the brightly coloured tissue paper. Hidden amongst the folds of canary yellow was a tiny t-shirt emblazoned with the phrase *Archaeology—I dig it*. It made Cassidy chuckle. Okay, sure she had rolled her eyes at first. It was a tad bit silly, but it began to grow on her as she had frantically searched, and came up otherwise empty handed, for a suitable present in the university gift shop.

A baby shower. It was a first for Cassidy Cane. She was wearing (and she couldn't quite believe it herself) a dress. Her hair was freshly curled and fell in soft waves that brushed against her shoulders. Her hands itched to haul it up into its usual ponytail.

The party was being held in one of the University's many function rooms, the organization of which had been delegated to a lowly research assistant in the Anthropology Department. Tables had been pushed to the sides of the room and chairs were lined up against the walls. Three blue and white balloons were tied to a podium; a hand written sign, taped on the wall beside the door read:

Welcome

Mateo Romero-Jones

to the Plainsfield Family!

Cassidy's eyes widened and she let out a low whistle.

Wow. Clearly they had spared no expense on the decorations.

Cassidy heard laughter and the low rumble of intimate conversation as she approached the room. She stood in the door way, hesitating. A few professors that she recognized from her own department were milling about inside, as well as a number of others that she did not know. Gamgee had been right to insist that she attend, of course. Between travel and work, her social status at the University, and well, if she was willing to admit it, her social status everywhere else, was at an all time low.

With a sigh, she stepped through the doorway.

Lars Economides from English waved a sandwich at her from the refreshment table; he held a red solo cup steady in his other hand. She was quite glad he hadn't tried to wave with that one. Lars was a bit of a klutz and he was wearing a light-coloured leisure suit. Etienne-Andre Durand, French Department, nodded politely when he caught her eye. He then glanced at his watch and resumed tapping his foot.

Annie Jones grinned in delight when she spotted Cassidy from across the room; she waved a hand and beckoned for Cassidy to come closer. Annie's wife, Ximena Romero, was cradling a blue bundle, her smile content as she swayed to and fro in a slow, rhythmic but gentle motion.

"I am so glad you are here, Cassidy! Meet Mateo!" Annie beamed with pride, gesturing toward her new son. "I haven't had a full night's sleep in what seems like forever but who needs sleep anyways, right?!"

Cassidy laughed. "I'm so happy for you both!"

"Thank you! We are just over the moon!"

"Dr. Gamgee sends his regrets. He's at home with a bit of a head cold today. He didn't want to pass it along to the baby, but he hopes to meet Mateo soon!"

"Of course! We completely understand. Please tell him we hope he gets well soon," Annie replied.

A tiny head dusted with wispy strands of raven hair poked out the top of the soft blanket in Ximena's arms. Cassidy peeked inside. Cocooned within, Mateo yawned and stretched laboriously, one tiny hand escaping its woolly confines. He blinked up at her. His dark, unfocused eyes were adorned with impossibly long lashes. They dominated his heart shaped, dusky-pink baby face.

"Adorable!" Cassidy exclaimed, and truly meant it.

***

Within the hour, the celebration was in full swing; the number of people in the room had increased exponentially. Someone from the Spanish Department had snuck in several bottles of wine and another, a middle aged man with a bright green Mohawk, had hooked a phone up to a small speaker, which had, inexplicably, started pumping out instrumental covers of theme songs from popular television sitcoms. A few ladies were dancing. Somehow baby Mateo was sleeping through all the ruckus.

Cassidy balanced a paper plate of assorted sandwiches and small cookies on her knee. She'd retreated to a far corner where she could sit and eat in peace. And to observe, of course. She liked to watch people in their natural habitats, to attempt to interpret their body language, to read their facial expressions; to try and figure them out—who they really were beneath the mask of social constructs.

Huh. So maybe *that* was why she didn't have very many friends. She'd have to give that a bit more thought later, when she was relaxed at home and fully prepared to psychoanalyze herself.

Hunger satiated for now, Cassidy left her plate on the chair to mark her spot and went in search of a drink at the refreshment table. She skirted around several small groups of people, clustered together in conversation, excusing herself as she stepped in front of them and around them. What a crowd! Had strangers just wandered in off the street? She wedged herself into the small space between the table and the wall, a small alcove created by the storage room door, and was pouring herself a glass of tepid lemonade into what she hoped was a clean cup, when a snippet of half-whispered conversation caught her ear.

"… us that we were the perfect candidates and just a few days later we had a call saying that our file had been chosen by one of their clients. By the end of the week, we were bringing Mateo home!" Annie's voice was low but animated.

Cassidy inched a little closer, keeping her back to the two women who were huddled together chatting quietly. She pretended to be looking for a napkin, while in reality she was eavesdropping with complete and utter abandon.

"Incredible! I have friends who have waited *years* for that call!" came the hushed reply.

"We were very lucky! We had to sign a non-disclosure agreement, if you can believe it. I probably shouldn't even be discussing this in public," she giggled and then continued, the wine clearly having loosened her tongue, "The amount of paperwork was just astronomical. Totally worth it of course, don't get me wrong! Rising Sun have truly made our dreams come true. We're just not supposed to tell anyone the details!"

Cassidy pleaded exhaustion and said her goodbyes shortly afterwards, once more congratulating Annie and Ximena on the adoption of their son before she left. If she was being honest, and Cassidy was often brutally so, she simply wanted to go home and ruminate on what she had just overheard.

She also desperately wanted to shed the dress.

Once home, she quickly changed into more comfortable clothing, some old sweatpants and a favourite but faded shirt from an 80's hair band. She plopped onto the couch and reached for her laptop, sliding it onto her legs and powering it on. The startup prompted her for a password; within seconds she'd clicked into the main screen of a popular search engine. Fingers flying, she typed *Rising Sun Adoption* into the box, hit enter, and waited for the results to populate.

Nothing.

Cassidy drummed her fingers on the arm of the couch. She typed *adoption agencies near me*. Again, no results.

Curiouser and curiouser by the minute. And like a dog with a bone, Cassidy was *not* letting it go.

Cassidy glanced at the time. It was late but not *that* late. She nibbled on a thumbnail and then, before she could change her mind, she grabbed her cell.

The phone rang once at Cassidy's end before Gamgee answered with, "Good evening, Cassidy!"

"Good evening, Doctor. I hope you are feeling better. I was wondering if I could ask you a quick question?"

"Not feeling too bad for an old man with a cold, I suppose!" he replied in a nasal voice. "And, of course, you may ask me anything! I trust you enjoyed yourself at the baby shower?"

"Ah, you bet! I sure did," Cassidy fibbed.

Gamgee chuckled, then coughed. "I am glad that you decided to go. Now, to what do I owe this pleasant surprise?"

"Well, I was wondering, have you ever heard of a Rising Sun Adoption Agency?"

He paused. "No, I don't believe I have. It doesn't sound familiar anyways, sorry."

"Oh, that's too bad. I was just—"

"Wait!" he interrupted. "Now that I think about it, it does sound a little bit familiar. Could it be The Rising *Son* Agency?"

"Oh! Yes! It might be! I may have just misheard."

Gamgee made a noncommittal noise and finally: "It's near my place but at the other end of Carina Heights, up in the old gated community, I believe. I rarely drive over that way; they're horribly slack with repairs you know. The roads are terrible. I've heard rumours there's even a big gap in their security fence. Imagine!" He sounded horrified at the thought.

"Yes, of course, that is quite unfortunate. I'm sorry to have bothered you when you're under the weather, curiosity got the better of me I'm afraid. Perhaps I will follow up in the morning."

"You know what they say, Cassidy: there is no time

like the present! Hope you enjoy the rest of your night."

"Thanks, Doctor G. You too."

Cassidy chewed absently on her lower lip, and glanced at the time again. Her hunch that something was *off* about the whole situation was sitting heavy in the pit of her stomach. And her gut had never led her astray before. Well, maybe a few times. Before she could change her mind, she'd run into her room to change her clothes. Moving with urgency, for reasons she could not quite explain even to herself, she grabbed her keys, pocketed her phone and hurried out the door.

She'd worry about the gates when she got there.

Locks had never stopped her before.

CHAPTER TWO

The crunch of gravel beneath the tires was reminiscent of the cracking of long buried bones as Cassidy pulled up as close as she dared to the closed, and presumably guarded, gates of Carina Heights. She left the car in a pool of darkness in between street lights and beneath a no parking sign she did not even acknowledge. She pulled a dark stocking cap low on her head and eased the door shut with a muffled click. Slipping around the side of a faded but once elegant welcome sign, breath misting in front of her face, she cringed reflexively as the crunch of leaves and the snap of twigs beneath her feet rang out like a shot in the night. She froze. Heart pounding frantically, yet in a way that she still strangely enjoyed, Cassidy paused only for a moment, and then plunged headlong into the darkness.

Gap in the fence. Was that right?

Cassidy ran, glancing over her shoulder frequently before she finally stopped to catch her breath. She could see lights off in the distance, not too far at all. She moved up close against the fence, following along the length of it. She crept by, hand trailing against the chain links. This was taking far longer than she had anticipated. But she was committed now.

Finally, there it was: the gap in the fence just as Gamgee had mentioned in that offhand way of his. Invigorated now with this convenient discovery, Cassidy rushed forward. She cursed elaborately as her jacket snagged on a jagged bit of fencing. Cassidy gritted her teeth and gripped the material, ripping herself free. Chastened, she now made sure to step carefully through the hole. Directly in front of her and across a plush, expansive lawn was a large squat building—and coming down the street in front of it was the flash of oncoming headlights! *Dammit!* She would be caught for sure. Cassidy's mind quickly calculated the list of criminal charges she had amassed thus far tonight. Not good. Not good at all. Crouching low, she made a dash for the cover of the darkened exterior of the building. She flattened herself against the back wall just as a private security vehicle drove slowly past. She needed cover. *Now.* Pulse quickening, Cassidy reached up behind her and, to her surprise, discovered that the window slid open easily. When no alarm immediately sounded, she hoisted herself to the ledge and dropped inside, feet first. She slid the window closed behind her and allowed an audible breath of relief to escape her lips.

She grinned. She was safe.

At least for now.

But that was all that really mattered.

Cassidy waited for her eyes to adjust to the too dark darkness. She couldn't risk using the flashlight on her phone. Too much light would make her much too noticeable, especially with security skulking around. Briefly, she wondered just what the hell she was doing here. But the thought was fleeting, swallowed up by the giddiness and thrill of the chase. She did this sort of thing all the time right? Slowly, shapes in the room came into focus. She was in someone's office. There was a desk, a chair, and filing cabinets. She picked her way gingerly across the room and towards the desk, slow going, taking her time in the unfamiliar surroundings. A cracked shin was something she did not need right now. Cassidy reached for her phone, deciding she would risk using the dull backlight of the main screen to illuminate the paperwork upon the rich mahogany surface. *The Rising Son Adoption Agency* read the letterhead.

Oh. Heck. Yeah.

Delighted, feeling as though lady luck was by her side tonight, Cassidy felt emboldened enough to leave that particular office and explore further in the building. The adjacent wall in the hallway outside the door was adorned with simple black picture frames that held photos of cheerful happy babies. Successful adoptees, Cassidy presumed. She tried the door across the hall only to find it was locked. As was the next one. The third door opened into a small kitchen. It was of little interest to her—she did not care to learn what their preferred brand of coffee was or how many tubs of expired yogurt the fridge held. By the time she had reached her fourth locked door in succession, Cassidy felt her frustration reach a pinnacle. Trespassing or not, she wasn't leaving without some kind of answer to the questions that had plagued her all night. But so far, she wasn't getting anywhere.

She very much did not want to go home right now. Especially since she had come this far. And broken so many laws. In pursuit of what exactly though, she wasn't sure. Just that feeling in her gut. Something was up.

Cassidy's eyes alighted on a door at the end of the hall. Like a moth to a flame, her attention was immediately drawn to the glow of a keypad. Security such as that usually meant that there was something behind the door that was worth hiding. So her hunch had been right after all. Her excitement mounting, Cassidy strutted boldly up to the door. It was a numbered keypad, simple for the most part, but how many attempts would she be allowed to try before it locked her out? There could be thousands of possible combinations. Suddenly she stifled a snort of laughter. Written in light pencil, just to the right of the keypad: 1015. Cassidy punched in the number and grinned in delight as the lock disengaged with a soft click. Things were going a lot easier than she'd imagined.

Maybe it was even a little too easy?

A buzz ran up her arm as her fingers lightly touched the doorknob and Cassidy flinched in surprise. What the hell was that? She wrapped her hand around the knob, turned and pushed. Before she was even fully in the room, she felt the thrumming along her veins, the pressure in her ears, that had, over the last little while, become so familiar to her. So intoxicating. But no. *It couldn't be? Could it?!* Brazen now, Cassidy felt along the walls nearest the door and, finding exactly what her fingers sought, she flipped the switch, flooding the room with a dim florescent light. She gasped.

How was this even possible?

She took a step forward, hesitated, not quite sure if she could believe her eyes.

Sure, she'd expected to find *something* inside The Rising Son Adoption Agency but she certainly hadn't expected that something would be a portal.

CHAPTER THREE

Cassidy shook her head as if physically trying to dislodge the image in front of her. It remained solid. She was not normally given to flights of fancy, it was true (and she knew it), but she was still reassured to know that she was not just imagining things. She took a step forward, her brow furrowed; her brain running a mile a minute.

"There's no one here, boss."

Cassidy jumped.

A crackle of static: someone was nearby. She moved closer to the door, straining to hear. "I checked all the offices. No signs of break and enter." More static, a mumble of words, then: "I'll make one more round. Something must have tripped it."

Dammit. There must have been a silent alarm after all. Cassidy cursed again beneath her breath. Such a stupid, rookie mistake. If the guard came any closer down the hall, he'd notice the open door; for certain he'd notice that the light was on. Cassidy wondered if she would have enough time to ease the door shut; if there would be time to hide.

The sound of approaching footsteps, then an excited:

"I think I've got something boss!"

Cassidy considered her limited options, but really there had only been one viable option all along. Even if there *had* been other options, the look on her face suggested she would not have chosen them anyways. A mixture of excitement and anticipation flushed her cheeks and she grinned widely.

"Here we go again!" she murmured under her breath.

As the guard began to step hesitantly through the door, Taser extended forward in a shaking hand, Cassidy turned her back on him and launched herself forward. She heard him shout "STOP!" in a nervous, quavering voice, but there was no stopping now. She plunged through the portal at a dead run.

Immediately, Cassidy wished she *could* stop. Momentum carried her forward into a tumble, a riot of colours blurred past her, and then the crushing impact as she hit the ground, bounced, rolled and then landed face first. She grimaced in pain as her right hand took the brunt of the skid; she felt a snap; heard a muffled crack, then, warm and sticky, blood began to flow freely and plentifully from a gash that spread across her palm. Cassidy clutched it protectively to her chest as she lay, winded, upon the uncomfortable uneven ground. Sound came back to her all in a rush and she could hear several timid voices speaking uncertainly around her. Someone was screaming.

Oh. Wait. That was her.

"Clear the way, children, please. Let me through now!"

This was not a hidden portal. No one seemed surprised to see someone come through either.

Beneath her eyelashes Cassidy saw the shadow of a figure walk forward and crouch down next to her, speaking urgently and with authority: "Are you able to get up?"

Cassidy gave a brief nod and, teeth clenched, was helped to her feet. Her left hand shading her eyes in the bright sunlight she blinked rapidly at the sight before her. A woman wearing a long flowing dress and a flower crown stepped forward, her salt and pepper hair nearly to her waist.

Was she dead?

"Well, this is not how we normally treat our visitors," the woman gestured towards Cassidy's injured hand and smiled. "But all the same, welcome to Lotus Lorea!"

No. Not dead.

"Thank you," Cassidy said, hesitantly sounding out the words, her speech slow and slurred from shock and pain. They spoke English here. Or at least this woman did, though it was with a slight accent; lyrical and pleasing to the ear.

"You've no need to be afraid, child. You are safe here with us. My name is Marcella; please, let us take care of that hand for you."

Cassidy glanced down and saw that the clothes she had changed into before leaving her house were saturated in blood. Her hand throbbed in time to the rhythm of her heartbeat. This wasn't her first injury and she was certain it would not be her last either, but she reckoned there was no reason why she should just stand there and bleed to death. She nodded her consent.

"Eliza, please bring some water from the fountain to the infirmary." A small tow-headed child sprinted away, clearly elated to have been chosen for this special task.

"Come along with me, Cassidy. I am sure we can find something clean for you to wear as well."

Feeling lightheaded, Cassidy heard herself mumble, "How did you know my name?"

"Oh, I am sure you mentioned it, dear."

And that was all Cassidy heard before everything faded to black.

***

Cassidy regained consciousness slowly, her world coming back into focus little by little. She was flat on her back beneath crisp white sheets, her head cradled atop a soft, fluffy pillow. She blinked several times, her vision still cloudy. A light breeze ruffled the sheer curtains in the window across the room. The scent of lilac drifted in, reminding Cassidy briefly of her grandmother. She could hear the voices of children outside, laughter and the low murmur of conversation between adults.

Lotus Lorea. That was what the woman had said, right? Marcella. Cassidy was sure that was her name. Her memories of her arrival were fuzzy and distorted.

Woozy, head still spinning, Cassidy relaxed back against the pillow. She squinted in the bright light as she took in her surroundings. The room was small but neat and tidy. That familiar antiseptic smell that assaulted her senses confirmed her suspicions that she was still in the infirmary.

Then, suddenly, she remembered! Her hand! She withdrew it from beneath the blankets and found it wrapped in a long length of gauze; it was thick and stiff with the bulk of a bandage beneath. Cautiously, she flexed her fingers and found that the pain was minimal. She was relieved. From what she had seen of it, from what she had *heard* of it, and combined with the significant blood loss, she had expected much, *much* worse.

She pushed back the blankets and swung her feet off the bed. She took her time, taking deep breaths. She did not want to faint and hurt herself again. These people would think she was some kind of klutz. She glanced down at herself in surprise. She was clothed in a long billowy garment much like the one Marcella had been wearing. Underneath that, she was wearing a pair of light-weight leggings. She saw that her boots, hat, and jacket were stacked neatly on a nearby chair. Her phone had been placed on top of the pile. She quickly hauled on the boots and picked up her phone. The screen had cracked from side to side. She sighed. Another one bites the dust. She knew there'd be no point in turning it on anyways since cell phones never worked within the worlds she travelled to. She left it where it was on the chair, crossing her fingers that it would work the next time she had a chance to power it on.

It was oddly quiet here. At least it was odd to Cassidy. If she'd been pressed to further describe it she might have even said it was peaceful. Cassidy noted the absence of the sounds of traffic, cars, horns or shouting. There was no construction, jackhammers or the raucous laughter of builders. There were no angry commuters, no road rage or cursing bus drivers. She couldn't deny that it was nice for a change.

There was a light knock at the door behind her. It slid open and Marcella's head appeared through the crack.

"Oh good, you are awake! How are you feeling, okay?" She beamed at Cassidy, who nodded and returned the smile. "It's nearly lunchtime. If you're feeling up to it, please come join us!"

A long table had been set up in the community centre. A simple white cloth ran the length of it. The table was laden with an impossible amount of food and Cassidy gaped in astonishment. Bowls of luscious deep violet-toned grapes, glistening trays of ripe cantaloupe and juicy pineapple; there were lychees and pomegranates, dragon fruit and papaya; parfait cups were filled with berries and clotted cream. There were several types of produce that Cassidy did not recognize and she thought, perhaps, these fruits (or whatever they were) were native to Lotus Lorea. Their diet, Cassidy couldn't help but notice, seemed entirely plant based. There were no meats in sight, though there were bowls of what appeared to be oatmeal or some type of cooked grain. Large bowls of vibrant leafy greens were placed in the centre as well as at both ends of the table; luscious tomatoes on the vine stood out next to them, begging to be sliced.

A hush fell over the crowd as they noted her arrival. The children stared wide-eyed with undisguised interest and there was an anticipation to the silence as the crowd held their breath and waited for the newcomer to do something … anything.

Cassidy felt a bit like a deer in the headlights but still she managed to smile and say hello.

They smiled back.

A few of the children waved.

"Please, won't you take a seat, Cassidy. Here, next to me, and we can have a bit of a chat."

Cassidy sat where Marcella indicated and, as if by some unspoken communication, conversation around the table resumed. The children re-commenced their bickering, and platters of food were passed around; plates were heaped high and smiles were broad and joyful. Cassidy would not have been able to guess as to the ages of those present. Wrinkled, smiling faces watched toddlers and teenagers alike with the same indulgence and tolerance; soft, creased hands patted the round bellies of several pregnant young women—eager to hold their grandchildren.

Quickly, Cassidy remembered her manners. "Thank you, Marcella. For everything you have done for me since my … unexpected arrival." She wiggled her fingers under the table, once again amazed at her recovery from what she was sure should have been a debilitating injury.

Marcella patted Cassidy on the arm gently, "It's been no trouble dear. We are glad to help when we can. I am sorry that you did not have a more pleasant welcome. Please, help yourself to some food! There is plenty for everyone!"

She didn't need to be told twice. Cassidy helped herself to everything within her reach and then to more as the platters were passed around. She was ravenous. Food had never tasted this good. A cold glass of mango juice appeared next to her plate and Cassidy drank deeply of the chilled beverage. She couldn't help but close her eyes

in ecstasy. It was as though all her senses had been height-
ened—especially that of taste.

"What brings you to Lotus Lorea, Miss Cassidy?" a
curious voice asked.

Cassidy's eyes popped back open, seeking the person
to match with the voice: a child with a bright, earnest face
regarded her with a friendly grin. Cassidy paused for a
moment, thinking, then: "Curiosity?" she offered ambigu-
ously.

Marcella laughed. "Well that's just as good a reason as
any, now isn't it? Once you have finished eating, perhaps
you would like to join me on a tour?"

"Yes, thank you! I would enjoy that very much."

The conversation flowed freely; Cassidy listened as
her lunchtime companions spoke of their day and the
work left to be done before night fell. As lunch came to
an end, the women rose together and began to clear away.
Others tended to the children; young mothers nursed in-
fants hands-free in complicated ring sling carriers while
they chased toddlers and carried empty bowls and plates.
Cassidy watched in amazement. They were like a well-
oiled machine.

As Marcella and Cassidy left the community centre
and strolled down the cobbled streets of Lotus Lorea, a
soft, fragrant wind lifted the hair from their faces; a warm
caress, soft as a mother's touch.

"It's very tranquil here."

"I'm glad that you think so." Marcella beamed. "We
constantly strive for calm. It takes balance and hard work.
We are very much about equality and there is no class
structure here. Everyone does their part; everyone chips

in and helps out, especially with the children. It takes a village to raise a child, you know. If you have any questions at all, please do not be afraid to ask!"

Cassidy nodded. Marcella was really selling it but something was nagging at the back of Cassidy's mind. Annoyingly, it stayed right there, just beyond her reach, an itch she couldn't quite scratch.

"Our homes are fairly large, as you will notice," Marcella pointed out, "but they are communal. Each floor holds one family and there are several families to a house. We have a school for the younger children as well as a training centre for our graduates where they can choose to learn from a wide range of vocations and trades. We encourage a love of reading and learning from a very young age! Our children are the future ... they will carry on the legacy of Lotus Lorea."

As they walked, Marcella gestured towards the cluster of homes and then the other buildings as she described each one and its purpose. They were by no means opulent but still quite impressive if for their sheer size alone. The school was a low, flat, nondescript building with bright murals painted on its facade; the training centre was attached to it by a short walkway and was quite similar, though it lacked the charm of the murals. The buildings were more functional than anything else; Marcella explained that despite their outwardly bland appearances, their training facilities inside were ultramodern with state of the art training equipment. Students there learned everything from cooking to engineering and nursing. There was also a gym and exercise centre; Cassidy noticed a yoga class schedule posted outside as they passed by.

As they drew near the large fields full of crops and plants, Marcella explain that they were completely self sufficient. They ate only what they were able to grow or make themselves. Cassidy took note of a small brick building, much closer to the wooded, undeveloped area than the residential space she was getting a tour of. Marcella did not mention it. Immediately Cassidy's curiosity was peaked.

"What's that building over there?"

Marcella paused. "Oh. That's just The Hut. Storage for gardening supplies and things like that."

They had nearly walked the entire u-shape of the village when they came upon the library. It was particularly splendid, with a gabled roof, brick façade and trailing vines that surrounded two large, carved wooden doors.

"The library is one of our more elaborate structures," Marcella announced proudly. "It is also our oldest building, having been built by the original founding members of Lotus Lorea!"

There was nothing nondescript about the library. Cassidy took it all in with wide eyes, delighted, and made a promise to herself that she would visit the library the first chance that she got.

Their outing ended in the town square. "Here we are then," Marcella remarked. "This concludes our tour! I hope you've learned a little about us and how we live and work. I am quite proud of all that we have accomplished."

She gestured towards the wide open space of the town square, and further still a small park and grassy area. Cassidy's attention was drawn to a girl who was reading contentedly, propped against the wide base of a weeping willow; a small child was flying a kite nearby. A picnic had been set up beneath the shade of a cluster of the low hanging trees.

Cassidy took it all in with a wide smile. She turned around to express her delight to Marcella but then gaped in wonder, the words dying upon her lips. In the very centre of the courtyard was the most beautiful water fountain she had ever seen. It was a solid grey concrete, smoothed with age but untarnished. It was large and impressive but somehow managed to not be overwhelming or ostentatious. In the middle of the fountain, a curved cement bowl—resting at a slight angle—was perched atop two Greek Corinthian style columns; water gurgled from within the bowl and cascaded downward in a clear, steady stream where it splashed and bubbled joyously in the pool. But the most incredible part was a small, delicately carved stone child who sat perched at the very edge of the basin, her tiny feet submerged in the water. Her hands were cupped beneath her face, her lips pursed as though she were preparing to blow a kiss; within the chalice of her hands she held a single lotus blossom in full bloom.

"This is … exquisite!" Cassidy had finally found her voice.

Marcella watched her with a knowing look. "Isn't it? We call it The Lotus Fountain."

"Incredible…" Cassidy could barely tear her eyes away from it. There was something about the fountain that was mesmerizing. She felt an inexplicable connection to it; the gentle flow of the water calmed her immediately; the statue of the child stirred feelings that she could not even explain.

This ambiance was something that many people strived to achieve in their own homes and gardens back in Cassidy's world. But they had all failed miserably in comparison to aura of The Lotus Fountain.

A squeal of laughter snapped Cassidy out of her reverie and she was catapulted back to the present. A small group of children dashed by, riotous with laughter, and as she watched them go she had a sudden moment of clarity.

"Marcella, remember how you said it was okay to ask if I had any questions?"

"Yes, of course, my dear!"

"Um … just exactly where are all the men?"

CHAPTER FOUR

Cassidy had been offered a room in what Marcella referred to as The Dorms. From what Cassidy had seen so far, it housed mostly young women who attended the vocational school or those at the cusp of adulthood: too old to still want to live with their family, but too young to be with a family of their own. Of course, she had accepted. She wasn't ready to go back home through the portal yet. Not even close.

The room she had been given was small but functional and, best of all, private. Cassidy was grateful for it; she knew that she would eventually have to earn her keep, had in fact offered to help out in whatever way she could. But for now Marcella had told her to try to relax; to recover from her fall and subsequent injury; to get used to her new surroundings. There was a single bed placed in a corner of the room farthest from the door. It was draped in a homemade patchwork quilt sewn with bright, cheerful squares and threads. Two plump, down-filled pillows in mismatched pillowcases were stacked against the headboard. There was a lamp and a washbasin on a nearby weathered antique bureau; a small, ornate brass mirror hung above it. Next to the basin was a beautiful silver comb and brush set, a small hand towel and a bamboo toothbrush.

A window overlooking the fields offered natural sunlight. Cassidy squinted in the brightness, eyeing the brick building she'd noticed earlier on her tour. A myriad of mouth-watering scents wafted in through the open shutters, disrupting her line of thought. Someone was baking something that smelled absolutely delightful. Scones perhaps, or a pie. Maybe even bread. Saliva flooded Cassidy's mouth. How could she possibly be hungry after the incredible feast she had consumed at lunchtime?!

Cassidy sat on her bed and mulled over the story Marcella had shared with her in the town square. Sitting together on a well-worn wooden bench, the two women had discussed things quietly and at length. Cassidy listened intently and tried not to interrupt, though she had many, many questions. Even though the information that Marcella had imparted was common knowledge to the people of Lotus Lorea, her and Cassidy spoke together in hushed tones. Marcella's voice was reverent. Cassidy lost hers in shock.

There were no men.

Lotus Lorea was a matriarchal society; founded by women, led by women for women and those who identified as them. The children were raised together in complex family homes—mothers, sisters, aunts, cousins, grandmothers—they all lived together and shared the responsibilities of a household. No one was forced to take on traditional roles assigned to them by a male-dominated culture. There were no expectations that they would marry or bear children or uphold an outdated standard of femininity if they decided that path in life was not for them.

Marcella spoke passionately, though not zealously. She was adamant that their world had achieved nirvana. They did not *hate* men, and had much respect for them she insisted; they just chose *not* to live amongst them. And they were not welcomed on Lotus Lorea.

It was a whole lot of new information to digest all at once.

Cassidy had definitely seen pregnant women at the communal lunch and there were a great deal of children running around but, still, Cassidy hesitated to voice the obvious question.

Awkward.

She chewed on her bottom lip, concentrating, her brow furrowed in thought.

Now that she looked back over the events of the day and the people that she had met, the inviting faces who had greeted and welcomed her at lunch had indeed all been women and young girls. She hadn't put a lot of thought into it and, if she *had* given it a fleeting thought, she might had assumed that the men were off working somewhere or perhaps they ate separately. There had been a large number of babies and toddlers at the community centre as well, but they were dressed in a variety of different colours. Cassidy had made judgements based on how children were dressed back in her own world. Pink for girls or blue for boys—that was the usual. Long hair on girls, short hair on boys. It was a concept that was completely foreign here, but it was such a common thing where Cassidy had come from that she had not even clued in. She knew the difference now. It made sense.

Cassidy got to her feet and tiptoed to the window. It was quiet outside. She could see in the fields in the distance that people had gathered to work on the crops; there were many different kinds—rows and rows of fruits and vegetables; wheat and different grains. The climate here was something else that peaked Cassidy's interest and she added it to the mental list of all the things she wanted to investigate. It never seemed to get cold. Her list was getting very long.

Lotus Lorea seemed to be perfect. But Cassidy didn't usually believe in the concept of perfection. There were too many variables.

A peal of laughter reached her ears from the distance. Everyone was so happy and had such positive attitudes. She had not heard a complaint or an argument, no negative, sarcastic or snarky words had been spoken since she had arrived here. Only the children had bickered. And most of that had been good-natured.

Could this really be paradise?

***

Her clothes had been laundered. By some miracle they had been able to remove the blood stains. The rips in the knees of her pants had been mended as well. The stitch work was immaculate; from a distance it would not even be noticeable. Back home she would have just thrown all those garments in the garbage, went out and replaced them with something new. It really was such a wasteful attitude. Shaking her head ruefully, she tucked the bottoms of her pants into her boots and felt more like herself now that she was back in her own clothes. She carefully folded the borrowed dress she had been wearing and left it at the foot of her bed. She noticed that a pair of pyjamas had been kindly laid out for her on a chair next to the bed. They really had thought of everything.

Despite all of this, a seed of doubt was beginning to take root in Cassidy's mind, sprouting weeds of suspicion. It was difficult for her to take things at face value and, from her experience, when people treated you *this* well (especially strangers) there was an ulterior motive. There was something in it for them, or they expected something in return. And when they called in that favour, well, she was sure they would make it difficult for her to say no.

Keeping that in mind, she vowed to explore the town later, without a chaperone—to check a few things off that mental list she had found herself compiling.

She flexed her hand experimentally. Hardly any pain at all. Incredible.

Her first stop was, of course, the library. She was nearly salivating at the thought of all that she would find inside. Books were an escape for Cassidy when a real getaway was not possible. While her house did not hold all that many personal items (she kept most of her prized posses-sions in her office, where she spent most of her time), her bookshelves were packed to overflowing. She'd read all of them at least twice. The people of Lotus Lorea clearly shared this passion for the written word, for the library was one of the most spectacular that Cassidy had ever seen.

Cassidy stepped inside, the silence embracing her as it

had done in countless other libraries that she had visited. Polished wood floors led to an open concept foyer; off to the side was the circulation desk although it appeared to be unoccupied at the moment. Books, books and more books, as far as the eye could see. And even further than that perhaps, as the far corners of the library disappeared into darkness. Just exactly how big *was* this place?! It was a remarkable feat, this clever use of architecture. The building seemed to go on forever inside while, at the same time, outside it did not appear to take up all that much space at all.

The familiar musty smell of ink and paper flooded her senses the further she walked into the building. She breathed deeply.

With time on her hands and no place that she needed to be, Cassidy wandered the stacks unhurriedly. She'd yet to see another person. Libraries back home were bustling; someone was always shushing someone else for making too much noise or arguing with them that they were hoarding too many books. This was an entirely new concept, this silence and calm. She approached the curved staircase that lead to the mezzanine. Running her hand along the ornate craftsmanship of the timeworn but smooth and polished railing, she put her foot on the first step and—

"Can I help you?"

Cassidy gasped aloud and nearly fell over the step. She placed a shaky hand over her pounding heart and … laughed. What was this feeling? This lightness bubbling inside her chest? She turned around, a grin spreading across her face.

"Oh! I am so sorry, my dear, I didn't mean to startle

you!"

"It's okay! I just didn't notice you there."

The woman smiled.

So *this* was the librarian. And was she ever a cliché. She was older, though Cassidy would have been hesitant to try and venture a guess on her age; she could have been anywhere from sixty to eighty years old. She was grey-haired and softly wrinkled, the lines around her eyes and mouth were deep and enviable, for laughter must have come second nature to this woman. She wore half moon spectacles that were attached by a chain lest they fall and break or so that she didn't misplace them. She wore a floral dress, and a light lace cardigan was draped across her shoulders; her shoes were sensible and appropriate for someone who likely spent a lot of time on her feet, finding books or putting returns back on the shelves.

"Can I help you find something, dear?" she repeated. She glanced at Cassidy's bandaged hand. News travelled fast in Lotus Lorea. It reminded Cassidy a lot of a small town. Everyone knew everybody else, so newcomers stood out like a sore thumb. No pun intended.

"I was just having a look around. Browsing your collection. I hope that's okay. Your library is incredible!"

"Isn't it?! Or at least I think so anyways! I have worked here for 47 years this spring so I may be slightly biased." She chucked. "My name is Virginia but everyone calls me Miss Ginny—the young, the old, even Doctors. That's what they all call me! Now, you take all the time you want to look around. I must ask though that you not enter the restricted section. It contains some rather… sensitive works. It's at the back of the library, near the reference books.

You would probably walk right on past it …if you weren't looking for it." She turned and began to walk away.

"Thank you?" Cassidy called quietly, perplexed.

The septuagenarian paused in her stride and then glanced back over her shoulder at Cassidy. "I'll be taking a break for the next thirty minutes or so, just grabbing a cup of tea and a scone. I trust that you will be able to keep yourself occupied?"

Her rubber soles squeaked as she walked away across the polished floors.

Did she just wink at me? Cassidy wondered.

CHAPTER FIVE

RESTRICTED.

The sign was attached to a thick rope which cordoned off the bookstacks at the back of the library. The area behind the rope was unlit; what lay beyond, saturated in a murky darkness.

Despite the pleasant temperature inside the building, Cassidy felt goosebumps rise upon her flesh.

She glanced around.

Alone again.

She ran her hand along the rope. It was rough, her bandage snagging in the bristles. She pulled it free and then threw one leg over, casually, then the other, the way she did most things: like she belonged there; like she owned the place.

A small flashlight sat innocently on a reading table.

Surprised but pleased at the timely discovery, she turned it on and panned it around the area.

The temperature was cooler behind the rope, as though heat would dare not risk encroaching the barrier for fear of angering Miss Ginny. Cassidy blinked several times, waiting for her eyes to adjust to the dimness. The flashlight illuminated only a short distance in front of her before the light was swallowed up by the gloom. There were wall-to-wall bookcases and each one was packed tightly with similarly sized volumes. The musty smell was more intense, leading her to believe that she was most likely surrounded by aged and, perhaps, very significant books in the history of Lotus Lorea. She stepped up to a shelf and gazed in awe. These books were ancient. She ran her fingers along the spines reverently, respectfully. A thick layer of dust coated the shelf and the books. No one had been in here for a long time.

Holding her breath, she peered closer to take a look at the titles, the gold words faded and worn:

Founding Mothers: A Walk Through Herstory
The Book of Sons
Letters Concerning the Gateway
Provenance and The Font

Pay dirt. But where to begin? Cassidy began to gently pull *Letters Concerning the Gateway* from the shelf. She didn't want to damage the old book so she took her time. Her heart was thumping excitedly—could the *Gateway* in this title be, in fact, the portal? It made sense. The slim hardcover was halfway out of its space when Cassidy felt a familiar tingle in her nose. She held her breath, turned away from the light, but it was no use. Pressure built up in her sinuses and then Cassidy let loose with a dramatic sequence of sneezes—her usual ten in a row. Dust stirred up from the violent exhalation of air and Cassidy sneezed again and again. She let go of the book and tucked her head in the corner of her arm to stifle the noise. The fit of sneezing now finally over, Cassidy eagerly reached for the book once again, her fingers pulled it forward and then—

"Cassidy?! Was that you? Are you back there?"

Dammit.

(What? Were you expecting a secret passageway or something?)

She pushed the book back in place, quickly turned off the flashlight, and nimbly hopped back over the rope. By the time Marcella had made her way to the inner sanctum of the library, Cassidy was sitting at a reading table far, far away from the restricted area, casually flipping through the pages of a book on tinctures, poultices and herbal remedies.

"Oh, there you are, Cassidy! One of the community elders said they saw you come in here."

Cassidy smiled pleasantly, though behind those curved lips she was gritting her teeth, silently cursing up a storm in her head. She'd been *that* close. "Yes, I love old buildings like this, and especially libraries. You just never know what you might find."

A flash of confusion and what might have been mild annoyance crossed Marcella's face but then quickly cleared. Cassidy wondered if perhaps she had imagined it. Her suspicious nature and all.

"That's so very true! Would you care to join us for afternoon break? I believe one of the girls has brewed some fresh *jaroot*, if you would like a cup!"

Cassidy accompanied Marcella to the community centre; she made agreeable noises and laughed or demurred at the appropriate times in the conversation but the wheels in her head were turning frantically. She munched on a lemon poppy seed biscuit; the *jaroot* Marcella had spoken of appeared to be the Lotus Lorea version of coffee. It was served piping hot and sweet, with a dash of rice milk. The constant flow of food and drink to her mouth was an excellent excuse for not joining in the chatter with the other women.

Soon, she tuned out the noise in the room, lost completely in her own thoughts.

Miss Ginny had most certainly wanted her to find *something* in the restricted section. But what exactly?

Cassidy was going to find out, even if it meant breaking all the rules.

And she was very good at that.

***

When evening arrived, as dusk began to fall, the chime of a bell rang out. Everyone stopped working, or studying; the children put away their playthings. They all gathered in the great community hall to take dinner together, as was the custom for all their meals. A large tureen of a thick and creamy wild rice and mushroom soup was centre stage; a rich, golden cauliflower and chickpea curry took up space next to it, surrounded by an abundance of other fragrant dishes: fritters made of lentils and potatoes, an entrée of stewed tomatoes, red beans and rice. In amongst all these other dishes were pots of different steamed vegetables; one that was similar to eggplant but the colour blue, another of purple corn, and a third full of what appeared to be a zucchini/carrot hybrid. It was a fact that no one went hungry on Lotus Lorea.

No mash turnip to be seen anywhere, though, thought

Cassidy. She felt an unexpected pang of homesickness.

This time Cassidy sat off to the side of the long table, trying to be as inconspicuous as possible, to fade into the background. It was something she was normally very adept at. This time, it didn't work. Everyone wanted to talk to the newcomer and all eyes were on her; everyone wanted her opinion on something. Finally, she gave up and joined in the conversation. It flowed around her like molten chocolate: warm, comforting and inviting. An embrace made entirely of words. Warmed by the soup and the repartee, Cassidy helped clean up and then, as another bell rang out signalling the end of day, she made her way back to her room.

And waited.

And waited some more, growing increasingly impatient.

An eerie silence descended on The Dorms as people settled in for the night. It occurred to her that perhaps it was only eerie to her, for she had less than noble intentions on her mind.

Cassidy lay on the bed, enveloped by the darkness, accompanied only by her thoughts and a jittery anticipation. What she wouldn't have given for an internet connection right now; a game of words with friends or a random Wikipedia article to pass the time, to distract her. She began to count off the minutes aloud, in a whisper. Cassidy waited a full hour. The time passed with excruciating slowness. Boots in her hand, she eased open the door, and listened. Silence. She tiptoed through the door in her stocking feet. No one in sight. It was go time.

She edged the door shut behind her and, keeping close

to the wall, she hurried down the steps and out the front door, taking much the same precautions as she had leaving the bedroom. The stillness outside was unlike anything Cassidy had ever experienced before. It felt as though she were the last person left in the world. The night air was sultry but not sticky; a light breeze lifted the hair off her shoulders. There was a marked absence of crickets and other creatures; no dogs barked; there were no late night revellers or couples out for a walk. The silence was absolute—save for the rush of her quickened breath.

She hauled her boots on and took off, stealthily, in the direction of the library.

***

Cassidy gave silent thanks for Marcella's passing remark that there were no locks anywhere. The library door swung open on well-oiled hinges and closed with a muffled *whoosh* behind her as Cassidy slipped inside. Orienting herself in the semi-pitch black, Cassidy left her boots near the circulation desk and tiptoed towards the stacks. She wasn't risking any noise at all, if she could help it.

The flashlight was exactly where she had left it, on the same shelf as the book she had come for; she didn't dare switch it on but it was an excellent marker. Earlier, she had tried to quickly memorize the order in which the books were placed on the shelf. She was sure that the third book to the right from where she had left the flashlight was *Letters Concerning the Gateway*. It was the one that interested her the most. She had to make a quick choice and hoped that it was the right one. She edged the slim volume out from its space on the shelf and slipped it beneath the waistband at the back of her pants, tucking her shirt in around it so it fit securely. She pulled her jacket down as far as she could, hoping it would cover any visible bulk. She knew that it was imperative that she keep the book hidden. If she was unlucky enough to get busted out of The Dorms and walking around past curfew, she would simply lie about not being able to sleep and needing some fresh air. She hesitated for only a second before she slipped the tiny flashlight into her jacket pocket.

It never hurt to be prepared.

Mission accomplished. Her heart beating frantically despite the outward calm she displayed, she once again put her boots back on and, channelling her inner ninja, crept back towards The Dorms.

She had a little reading to do.

***

Adrenaline still pumping through her veins, Cassidy tumbled back into her room. She laughed breathlessly to herself and followed it up with a huge sigh of relief as she eased the door shut behind her. She'd met no one along the way—not that she'd expected to anyway, but her heart was pounding nonetheless, the sound of blood pumping in her ears. The rush was beyond compare.

She tossed the purloined flashlight and book onto the bed, slipped out of her coat and boots and climbed beneath the patchwork quilt. She made a platform with her knees, snapped on the flashlight and stifled a loud groan at what she saw in her hands: she'd stolen the wrong damn book. Of course she did. What she held in her hands was *Provenance and The Font*—of similar colour and size to *Letters Concerning the Gateway* but definitely *not* what she had risked sneaking out for. She swore elaborately and then finally sighed in resignation and accepted it for what it was. Perhaps all was not lost, she might learn something new after all. She definitely could not risk going out again. If she were caught this time, who knows what might happen. She had developed a repertoire with Marcella and she did not want to rock the boat. She was here for a reason; of that she was certain, even if that reason wasn't quite clear to her yet. It was not a good time to make enemies. And she was sure she would indeed make them if she was caught doing something untoward.

Opening the book, Cassidy directed the mediocre glow of the small flashlight toward the pages, and she began to read.

By the third page, Cassidy was more confused than anything else. The book was very, very old. It was handwritten and near impossible to decipher. There were a lot of what appeared to be formulas and incoherent ramblings scribbled along the margins. She could pick out a word here or there (*saved; spring; fountain*) but the faded ink and spidery cursive was sending her cross-eyed. She ran a hand through her already (perhaps permanently) dishevelled hair. All had been for naught. Disappointment swamped her. Hoping to at least salvage something from her nightly adventure, Cassidy flicked swiftly through the pages, careful to not damage them; scanning each page with a discerning eye lest a word might stand out to her as important.

It was a fruitless endeavour. She had learned nothing new and now she was in the possession of stolen property.

She grinned ruefully.

She had pulled a classic Cassidy.

CHAPTER SIX

She awoke bleary-eyed and disoriented, having fallen asleep mid-thought. It was a feeling she was used to, as she was so often beleaguered by jet lag. She waited until the fog cleared and the spinning stopped before she even considered moving from her prone position. She was sprawled across the rumpled bed; an uncomfortable lump digging into her ribs turned out to be the misappropriated flashlight. She remembered slipping the contraband book inside the pillowcase just before she'd finally succumbed to the exhaustion. The pillow, however, was somewhere on the floor. She groaned and rolled over, stretching sore muscles.

Abruptly, with a stunning clarity that sent her leaping from beneath the tangled sheets, she remembered the final words she'd been able to decode from the book before she'd passed out: *power* and *healing*.

She glanced down at her hand.

Eliza, please bring some water from the fountain to the infirmary. Marcella's voice came through clear and crisp in her mind, the memory bursting to the surface; her subconscious finally catching up.

She unwound her bandage and stared for a moment in stunned silence.

There was no mark on her hand at all. No indication that there had ever been an injury. No cut, no scab, no scar... just smooth, unblemished skin. She had seen the laceration across her palm. She had seen the blood. It would undoubtedly have required stitches. A scar would have been inevitable. Cassidy knew scars, she had many from her numerous adventures. She knew the drill.

This just was not possible.

Fuelled now by an insatiable need for answers, Cassidy dressed quickly, slipped from her room, and hurried down the stairs. She was fast but quiet, though she wasn't sure why—nearly everyone was in school or at work. Still, she crept past the shared living room area with its many shelves, heavy with books; the side tables stacked high with board games. There was knitting and cross stitch and any number of other crafts or hobbies one could choose to learn. Yes, she had been welcomed to Lotus Lorea with open arms and its residents had been nothing but cordial, warm and inviting—but a frisson of unease slithered down her spine. She glanced down at her hand once more and with a stubborn set to her shoulders, she slipped through the front door and stepped out into the sunlight.

Shielding her eyes against the glare, Cassidy tried to remember which route she needed to take that would bring her to the centre of town; was it left or right? Setting off at a steady, no nonsense pace, Cassidy's heavy boots scuffed louder than she would have liked. She sent furtive glances over her shoulder. Was Lotus Lorea the type of place to have surveillance? Probably not. But Cassidy was hardwired for paranoia.

She soon found herself in a small alleyway between two buildings. She had somehow taken a wrong turn. She closed her eyes and tried to centre herself. She had an excellent sense of direction normally but she felt jumbled and out of sorts; like her brain was waging a war between the Cassidy she was when she first arrived here and the Cassidy that was becoming inextricably linked to Lotus Lorea.

She began to retrace her steps.

Cassidy plunged back out of the opposite end of the narrow alleyway, her gaze fixed straight ahead, her focus entirely on the task at hand; she took no notice of the young girl observing her from the doorway of the library. With her earth-toned clothing she had blended in with the surroundings; Cassidy would never have known of her presence if not for the low bird-like whistle the girl gave; she inclined her head at Cassidy once she had gained her attention, and then, ever so slightly, pointed a finger to her left. Then she slipped back through the library door and out of sight. Quiet as a mouse.

That was... interesting to say the least. There had been something vaguely familiar about the girl, with the heart shaped face, the dark hair and the thick, impossibly long lashes. Cassidy filed the incident away at the back of her mind to mull over later when she had time to think it though, and then trotted off down the path that the girl had indicated. Within minutes, she emerged from the grass-lined trail and into the park that was adjacent to the town square. It was deserted, the only sounds those of the native birds that flittered from tree to tree, indulging in the sweet and sour berries produced by the domestic foliage. Their bright blue and ruby-red feathers stood out, easily visible against the green of the trees; their soft pitched calls to one another clear and pleasing to the ear. Like everything else here.

Trying to catch her breath, Cassidy bent at the waist, resting her hands on her knees. While she was down there her eyes roamed the grass, searching. She gave a small satisfied but short-winded grunt when she found what she was looking for. *Yes. That would work just nicely.* The rock was thin; not jagged but definitely sharp enough. She gritted her teeth and took a deep breath: no one could ever say she wasn't thorough in her research or committed to the cause. In one quick motion—before she could change her mind—she dragged the whetted edge of the rock across the palm of her left hand. She grimaced, her breath all at once hissing out through her front teeth at the sudden explosion of pain. White spots danced behind her eyelids. She closed her fingers over the quick deluge of blood that arose from the wound. Without hesitation, Cassidy sat on the edge, next to the stone child, and plunged her hand into the fountain. She spread her fingers wide and wiggled them around, watching as the whorls of crimson spread out across the surface of the water. The coolness of the water dulled the pain in her hand almost immediately. She glanced around to make sure she was still alone. How long should she wait? Her palm tingled. A pleasant warmth spread across her hand and out her fingertips. Heart pounding, Cassidy forced herself to remain still. She closed her eyes and silently counted to twenty, then forty, then sixty. Forcefully she made herself count as much again. Then, finally, unable to bear the suspense any longer, Cassidy withdrew her hand from the fountain and gazed in astonishment. Other than a small, thin red line, her hand had been mended. Within a day that line would most likely disappear and no one would ever know she'd been injured.

What the hell was she supposed to do now?

Wiping her still dripping hand on her trousers, Cassidy's mind whirled with the possibilities—though it was a cliché, those possibilities, right now, seemed quite endless. A fountain that …healed?! Gamgee would lose his mind over this.

Then it hit her. She laughed mirthlessly. *This* was why she was here.

He already knew.

Like the proverbial horse, she had been led to water.

CHAPTER SEVEN

The low-frequency siren whooped loudly through the town square, startling Cassidy as she sat, ruminating, on the same bench that she had sat on earlier with Marcella. She was so wound up from her shocking discovery, that the sudden barrage of sound made her jump and look around guiltily. Had she tripped some sort of alarm by touching the water in the fountain? Were they coming for her? Who would *they* even be? Her pulse raced.

"Don't be foolish," she muttered to herself. Her face coloured. She'd actually managed to embarrass herself with her ridiculous line of thinking. Maybe she had hit her head harder than she'd thought.

The rising cadence of the siren now sent people scrambling from everywhere; doors swung wide and Cassidy saw women running from all directions, some had not even paused to put on shoes. They all streaked past her and Cassidy, caught up in the urgency and the chaos, followed along.

Whoop, whoop, whoop.

Cassidy cringed. "What's going on?!" she shouted to the woman running next to her.

The woman gave her a strange look. "It's *a delivery*."

A delivery?

And then suddenly it all became clear. The medical centre loomed up ahead. Oh. It was *that* kind of delivery.

Cassidy rushed on forward, caught up in the crowd.

There was standing room only. People were huddled outside. In the main entryway a clique of teens was gathered together, chattering noisily and excitedly amongst themselves. An elderly lady shushed them, wagging a finger in their direction as she pushed past, into the lobby. Cassidy followed closely behind her, taking note of the teens' chagrined faces. There was the electric buzz of excitement in the air inside; hushed adult conversation was punctuated by barely stifled childish giggles and a rousing game of tag by the younger children that only added to the pandemonium. Cassidy made her way to the front of the throng, murmuring apologies, doling out smiles as necessary, as she excused herself past group after group of waiting women. They were all here to support each other. It was clearly a community event and it all seemed quite remarkable to Cassidy, this unique bond they all had— like something tied them together as one.

She spotted Marcella immediately, speaking to a tall bespectacled woman wearing a set of sparkling white scrubs. They both looked concerned, gesturing with their hands and frowning repeatedly.

"Is there anything I can do to help?" Cassidy interrupted. *This might be my way in.*

"Oh! Cassidy, hello! I didn't see you there."

"Is everything okay?"

"I'm afraid not, my dear. Well, nothing life threatening of course, just more of an inconvenience at the moment. This is Laura, she's our head midwife. She's been telling me that we are a little short-handed today."

"You don't have a doctor here?"

Marcella observed her curiously. "No, we have several trained midwives and a number of doulas."

A memory fired in Cassidy's synapses: *Hadn't Miss Ginny mentioned a doctor?*

Snapping out of it, Cassidy offered: "I have first aid training... if that's of any help?"

Marcella brightened. "Goodness yes! You are a lifesaver!" she gushed. "Just follow Laura to the back, that's where the birthing suites are."

Cassidy spared a glance over her shoulder and saw the looks of interest on the faces of those gathered in wait. Many were nodding and smiling in approval. She turned and followed Laura, leaving the whispers behind.

The deeper she went into the hospital, the more it became apparent that someone was in a great deal of pain. Cassidy did not have a great deal of experience in this sort of situation. In fact, what she knew of birth was in medical terms, from text books and, of course, from movies and television. The pain and screaming she had most definitely expected.

"Everlee is in active labour. We are getting quite close to the end now. I could definitely use a second pair of hands, just in case," Laura offered, smiling. "Now, you're not the queasy sort are you?"

Cassidy's eyes widened but she shook her head no and did not falter in step as she trailed along behind Laura. The screaming got louder. Cassidy winced. Together, the two women entered the small but clean and functional room that was, as Marcella had said, the birthing suite. Upon the bed at the centre of the room lay a young woman (Cassidy estimated her to be in her mid-twenties) drenched in sweat; tendrils of curly brown hair clung to her forehead and trailed into her eyes. She was breathing raggedly, bent forward over her knees as best she could, considering the large belly she was sporting in front. Holding her hand was the young girl Cassidy had encountered earlier. The same one who had shown her in which direction to find the fountain. Cassidy tried not to react.

"This is Everlee. Everlee, meet Cassidy. She's going to be giving me a hand since Lenora and Elsie are out with the flu. And Cassidy, this is Everlee's sister Ella."

Their eyes met briefly; an unspoken communication. "Nice to meet you, Ella."

"You too …Cassidy."

"Things will move quite swiftly now, Everlee," Laura said, stepping back from the bed where she had just administered a short examination.

Everlee grunted in reply, resumed her deep breathing and closed her eyes in concentration. Ella, stoic and glued to her sister's side, smoothed the damp hair back from her eyes and murmured what Cassidy assumed to be words of encouragement. Everlee quieted and nodded her head.

Laura guided Cassidy to the side of the room, showing her where to wash up and handing her a set of scrubs. "You can change into these in the room next door. It won't be long now so try to make it quick."

Everlee was already pushing, her face red and blotchy

with effort, when Cassidy returned to the room.

"Cassidy, are you ready?" Laura asked.

Cassidy took a deep breath, "As I'll ever be…"

***

The frantic high-pitched newborn wails filled the room and echoed off the walls. Cassidy stepped back in astonishment. She had never in all her days witnessed anything like this. She felt empowered and in complete awe of what Everlee had just accomplished. Everyone breathed a sigh of relief at the baby's cry—Everlee fell back against the pillows on the bed, her exhaustion apparent; Ella grabbed her hand and they smiled at each other. Both were crying.

"It's a boy," Laura announced quietly and Everlee gasped.

"No," breathed Ella. "Not again."

"Would you like to meet him before…?" Laura enquired.

Everlee turned away, her eyes full of unshed tears.

"Are you sure you don't want to? It is permitted. Many women choose to do so." Laura glanced at Ella as if looking for guidance but Ella shook her head curtly, and Everlee's only response was to curl onto her side and face the wall.

Cassidy, bewildered at the scene unfolding before her, watched as Laura wrapped the newborn in a soft blue blanket. She hummed under her breath and rocked him in her arms until he finally settled. Marcella appeared in the doorway, an eyebrow raised in question. Cassidy watched as she took in the scene, as she very quickly noticed the blue blanket. Her face fell. Laura walked to her and handed over the swaddled child.

"A boy," she said. Then, "Healthy. Strong lungs."

Marcella saw Cassidy looking at her and smiled softly, almost apologetically. "It is our way." And then she left with the baby as Everlee began to softly cry.

"This is bullshit!" Ella shouted as she ran from the room, knocking into Cassidy as she passed.

Laura shook her head, frowning. She seemed more upset at the language than the situation she'd just witnessed. She turned her attention back to Everlee, and Cassidy slipped unnoticed from the room. The medical centre had gone silent.

Everyone else had left.

The blue blanket—a signal.

Life would go back to normal now for everyone. For everyone, perhaps, but Everlee. And Ella. Cassidy was shaken. They'd taken the baby away. Just like that.

Cassidy heard muffled voices further down the hall; a door had been left ajar. She crept down the corridor, sidled up to the doorway, and strained to hear what was being said.

"Have they been chosen yet?"

"Yes, an older couple. They'd been waiting a long time before they found us. I've already made the call," came Marcella's voice.

"Wonderful! I'll leave with him shortly then."

"Yes, that sounds perfect! They'll take care of everything else back at The Agency. Out of necessity, this one will be heading out of state."

Footsteps approached; Marcella was leaving. Cassidy

looked around for a hiding spot and quickly slipped into a supply closet, coming face to face with mops, brooms, cleaning supplies, toilet paper, and the tear-stained face of Ella. Widening her red-rimmed eyes, her long dark lashes glistening with moisture, Ella quickly raised a finger to her lips, pursed them and emitted a small whisper of breath: *shhh*. Cassidy nodded once, a brief acknowledgement of her understanding and, with the greatest of care, she eased the door shut behind her.

She already had the answers to some of her questions.

She had a feeling she was about to find out a whole lot more.

CHAPTER EIGHT

A dim light came on overhead; a single bulb hanging on a thin string swung lazily to and fro, briefly illuminating their faces and then plunging them back into shadow. Cassidy averted her eyes and waited for Ella to compose herself. She didn't want to embarrass the girl anymore than she already was, having interrupted her in a private moment of loss and grief. Ella took deep shuddering breaths and swiped at her face with the sleeve of her tunic.

"Please. Don't tell them I'm in here!" Her high panicked tone raised Cassidy's hackles.

"It's cool. Don't worry. I won't say a word."

"Thank you," she replied with obvious relief, her shoulders visibly relaxing.

Cassidy eyed her curiously; she couldn't help but ask: "What happens if you're caught in here?"

"Caught spying? They'll send me to The Hut." She shuddered.

The Hut? Cassidy's thoughts drifted back to the small building she'd asked about while on the tour with Marcella. *The storage shed?*

"You don't want to know," Ella offered tremulously.

Oh, but Cassidy *did* want to know. She wanted to know very badly, but seeing the distress it was causing the girl, and along with everything else she had just had to deal with; Cassidy held her tongue, and her questions. Another time. Another place.

Ella gulped several deep breaths of air, swallowing her sobs.

In a faltering voice she whispered: "He's already gone isn't he?"

"Yes. I'm so sorry."

She sighed shakily but nodded her head, resigned. "It's for the best, I know that. But we still cared about him, you know? He'll be happy won't he? He'll go to a good home too, right?" she implored.

Cassidy wanted nothing more than to reassure the young woman. She knew that if all of the other parents chosen by The Rising Son Adoption Agency were anything at all like Annie and Ximena, the baby would have a wonderful home and would never want for anything. Cassidy knew that love was plentiful in the Romero-Jones house and Mateo would be cherished there.

"He will be loved. That's what they told me."

"He will," Cassidy answered; in her heart she felt it was the truth and she desperately wanted Ella to stop crying. She wasn't quite sure how to comfort her. And she didn't want to say the wrong thing. She was a bit out of her league with this whole entire situation; she just was not good with people and their emotions. Cassidy was accustomed to climbing mountains, tumbling out of cars, and breaking through windows; dodging bullets and belligerent aliens; exploring new worlds. Yet here, in this supply closet with this heartbroken girl—it was one of the scariest moments of Cassidy's life.

"Ella..." she began gently, questioningly.

Ella watched Cassidy intently, looking for signs of sincerity, clearly wanting to confide but also bound by what she had been taught her whole life was a secret. "It is our way."

"I've heard *that* before," Cassidy remarked dryly.

"It's better like this! Better than ways of old when..." She stopped, choked back another sob, unable to go on.

Cassidy was certain she understood what the *ways of old* might have entailed. She shivered. It was unimaginable.

The girl sniffed and wiped her nose on her arm again. Cassidy had been biting her tongue but curiosity had quickly overcome her.

"How often does this sort of thing happen, Ella? Baby boys being born here, I mean."

"Um…" she hesitated, her face darkening. "Not all that often. A few times a year maybe. Something goes wrong I guess. Usually when we… The fountain doesn't…" she trailed off. Her eyes widened, she flushed and an unreadable emotion flickered across her face.

"The fountain? What does the fountain have to do with this?" Cassidy jumped eagerly on what was clearly a slip up. She was eager for the big reveal.

Ella stared at Cassidy again for a few moments and Cassidy wondered if perhaps she'd spooked the girl, been a bit *too* eager. And then with a resigned look Ella began to speak, her voice taking on a reverent tone as she recited by rote: "At the time of the month, when the moon is high and the flower blooms, when we are of age and the time is right; when it is the path we have chosen to follow: we drink of the Lotus Fountain. It is our duty."

"But… what does that even…"

"It is our greatest blessing but also, sometimes, it is our greatest curse."

And then she slipped through the door, not making a sound, and was gone before Cassidy could say anything else. She didn't dare call out to her.

Cassidy sat abruptly on an upturned bucket—what the hell was going on in this place?! How did the fountain tie in with everything? And just what went on in that storage shed? Her mind whirled with all the snippets of information she'd gathered throughout the day, all the things she had learned about Lotus Lorea and the people who lived there.

Perhaps, after all, it was not nearly as perfect as it seemed.

Not one single bit.

She tiptoed to the door, opened it a crack, and waited until the coast was clear.

***

Walking back towards The Dorms, Cassidy gazed in wonder as the women around her carried on as though nothing remarkable had happened just a few short hours ago. As if a child had not been born. As if that child had not been whisked away …and then never spoken about again. Cassidy did not consider herself to be an overly maternal type but surely this wasn't normal behaviour, was it? No, not normal in her world, she realized, but perhaps this was nothing new here.

"Cassidy?"

The questioning voice broke her train of thought, startling her back to reality.

"I wanted to thank you for your assistance today. Laura was very grateful, as I am sure Everlee was as well."

Marcella smiled at Cassidy as she turned around and faced her. Marcella took a step closer.

"I see something in you, Cassidy. You are a strong, intelligent woman, one who knows what she wants out of life; one who grabs it by the horns and doesn't let go. We need more people like you in Lotus Lorea. Someone our young girls can look up to …like Ella does already." She paused. "This is rather unorthodox, and please, take all the time you need to consider my offer."

"Your offer?" Cassidy interrupted.

"Yes, my dear," Marcella continued. "Myself and the other elders have conferred and we would very much like it if you would stay on here. To join us permanently on Lotus Lorea."

At the look on Cassidy's face, a mixture of shock and bewilderment, Marcella quickly added: "Of course you could visit your own world as often as you like—the portal would remain open and at your disposal. But, your place, your *home*, would be here with us. There's a beautiful house just at the outskirts of the village. It could be yours. We are certain that, with a little bit of work, it could be turned into a lab or a research facility or whatever you want it to be! You would become an important part of our herstory."

"I… I don't…"

"Think about it, Cassidy, please. Take your time. Get

to know us, take your time and look around as much as you would like and then you can make your decision."

Marcella nodded at her, smiled a smile that seemed almost apologetic for having put her on the spot. She walked away in the direction of the town square, a slight droop to her shoulders.

Cassidy, still stunned at the proposition, made her way back to her room at The Dorms, lost once again in thought.

She felt disconcerted, perhaps even a little bit angry. Okay, she was a lot angry.

But mostly it was directed at herself.

Because, in the back of her mind, in the dark recesses that she kept hidden from everyone but herself, she was actually considering the offer.

***

She threw herself on the bed. She was being overly dramatic, she knew. Her mind flashed back to her teenage years when this very thing was a regular occurrence.

A long walk through the strawberry fields had helped to lessen her anger; the warm, fragrant breeze lifted the hair from her face and also helped to ease the tension from her shoulders. She'd stopped to watch some of the women as they prepped the soil for a new round of planting, and with some mild encouragement she found herself down on her knees, digging in the dirt and, to her surprise, thoroughly enjoying herself. Traces of soil still remained under her nails despite repeated scrubbings.

She had inspected The Hut as much as she dared, unable to resist the opportunity, being in such close proximity to it. Much to her disappointment, she wasn't able to get close enough to take a look inside one of its grubby windows. There was no way to bring up the topic without raising suspicion either, but the women were keen to keep a healthy distance from the building and that was something that did not escape her notice.

As the day wore on, she found herself invigorated by the work, and by the conversation and companionship of the women. She'd been invited to go around to Maggie's house for tea and a game of cards; Johanna insisted she come by and raid her closet, as Johanna was sure she had some things that would fit Cassidy perfectly. She glanced pointedly at Cassidy's now dirt smeared clothing and laughed. While they took a break in the shade of another weeping willow, sharing rich flaky scones slathered with a deep red berry jam, Cassidy enchanted them with stories of her own world. They seemed most interested in learning about cats and dogs, neither of which was native to Lotus Lorea.

"And you keep those things in your house? These animals with teeth and claws? Do people not fear it might gobble them up?!" asked a young girl named Ruth.

Cassidy laughed and then explained the deal with domesticated animals. They all listened intently with mouths agape, completely enthralled. Cassidy couldn't remember the last time she had been this relaxed; had spent this much time with people outside of work; had made friends. It was sobering. And invigorating. A different kind of adventure.

Here now, alone in her room once again, she stared at her dirty nails and everything rushed back to the forefront: the fountain, the birth; the adoption; Marcella's proposition, and the fact that she was actually thinking about staying. What was she thinking?!

She recalled all the occasions where, despite her level of education and her expertise in the field of Archaeology, and despite years of hard work and countless accolades for her accomplishments, she was still no where near on the same scale as her male counterparts. She was, of course, successful in her own right, this was true, but she could still imagine how it would feel to be at the top in her profession and *not* be ridiculed for her ideas simply because she was a woman. She read the hateful comments online even though she knew she shouldn't. She overheard the not-so-whispered remarks behind her back at conferences and the *can you believe this chick?* chuckles from the male dominated audiences as she gave keynote speeches. She shook her head, no, she would not be sad to leave *that* behind, of that she was certain.

She could have everything she had always wanted.

Here on Lotus Lorea.

But that was the catch.

Could she leave her old life behind?

Tangled up with all this disillusionment about what she should do were also her heavy suspicions that Gamgee was more than aware of the portal she had used to get here, that he'd known what was on the other side and that he'd had his own motives for encouraging her to investigate the mystery of the adoption agency when she'd brought it up to him. She could not understand all this subterfuge, these games, when it had never been necessary before.

Then again… there was The Lotus Fountain to consider. It was quite remarkable, was it not? And that meant that there was a lot more at stake this time around. It also meant greater consequences. The burden of those consequences would now fall to Cassidy, and Cassidy alone.

She once again considered the possibilities and was wracked with indecision. Didn't she owe it to her world to bring back, at the very least, a sample of the water from the fountain? Gamgee… he could reproduce it. It would change everything, save countless lives.

But if she did that, well, surely she would have to destroy the portal. There would be war between the worlds otherwise. But then, The Rising Son Adoption Agency would be no more once the portal no longer existed. Cassidy would cut off their connection. What right did she have to do so? Surely they would then revert back to their *ways of old*. Cassidy couldn't bear the thought.

She arose from the bed and paced around and around the small room, chewing on her thumbnail, furiously cursing under her breath as she did so. See, that was the problem: she had too much time to think. Yes, that's definitely what it was. She was a woman of action and all this inaction was the foundation of her problems. She prided herself on *not* thinking—which, she was fully aware, sounded like quite a bizarre mantra, but she was a person who just went for it, consequences be damned.

Maybe it was time to take that leap.

Just go for it.

And that was when the knock sounded at the door.

CHAPTER NINE

"I'm afraid we have a bit of a problem."

Cassidy opened the door wide to allow Marcella to enter. The normally composed matriarch rung her hands. She was very visibly upset; there were beads of sweat gathered on her temples and her hair was in disarray. She looked at Cassidy imploringly; having stated that there was a problem she now appeared lost for words, or maybe even afraid to speak them.

"What's wrong?!" Cassidy exclaimed.

She bit her lip, then squared her shoulders before she began: "We cannot find Ella or Everlee. Laura has told me that Everlee left the clinic not long after the birth. No, it is not unheard of for women to check out early if they have family at home who can care for them but… we think they may have…" She swallowed with difficulty, struggled to get the words out. She finally met Cassidy's eyes and took a deep breath. "We think they may have accessed the portal." Then, all in a rush: "It is *strictly* forbidden."

"Don't you have a guard or something posted to it?!"

"No. There has never been a need. No one leaves. It is paradise. Why would they ever want to?"

Looks like someone did, Cassidy thought ingeniously.

"What do you need me to do?"

"Thank you, Cassidy! I knew you would help." Marcella sighed in relief and managed a flicker of a smile. "Would you go after them? They are not prepared for your world. It is so unlike ours. I am very worried for their safety! And who better to navigate it than you?"

Marcella had every right to be worried. Those two girls, ingénue as they were, would be sitting ducks, especially if they ventured outside the gated community of Carina Heights. And maybe even *inside* the gates if they ran into the wrong people.

"How much of a head start do you think they had?"

"We can't be sure. An hour, perhaps longer, but not much more than that."

"I'll go."

Marcella's appreciation was evident. "I knew you would help. Please… bring them home."

***

Cassidy rushed into her room at The Dorms and quickly gather up what little possessions she had with her. She jammed her useless cell phone in a back pocket, crammed the random bits she'd carried with her—lip balm, keys, a few dollars in coins, a roll of breath mints—back into another pocket. There was an urgency to her movements and she was back out on the street within minutes. A small group had gathered: Marcella, Laura and a few other faces Cassidy recognized from those she'd encountered, the friends she had made. Johanna, Maggie and Ruth.

They looked at her expectantly.

"I'll find them."

She nodded resolutely, meaning every word she had said, and took off at a run, heading along what was now a familiar route. The portal was midway up a cliff side on the south border of the village, a short distance from The Lotus Fountain. A set of stone stairs had been roughly hewn into the face of the rock—stairs that Cassidy had tumbled down unceremoniously when she had first arrived in this world—but had, over the years, from weather and use eroded into smooth, uneven edges. It hadn't been that long ago, but it felt like forever. She ascended the steps without hesitation, feeling the familiar thrum, that pulsing along her veins, the closer she got to the portal. She was high on the thrill of the chase; gone was the calmness and serenity she'd achieved during her brief stay on Lotus Lorea.

She felt useful.

Alive.

It was glorious.

Cassidy burst through the portal; the baby-fine hairs on the back of her neck and along her forearms quivered and stood at attention as the brief zap of energy flowed through her in a rush. It was not an unpleasant feeling. More so, it was something Cassidy associated with action, adventure and, yes, a whole hell of a lot of fun.

Unfortunately, fun was the one thing she was not having right now, even if on some level she was enjoying the thrill of the chase, the sense of purpose.

Her unexpected appearance in a back room of the adoption agency, which had now opened for business, startled those who had already started their workday, their office doors open wide and ready for clients who would soon arrive. There they sat in front of their computers, mouths agape in shock as Cassidy, who had seemingly appeared out of nowhere, strolled past. The existence of the portal was definitely on a need-to-know only basis in this place and these folks definitely did *not* know.

A cluster of minions had gathered near the water cooler, shooting the breeze. Ignoring the file folders in their hands, they seemed quite relaxed and utterly unaware of the hellfire that was about to rain down on them.

Cassidy—the aforementioned hellfire—fists clenched by her side, face flushed with suppressed emotions, shouted: "Two girls! Have two young girls gone through here?"

One woman squeaked in fright and dropped the folder she'd been holding. Another sloshed a small paper cup of water down the front of his suit and tie as he reacted to the squeak.

"Where in the world did you come from?!" The startled exclamation came from a ginger bearded man sporting thick black rimmed glasses and holding a clip board. "There isn't supposed to be anyone back here but employees of the agency!"

Cassidy rolled her eyes. "Listen, pal, I don't have time for your crap right now. I'm looking for two girls. Young, most likely scared. Have you seen them in this building or anywhere near here?"

"We haven't seen anything," he replied indignantly.

"How long have you all been here?!" Cassidy questioned, eyes narrowed.

"Ten... maybe fifteen minutes," sputtered the squeaker and dropper of file folders. "We haven't seen anyone other than our coworkers, I swear. And, well, now you too." She faltered, bit her lip nervously and looked away from Cassidy's penetrating gaze.

She seemed scared, Cassidy suddenly realized, like she expected Cassidy to haul out a weapon and start shooting. Cassidy had the grace to feel chagrined for her aggressive behaviour, but the moment, and the thought, was fleeting.

"Dammit all."

Cassidy ran past them all, ignoring their confusion and their rapidly burgeoning curiosity. They flattened against the walls, allowing her quick, unfettered passage down the hall. One man reached out as if to stop her but then reconsidered, his hand left dangling there in mid-air as Cassidy shot him a dark cautionary look over her shoulder, warning him in no uncertain terms, hands off.

Unlike the night before, when she had had to be clandestine and sneaky, when she had crept in through a back window like a thief under cloak of darkness, Cassidy blew past the reception desk and out through the front door as bold as brass, exploding out into the stark bright light of day, her mind on one thing: the mission to bring Everlee and Ella back to their home. It would be a bittersweet endeavour.

It smelled different here. And not in a good way. That was her first coherent thought of her own home as she hit the ground running. It wasn't that she had really been gone all that long but her senses had already adjusted to the absence of exhaust fumes, heavy perfume, cleaning chemicals and other offensive scents that were not native to Lotus Lorea.

She chose to ignore a pang of something that felt remarkably like home sickness.

She was missing something she had never really had to being with.

So, where to now?

Directly across the road from where she stood, an older woman in a voluminous purple coat was walking a ridiculously small dog along the sidewalk. Cassidy trotted down the curved driveway at the front of The Rising Son Adoption Agency, waved at the pedestrian and then, when that failed to catch her attention, she shouted: "Hey! Excuse me! Ma'am?! Can I speak to you for a moment?"

The woman stopped and regarded Cassidy with suspicion. Cassidy didn't blame her. The lady's tiny furred companion sent up a raucous yapping at her approach, spinning in circles, tangling both itself and its owner in the short bejeweled leash attached to a gem encrusted collar. Cassidy imagined how intrigued her new friends on Lotus Lorea would be by this chipper creature.

"Hush, Kevin!!"

Kevin?

Cassidy raised her voice over the enthusiastic barking that showed no signs of slowing down. "Have you seen two young girls anywhere near here? One has long, straight black hair, the other is a curly brunette. Very pretty. Maybe 5'3" or thereabouts? One may need immediate medical attention."

"I'm sorry, no, I haven't seen anyone other than a few other dog walkers and a couple of joggers. But I see those people nearly every day when me and Kevsie get out for a trot. Don't we, Kevin?! You like going walksies don't you, my good boy?!"

The lady continued to speak in a chirpy, singsong voice to the dog. Cassidy raised an eyebrow and backed away quickly, muttering a thank you under her breath as she made her escape. The woman didn't seem to notice. She was fully absorbed with Kevin.

Cassidy scanned the area. Where would they go? *Come on, Cassidy, think!* She hauled her damaged phone out of her pocket and powered it up.

"Please, please," she murmured, mentally crossing her fingers, hoping against hope that it would work, and that there was enough charge left for what she had in mind.

Victory. The easily recognizable logo popped below the shattered screen as the phone gloriously glowed to life. Battery at 13%. That would have to do. She scrolled through her contacts and crossed her fingers that this one phone call wouldn't completely deplete what was left of her battery.

"Hello there, Cass—"

"Are there any vacant houses in Carina Heights?" Cassidy broke in, her abruptness not completely out of character.

"Well, good morning to you too, Ms. Cane. Planning a move are we?" came the immediate response.

Cassidy was not in the mood for a witty repartee. She took a deep breath. Gamgee would be dying of curiosity; Cassidy was absolutely sure of it—especially if her suspicions were on the money. She wasn't giving up anything right now. Let him think she had not fallen for the bait.

She forced a laugh. "Not anytime soon. Just out for

some fresh air and a bit of exploring, you might say."

"I see. Well, it's not the best neighbourhood, I'm afraid. At one time it was very family oriented. There is an old cul-de-sac, I believe; development was eventually abandoned on it. It's on the Southside. Frecker. No! Fraser Place, that's it. Perhaps that would suit your needs?"

Perhaps it would indeed.

"Great! Thanks so much, Doctor! Bye for now."

"Will I see you at the university later?"

Cassidy paused; shook her head to herself. There was no time for this idle chat. "Sorry, my phone is about to die!" The words came out in a rush and Cassidy very quickly ended the call before Gamgee could interject again.

She accessed the maps application on the phone, tapped in Fraser Place and quickly memorized the route she would need to take to get to the subdivision.

Nine percent.

She shoved the phone with its worrisome low battery percentage back into her pocket and took off at a run through the park. If she was right, it would be a shortcut and her destination time would be cut nearly in half.

Cassidy was a fast runner. A skill born of necessity and well cultivated over the years from dodging bullets and escaping bad tempered nasties—both of the alien *and* human kind.

It was much better than a gym workout.

She vaulted a bench, not just because it was in her way but simply because it was there and she could. She grinned, pleased that she was still agile enough to do such things. Blood pumping, now that the adrenaline had kicked in, coursing through her veins. Sweat beaded on her forehead and the back of her neck; parched, she longed for a cold bottle of water. Her breath rushed in and out of her mouth and she felt the hit in her calves as the lactic acid she was producing flooded her muscles. The slapping of her feet on the ground matched the hammering of her heart and as she exited the tree line that encircled the park, Cassidy finally hit her stride, that runner's high that everyone talked about. Her body pumping like a well oiled machine now, Cassidy began to calculate all of the likely scenarios she might possibly face when she reached her final destination. Everlee had only just given birth. There could be any number of complications and she could require immediate medical attention. Not to mention the repercussions for the both of them from having gone through the portal. Even Cassidy, after her many travels, still felt the jolt to her very core as she passed through the doorways between worlds. Cassidy hoped there would be enough charge left on her phone to call 911 if it was necessary. She would worry later about the consequences of two undocumented females, without medical cards, insurance or any sort of ID. She'd figure something out. She was good at flying by the seat of her pants.

As she mulled over the situation, she wondered how the girls had managed to make it past the guards at the agency; how they had been able to make it as far as they'd gotten, given their lack of experience outside their own world. It took some planning, ingenuity and cunning. Cassidy suspected that Ella might have spearheaded the whole escape.

Inside, Cassidy was secretly impressed.

She hit Fraser Place at a dead run; the cul-de-sac was

larger than she expected but was still spread out before her as she had expected, its typical semi-circle shape coming to an abrupt end where construction had ceased on new houses. She slowed to a jog. Carina Heights had, at one time, clearly expected to grow by leaps and bounds. She stood facing several fully built houses, a few on each side of the street, with for sale signs still pegged into their front lawns, though most now sagged at a jaunty angle. At the very end of the road, foundations had been laid down for at least five more structures. Those basement spaces were now overgrown with weeds, filled with garbage and whatever else had blown or rolled in. Heavy equipment sat dormant, deserted and rusted on the gravel driveways and atop bare patches of dirt that, had the neighbourhood come to fruition, been covered in lush green lawns. All was quiet save for the soft rustle of the breeze through the trees and the occasional whistle of a bird. Cassidy was far enough away now that even Kevin's sharp yaps were no longer audible.

She surveyed the houses, wheels churning in her head. Ella was a clever girl; she'd pick a hiding place that would be safe for her and her sister. Which house would she choose? Cassidy bit her lip. Then it clicked. Ella would want electricity if possible, running water, a working toilet—amenities Everlee would need as she recovered from the birth. Angling her head skywards, Cassidy eyed the power lines running from the poles; she followed their serpentine trails straight from the pole to the one and only house where they had been connected, and where, presumably, electricity still flowed. Number 1 Fraser Place.

"That's it," she whispered to herself.

Cassidy made a beeline for the front door. She saw no sense now in playing coy. There was no need to knock. Instead she simply twisted the handle. It was locked. Because of course it was. She took a step back and squinted in the glaring sun, glancing upwards at the second floor windows. A curtain twitched.

Cassidy smiled.

Gotcha.

CHAPTER TEN

"Have they been located?"

"Yes, ma'am. They'd gone for a walk along the south fields and stayed there, near the water, for a while to rest and eat."

"I expected as much. Thank you."

"And, what of the visitor?"

"It's been… taken care of."

***

The top step creaked as Cassidy leaned forward to peer through the grubby window. Cupping her hands around her eyes, she squinted in the low light that extended beyond the door. No movement. No sign that anyone at all was staying there, as a matter of fact; no stray shoes scattered across the floor or a jacket abandoned over the back of a chair, no backpack or purse… nothing like the permanent "lived in" look that was the constant esthetic at Cassidy's house. Ella, or Everlee, or whoever it was who had peeked through the curtain in the upstairs room, already knew that she was there, but still Cassidy shrugged and raised a hand to knock firmly on the door.

"Everlee? Ella? It's me, Cassidy!" Impatiently she

waited; was met with silence. She knocked again, sharply. Concern furrowed her brow.

"It's okay, I promise! I'm just here to help! You can let me in!" she shouted, hoping she had been loud enough to be heard inside.

Another flicker at the window upstairs. The blue floral curtains swayed ever so slightly, as though having just been kissed by a light summer draft. There *was* someone there—she had not just imagined it.

Concern was quickly giving way to suspicion now. There was absolutely no reason for Everlee or Ella to be afraid of her. Why would they continue to hide and ignore her calls?

Cassidy took a step back. And then another. A frisson of awareness trailed its frigid fingers down her spine. A dog howled shrilly in the distance.

Something wasn't right.

Her gut instinct was telling her to run, to run now and not stop—and she trusted her gut implicitly. She'd gotten no further than fifty feet up the road when the explosion ripped through the house, sending flames shooting high into the sky and echoing with horrifying certainty throughout the gated community of Carina Heights. The colossal blast hit Cassidy in the back, a blazing hot smack that lifted her unapologetically off the ground and tossed her like a ragdoll. She tumbled through the air, an agonizing slow motion freefall that ended abruptly as she smashed into the ground, the landing leaving her winded on the grass of a house all the way on the other side of the road.

Flaming debris, glass, and metal shrapnel showered

around her and she instinctively covered her head and face with her arms as she tried to catch her breath. Chunks of scorched wood thumped onto the ground around her and she counted her lucky stars that none of them had hit her. When the worst of the explosion and the fallout seemed to have passed she did a quick army crawl to the safety of the houses covered porch.

What in the actual hell had just happened here?

Breath coming in wracking gasps that bordered on hyperventilation, Cassidy dragged herself up the steps and collapsed against the emerald green door of number 7. She winced in agony at the high pitched whine that was a constant ringing in her ears, and the pain at the base of her skull that throbbed in time to the beat of her heart. She assessed her injuries, of which there were many, and grimaced: the hand that came away from her scalp was slick with her own blood. Her eyes streamed; she wasn't sure if they were tears of pain or from the thick smoke that stung them.

For a brief moment, Cassidy thought of the healing powers of The Lotus Fountain and found herself giggling hysterically.

Then she slumped to the ground, bleeding and unconscious.

***

The wailing of sirens roused Cassidy to awareness. She groaned loudly as she pushed herself back into a sitting position. How long had she been out for? The smouldering ruins of the house on the cul-de-sac still sent dark whorls of smoke spiralling into the cloudless cerulean

skies above Carina Heights, turning them murky and ash-
en. Small areas of fire still burned; hungry for fuel, fingers
of flame reached out for the woods beyond what once had
been someone's home.

A home that had just been completely obliterated.

Her head was spinning, but if Cassidy knew one thing,
it was that she did not want to be here when the emergency responders arrived. They would have a lot of questions and the one thing she did not have was answers. She
gingerly assessed the wound at the back of her head and
deemed it to be not life threatening. Rising slowly to her
feet, she fought back brutal waves of nausea and dizzi-
ness. She took deep shaking breaths and focused on the
act of standing and remaining upright. The acrid smoke
from the explosion and continuing blaze wafted in her direction; she coughed and gagged, retching on the scent,
vomiting over the side of the front steps into the hydran-
gea bushes. Well, at least that was out of the way. Swiping a hand across her mouth, Cassidy stumbled down the
steps, reoriented herself, and set off at a slow agonizing
jog, putting distance between herself and Fraser Place.
She ducked under the cover of trees in the park that occupied the centre of Carina Heights; she paused beside
an American elm, leaning against its trunk to catch her
breath, her hands and knees shaking—a delayed reaction
to the shock of what had just happened. Still beneath the
leaves, she watched as a long string of emergency vehicles
flew past where she stood and on up into the cul-de-sac,
sirens screeching and lights flashing red and white. The
shockwaves of the explosion had no doubt been felt for
miles around.

If there had been anyone in that house… Cassidy didn't even want to think about it.

Couldn't think about it.

She turned her back on the scene, pushing it from her mind and plodding on forward, as she always did. She took stock of her ripped and stained clothing. The heavy scent of smoke clung to her hair and skin; her hands were bloodstained, her nails filthy.

She was a sorry sight.

And the person who orchestrated this whole thing too, once she got her hands on them, oh yes, they would be a sorry sight as well.

Cassidy burned with the need for revenge. Someone would pay for this. And she had a pretty damn good idea who that person would be.

***

Cassidy walked in through the door of The Rising Son Adoption Agency just like she owned the place. She heard the gasps of shock from the young woman on the front reception desk, saw her push back her chair to rise, but Cassidy did not pause in her stride. She chortled to herself, imagining what the poor woman must be thinking at the sight of her, like an extra from *The Walking Dead*. Cassidy continued beyond the outer foyer and towards the inner offices and then, down that now familiar hall. She had no trouble finding it now, and as people poked their heads out of various office doors she tipped an imaginary hat at them, smirking as they quickly ducked back inside and shut their doors. A lot of people felt that way about Cassidy even when she *wasn't* covered in soot and blood. She was surprised no one had called the cops on her yet.

Cassidy punched in the security code on the pad with only the briefest of glances. She threw open the door to the room holding the portal and slipped inside. The door swung shut behind her, the lock mechanism clicking securely. She wouldn't be bothered this time. She headed straight through the portal without pause, the zap of energy running through her; it was much needed energy that would fuel her for what was ahead. It was time for some answers—she would demand those answers, dammit—and she was going to be the one asking all the questions.

This time when she arrived there was much less fanfare, but she wasn't in much better shape. To Cassidy, blood and Lotus Lorea seemed to go hand in hand. She quickly and deftly descended the stone steps and planted her feet on the now familiar cobbled pathways of the world of Lotus Lorea.

There wasn't a soul in sight.

She would take a direct approach, for there was no need for subtleties. In all honesty, Cassidy could not have been bothered. She was too tired to be subtle. The time, the energy—she was far beyond that right now. In spite of all their insistence that they were the embodiment of tranquillity and peace, Lotus Lorea was not nearly as perfect as they wanted everyone, and especially Cassidy, to believe. She set off at a steady pace along the path that would take her to the centre of town. There would be no healing waters for her this time around, no mending of clothes, no welcoming party or lavish meals. If her suspicions were correct, the Lotus Loreans were more about hurting than healing.

As she began to near the centre of town, as she strode past the housing units and along the main thoroughfare, Cassidy began to come across more and more people. They filed out of doorways as if they sensed that something big was about to happen. They huddled together in small groups, whispering; their faces aghast at the sight of her and, perhaps, even a little fearful. She did not blame them one bit. They had a right to be afraid. And she was willing to take each and every one of them on if she had to. Not only had they messed with her—and very nearly gotten her killed!—but they had also messed with someone she cared about.

Cassidy saw Marcella, had a moment to assess her, before the matriarch saw her. She was chatting animatedly with another woman, laughing and smiling as though she had not one care in the world. That was about to change.

How dare she?! What kind of monster is she?! wondered Cassidy.

"Did you try to blow me up?! What about Ella and Everlee?! Do you realize what you have done?!" Cassidy demanded, her voice dripping with malice and rising higher and higher in octave, raging with each and every word, until the final one came out as a scream, the cords in her neck straining with the force of her emotion.

Marcella recoiled as though she had been physically struck. Her reaction from the shock of seeing Cassidy in front of her and the onslaught and venom of Cassidy's words—they were like a slap in the face. "I… I don't know what you are talking about!" she stammered, feigning innocence.

"Like hell you don't!" Cassidy sneered, spitting out each syllable as through it had left a bad taste in her mouth.

A small crowd had begun to gather in the square behind Cassidy. They all watched with a keen interest and there was a sizzle of anticipation in the atmosphere.

How long before someone showed up with the popcorn?

Marcella had backed up against the fountain, her hand upon her chest—Cassidy thought for sure that if Marcella had been wearing a string of pearls around her lying neck, she would have been clutching them, meme style. In spite of the seriousness of the situation, Cassidy felt a giggle bubble in her chest. Maybe she *had* acquired a head injury in the blast.

Cassidy licked her lips, ready for a war of words; her weapon of choice. She took one step closer. It was war she was sure she could win. "Why the hell did you try to kill me?!"

Marcella began to shake her head in denial. Her eyes moved frantically, searching for an ally or a way out; she was like a rat trapped in a corner and Cassidy was the hungry cat, claws out. Marcella murmured 'no' over and over again, repeatedly, under her breath.

"Hey!" Cassidy shouted, moving forward to snap her fingers right under Marcella's nose. Marcella's eyes popped open and the tears began to tumble down her face.

Marcella stammered; the words inaudible, barely above a whisper. She was a shell of the woman Cassidy had met when she first arrived. Absolutely pathetic.

"Speak up!!" Cassidy demanded, disgusted. The growing crowd behind them leaned forward nearly in unison and held their breath in anticipation. They appeared to be just as invested in these answers as Cassidy was.

Marcella began to sob inconsolably as, bit by bit, her voice wavering and cracking, the story tumbled out.

"They were only supposed to scare you! That's all! Just scare you! Not hurt you, I swear. I never wanted that. My goddess almighty, they were never ever supposed to try and kill you! What did they do?!"

"They?" Cassidy breathed menacingly.

"I... I can't... No."

"Oh you can, and you bloody well will."

Marcella once again dissolved into tears. "Cassidy, I cannot apologize enough to you... "

"You can take your apologies and jam them up your..." Cassidy took a deep breath. "Who are *they*?" she repeated.

Marcella clammed up and shook her head.

Miss Ginny stepped forward from a throng of people standing outside the library. Cassidy hadn't even noticed her there; she was so blind with rage she might not have noticed anyone.

"Marcella! What is going on here?!"

Marcella glanced at Miss Ginny, their gaze met. Marcella took a deep shuddering breath and finally nodded her head. Out of nowhere someone handed her a handkerchief. She blew her nose loudly. Her red-rimmed eyes met Cassidy's fiery expression. Finally, beaten at a game she should never have tried to play, she spoke.

"They were only supposed to scare you. The security

team that was hired to protect the agency, to keep strangers away, to discourage snooping from the people who work there. They were *never* meant to harm you!"

"And what about Everlee and Ella? Were *they* supposed to just *scare* them as well?! *They* blew up a house!"

"No! No! They were never missing to begin with!"

Cassidy flinched in shock. "What did you say?!"

"It was all a ruse. A lie to get you to leave. It was the only way I could think of to get you away from here. I am so sorry."

"Where are they? Have you put them in your Hut?" Cassidy spat, making no attempt to hide her disgust.

"No! I swear, they are safe. And no, before you ask, they were not in on this deception at all. Ella would never have consented to that. She has taken a very real liking to you," Marcella finished sadly, lowering her head, her voice thick with suppressed tears and emotion; she was defeated.

Cassidy ran her grubby hands through her hair. It was a tangled mess, sticky with half congealed blood at the back. She probably needed stitches. She would worry about that later… once this place was in her rear view mirror.

"Why?" The question came out softly. There was no malice now, just a need to know. Cassidy was tired. So very, very tired. The fight had gone out of her now that she knew that Ella and Everlee were safe.

Marcella sniffled. "You would *not* have stayed, I could see that—and we really did want you to! But we knew what would have happened once you left here. In all good conscience I could *not* let you do that to us. We needed to scare you away somehow. Sacrifices had to be made for the greater good."

The portal. Marcella knew that if Cassidy had decided not to stay, if she had left Lotus Lorea for good, the portal would have had to be destroyed. Somehow, she knew the drill.

Cassidy felt a burning sense of betrayal; a twinge of humiliation and the paralysing rush of guilt. Because that is exactly what would have happened.

As she felt her legs crumple beneath her, her last coherent thoughts were disappointment commingled with sadness for all that could have been and all that would never be.

CHAPTER ELEVEN

A cup of strong, sweet *jaroot* with what appeared to be quite a liberal dash of rice milk sat waiting for Cassidy on the small table in her room. Beside that, on a tray, a thick slice of almond cake similar to Norwegian Kransekake; generous morsels of sharp goat's milk cheddar, and a bowl of large luscious blueberries lightly drizzled with lavender honey.

Cassidy wanted to partake of the lavish spread before her but her heart just wasn't in it; neither was her stomach. It was almost as though she felt nothing at all, a weird muted non-feeling that was entirely unique to anything she had ever experienced before.

She had returned after a short walk and had been left here alone simply because she had asked to be, really *had* wanted to be alone, but when a knock came to the door presently, she sprung quickly to her feet, eager to see what she hoped would be a friendly face. She cringed at the insistent pain at the back of her head, the wound having not quite healed, and the agonizing twinge of her still stiff and sore muscles, her aching joints.

"Come in!"

A head peeked around the door. It was Ella. Of course it was.

"Hello," she offered tentatively, flashing a shy grin.

"Hello."

Ella's concerned gaze brushed over the untouched food, Cassidy's defeated demeanour. She quickly took stock of the myriad of cuts, bruises and abrasions on every visible inch of Cassidy—her imagination filled in the injuries she could not see. Ella shook her head at the stubbornness of her new friend.

"You should at least drink your *jaroot* today, Cassidy. I made it myself, especially for you. I think you will feel a whole lot better afterwards." She smiled teasingly, winked, and backed out of the room. "I'll check on you in the morning. Bright and early as usual okay?"

Cassidy nodded. And after the door was closed behind Ella, Cassidy finally gave in and drank the *jaroot*.

Then she ate the cake and the cheese and the berries—devoured it with relish. Belly full, she returned to the bed, lying back on the feather down pillow, luxuriating in the relief as the stiffness seeped from her weary, bruised and battered body; there really was no greater feeling than the cessation of pain.

In repose, her mind wandered and ruminated over her exploits of the last little while. And the final confrontation with Marcella.

Cassidy had not returned to her room at The Doors. Once she had recovered well enough to leave the infirmary she had been made welcome at the home of Ella and Everlee. She was comfortable there as she recuperated, having been kept company by their elderly grandmother

Diana and a younger cousin, Melody.

Marcella, her lesson learned, had stepped down from her tutelary role. A decision would be made later, once the community came to terms with what had happened, on who would take her place. Her last instruction had been to order a decommissioning of The Hut, a place of punishment that had been largely kept secret from the population of Lotus Lorea, save for those who had been disciplined by being locked inside.

At least some good had come out of it all.

Everlee, who had since recovered from the birth (something she still refused to speak of) had applied to the vocational school, hoping to be educated in the field of midwifery. She wanted a better experience for the other women who gave birth on Lotus Lorea. That was something that would never change. It was an integral part of who they were.

Ella found herself thinking that she might eventually train to become a nurse. Between caring for her grandmother, Everlee, *and* Cassidy, she had learned it was something she enjoyed and had a flair for—helping people, making them well again. The book that Cassidy had been reading in the library on tinctures, poultices and herbal remedies had been checked out so many times that Miss Ginny finally told Ella she could just keep it.

Miss Ginny. She was a mystery, that one. And Cassidy supposed that some mysteries were better left unsolved. Cassidy had some ideas, naturally, but decided to keep the conjecture to herself.

Cassidy flashed back to the day she'd stumbled upon the secret of The Lotus Fountain. How it was such a strange coincident that Ella had happened to be in the right place, at the right time, right there outside the library, directing Cassidy along the right path. Suddenly, something finally clicked in her head, two and two came together at last in an explosive revelation and Cassidy's eyes popped open with a start. Ella. The dark hair. The heart shaped face. Those impossible lashes. A wave of sadness rocked her to her core. *Oh dear god no. That poor girl.*

Then, as the *jaroot* worked its magic, a pleasant drowsiness overcame her and, though she fought it, she finally succumbed to the oblivion of sleep.

***

She left while everyone else was still in bed. She was not the sort of person who was very good with goodbyes and she did not want to delay the inevitable now that she had made her final decision. A note for Ella was left behind, on the bed next to the pillow where Cassidy was sure that her friend would find it when she came looking for her in early hours of morning. It was so much better, much easier this way. For everyone involved. Cassidy felt the vestiges of regret but pushed them deep down inside as she snuck out of the house and into the silken embrace of night.

Dear Ella,

You are such a strong person. Thank you for everything; for taking care of me while I recuperated, but most of all, I want to thank you for being a friend. I know now that despite everything, I belong in my own world and it is time for me to go back there now. Come to the stone steps at the base of the cliff. Come alone. There will be something waiting there for you. Keep it to yourself. It is the only way I can think to repay you.

C.

A sullen moon gave very little in the way of light as Cassidy's battered boots scuffed along the cobbled stone path that would lead her to the cliff side and, eventually, to the portal. She would go back to her own world with its trials and tribulations and perfect imperfections because, even with all its faults, it was still *home*.

The building that occupied The Rising Son Adoption Agency was dark and quiet save for the drone of machines and the light of computer screens left running with their screensavers dipping and swirling, as Cassidy arrived back Earth side. It was evening here—the fluidity of time, the flip flop of day and night between here and there threw her off balance every single time, her body and mind struggling to adjust to the fluctuations. She punched in the lock code and when the mechanism clicked, she exited the room, her shoulders set, a sense of purpose to her step. The door swung shut behind her. She strolled down the hallway and made her way to the office she had entered on that very first night.

The door was locked.

"Goddammit all!" she muttered under her breath.

There was no keypad with which she could gain entry but Cassidy was as determined as she ever had been. She refused to let a flimsy little lock like that stop her. She put everything she had left into it, all the pent up anger and emotion, and with one swift, well aimed kick near the doorknob, the wood panel door splintered and Cassidy shouldered her way in through, booting detritus and debris out of the way as she entered the room. She flipped the light switch and headed straight for the desk, not even remotely concerned about the silent alarm or anyone who might notice her presence.

The inbox that sat atop the heavily polished workspace was neat and orderly: only one file sat askew, like it had been tossed there at the end of the day, when it's owner had decided enough was enough and a glass of wine at home sounded better than pigeonholing this last tedious bit business.

Cassidy figured that was the sort of thing that happened when your carefully laid plans suddenly went awry. She grinned a little, taking full credit for the upheaval her presence had caused.

The filing cabinets were not locked. Cassidy browsed leisurely through the files in each drawer; they were conveniently alphabetized so It did not take long before she had found what she was looking for. There it was, filed under *R* for his adoptive parent's surname.

She stared at the tan coloured folder in her hands for a moment before she took a deep breath and, nodding her head, for she know in her heart what she was doing was right, she opened it. Pinned to the inside flap with a bright blue paperclip was exactly what she had been looking for. *Those impossible lashes.* She slipped it out from beneath its confines and replaced the folder back into its slot. She flopped into the ergonomic office chair and began to methodically search through the desk drawers until she found the item she sought. A simple envelope, a simple inclusion; it felt heavy in her hands. Sealing the picture inside, she grabbed a sharpie and scrawled *Ella – He IS Loved* across the front in her bold cursive script.

This one last time she would go through the portal. One last time would she set foot on Lotus Lorea; a brief excursion to repay a kindness, to try and somehow right a wrong when her options were limited. It was the only way she knew how.

Errand completed, Cassidy stood in front of the portal entrance, wracked with indecision. The fine hairs at the back of her neck and on her arms were raised in response to the thrum of the portal. Even now, she could feel it, the inexplicable pull of its siren song.

It would not take much to put an end to it all. There weren't any people in the building right now. If she took it down, the destruction could easily be linked to the earlier explosion on Fraser Place. Random acts of violence that were becoming more and more common these days. Some minor faction who was angry about something. There was *always* someone angry about something these days.

She could think of no other way to break the link, to cut the cord. Could she really go through with it though?

The ways of old.

The words echoed around the empty room, as though someone had spoken them out loud. Perhaps she had.

No, she would not be able to bear that burden, knowing that she would leave them with virtually no other choice. Cassidy backed out into the corridor and closed the door behind her with an air of finality. She nodded once, her decision made. And then she walked away.

There was a lightness in her step as the weight was lifted off of her shoulders. She had done what she thought was best. And there was no burden left for her to carry.

She glanced ruefully at the office door she had obliterated a short while ago. She shrugged. Collateral damage. Sorry not sorry.

As she pivoted to exit the building, a sense of whimsy overcame her. She thought, why not? If for nothing other than coming full circle, putting an end to her adventure. She stepped back in through what was left of the office door, chuckling to herself as she kicked her way through the debris. She slid open the office window and hoisted herself up to the ledge. She swung her legs around and, without so much as a backward glance, she dropped to the ground outside, landing lithely on her feet. Still in a crouch, she paused. And in a moment of uncharacteristic charity, Cassidy turned back around and shut the window behind her before she ran off in a crouch, heading towards the gap in the fence.

Taking a deep lungful of the cool evening air, Cassidy shivered as her body struggled to adjust to the change in core temperature between here and Lotus Lorea. Cassidy picked her way through the maze of fences and trees, stumbling through the darkness, tripping over rocks and exposed tree roots. She thought longingly of a hot shower and a generous pour of red; the peace and quiet of her own home.

One foot in front of the other. It kept her going.

Finally, she emerged from within the woods. She was back to where she had started; before she knew what she would come up against. She peered suspicious from behind the Carina Heights welcome sign, always on alert and—

Darn it.

Her car had been towed.

And it was a long walk home.

CHAPTER TWELVE

Back in her old bed at last, sleep had found her quickly, and so had the dream. The dream unfolded rather pleasantly at first, Cassidy was playing fetch with a Labrador Retriever, the golden dog bounding joyfully though a sweet-smelling meadow in agile pursuit of a bright yellow tennis ball. The grass was tall, fragrant and a beautiful emerald green, still damp with morning dew. The sun was shining brightly and Cassidy had to use a hand to shield her eyes. In the distance, a red and white checkered picnic blanket had been spread out on the ground and Cassidy could see sandwiches, salads, fried chicken, chips and cookies laid out, waiting to be eaten. The dog returned to her feet, dropped the ball and demanded her attention. He barked happily and waited, tail wagging, panting in anticipation.

Somehow Cassidy knew that his name was Fred.

Cassidy picked up the ball and launched it in the direction of an old oak tree; it disappeared amongst the grass, and Fred zoomed after it. His pure joy at such a simple game made Cassidy laugh, a carefree sound that echoed in the stillness of the field.

She'd definitely had worse dreams.

A low rumble of thunder drew her gaze skyward: deeply bruised Cumulonimbus clouds steamrolled towards her, bringing with them a cool, charged breeze and a whiff of rain and ozone. A thunderstorm was brewing. She looked around for an umbrella. She did not have one.

As dreams are often wont to do, time shifted swiftly and Cassidy soon found herself sitting Criss-Cross Applesauce on the picnic blanket. Fred had not returned with the ball and she whipped her head around frantically, searching for the errant pup. She couldn't lose him. Thunder rumbled overhead; the storm had moved in quickly. Cassidy looked down to find herself holding a triangle sandwich. It was ham and cheese. There was a plate on her lap filled with lush raspberries. The juice from the berries had seeped through the flimsy paper of the plate. Red stains had spread across the white linen pants she was wearing. She swiped at it ineffectively with a paper napkin.

"Would you like some lemonade, Miss Cane?"

She startled at the sound of the voice, having assumed she was alone in the dream now that Fred had gone missing. She turned towards the sound.

"Dr. Gamgee!"

"Would you like some lemonade, Miss Cane?"

For a second time he offered her an empty pitcher, his voice low and devoid of intonation or emotion; his gaze was fixed on a point somewhere above her head.

"Dr. G, are you feeling okay? There's nothing in your jug."

"Lemonade. We need to make the lemonade."

"Sure. Let me help you with that!" She tried to get up but found that her movements were sluggish, as though she were walking through a pool of thick syrup.

"We need water to make the lemonade. You have the water."

"What... I don't..."

"THE WATER!" he shouted. An intense flash of lighting ignited the sky and suddenly Gamgee was right next to her, his eyes frantic and boring straight into hers. He thrust the jug insistently into her hands.

"THE WATER MAKES THE LEMONADE AND THE LEMONADE QUENCHES OUR THIRST!"

Cassidy tried to back away from the onslaught, shaking her head in confusion and fear. *Wake up! Wake up!*

"SAVE US ALL, CASSIDY! GIVE US THE WATER! WE WILL DIE OF THIRST!"

The voices multiplied, rising in volume and ferocity, as behind Gamgee there winked into existence every single person Cassidy had ever known and loved in her life. Before her very eyes, one by one, they began to shrivel, dry up, turn to dust.

The air heavy with the ashes of her friends and family, Cassidy coughed and blinked rapidly to clear her vision. Gamgee shuffled closer towards her, his voice rasping, "Water, water!" His lower jaw slackened, widened and his eyes sunk back into his head; Gamgee reached for Cassidy imploringly, holding out the jug. Cassidy tried to back away, she closed her eyes, willing herself to just wake the hell up. She heard a dog yelp in the distance, a cry of fear and pain. Her eyes popped open and suddenly she was face to face with the nightmare Gamgee. As his fetid breath washed over her, an overwhelming odour of sickness and decomposition, a deafening explosion of thunder rocked the meadow and Cassidy exploded from her bed, breathing heavily and covered in sweat. She threw back the blankets and jumped to her feet. Stumbling to the ensuite, she accidentally knocked over the toothbrush holder and soap dispenser in her haste to grab the tumbler next to the bathroom sink. She ran the tap until cool clear water overflowed the cup and then she drank it down.

It wasn't difficult to interpret *that* dream.

Cassidy refilled the glass and, leaning against the vanity, gulped it greedily. She splashed water on her face and stood there, dripping, staring at herself in the mirror.

There was no amount of water that would be able to slake her thirst tonight.

And she was never eating pizza before bed again.

CHAPTER THIRTEEN

Cassidy marched into the office, takeout coffee cup grasped firmly in hand, the highly recognizable mermaid logo of the coffee shop emblazoned across the front. She took a nourishing slurp of the hot frothy concoction and smacked her lips in satisfaction. It was no *jaroot*, that was true, but the latte was fantastic enough in its own right. And she definitely needed all the caffeine she could get. She dropped her messenger bag on the floor of the office, next to her desk, and placed her laptop case carefully next to it. She slipped her new jacket off her shoulders and slung it on the back of her chair. She cleared a small space for the coffee cup amongst the wild disarray of her desk and sat down to mournfully regard the mess in front of her.

Where did she even start.

She dragged her dishevelled hair into a low ponytail, swiped a hand across her face, and began to rummage through the pile of paperwork and mail that had accumulated in the inbox on her desk. Though most of it would end up in the recycling bin, there was an invitation to speak at the International Conference on Archaeological

Anthropology and Human Cultural Experience in Kuala Lumpur, Malaysia that Cassidy filed away for later consideration; there was a thank you card from Annie and Ximena for the baby shower gift, and also several memos from the department head asking if she had picked a research assistant for the summer based on the student resumes he had forwarded to her. Resumes? Cassidy made a face at the stacks of files and paperwork and uncorrected term papers on her desk.

Probably under there… somewhere.

Restlessness overcame her. She pulled the elastic out of her hair and swept the locks to one side. She leaned back in her chair, clasping her coffee cup in hand as though it were a life preserver; she sipped and speculated.

Maybe it was time for her to get away for a little bit; a getaway that was a *vacation*, one she planned on her own terms where there were no tasks to complete, no ulterior motives. When was the last time she'd gone on a holiday?

Cassidy needed this destination to be a faraway place where she could get out and explore; she wanted to try new things and meet new people. Rest and relaxation was not the most important factor, so beaches were not up for consideration. Cassidy popped up from the swivel chair and grabbed a well worn map of the world from the box that sat beside her bookshelf. She smoothed it out and tacked it quickly to the wall, visualizing all the places she had travelled around the world... and around other worlds as well. There were still so many endless possibilities.

From atop a filing cabinet, Cassidy picked up a single,

brass tipped dart from amongst the trinkets and artifacts she kept there, those she had collected on her travels, things that were dear to her, that brought back fond memories of her many exploits. A cheeky grin played across her lips. She crossed the room and turned to face the map. Closing her eyes, she took a deep breath and threw the dart, aiming nowhere in particular, dreaming solely of escape. She heard a satisfying *thunk* as the sharp point buried itself deep in the dense wood of the wall. She drew closer to the map and squinted at the tiny Canadian island her dart had landed on. She sounded it out, the name rolling off her tongue: Newfoundland. The shape of its rugged coastline appealed to her. She slipped her laptop out of its case.

A quick internet search showed bright, jelly bean coloured row houses; there were zip lines excursions, world class restaurants, and incredible hiking trails. She'd already heard talk of the Viking settlements in L'Anse aux Meadows from her peers and grinned in anticipation of what she might discover there. There were breathtaking ocean views and a wild, untouched beauty. She quickly booked a flight, more excited than she had been about anything in quite some time.

A brisk knock at the door was an unwelcome intrusion as she daydreamed about her upcoming jaunt, but was not entirely unexpected at a busy university. Cassidy closed the lid of her laptop, sliding it back into its satchel. A second knock sounded before she had a chance to respond. She sighed.

"Come in."

Doctor Gamgee poked his head around the door, a

broad grin on his face. Cassidy was impressed that he had paused long enough to knock and wait this time, rather than just barge in as was his normal entrance style. It was some progress at least.

"Miss Cane. So glad to have you back with us! May I come in for a moment?" he said, already making his way through the door and into the room.

"Of course," Cassidy replied dryly.

"I trust you have, err, recuperated from your little... experience the other night?"

Cassidy had had to fabricate a story to explain, well, everything that had happened to her. There were lots of questions. Her car had still not been recovered. She'd called numerous towing companies but none had a record of her vehicle in their lots. Her missing phone, which had now been replaced, had required the distribution of a new phone number to her colleagues and friends. And then there were the injuries she'd sustained. No amount of makeup or long sleeves could hide the still healing scrapes and bruises that peppered her face and hands.

She tried to keep her story simple, Occam's razor and all that jazz. She stuck with the story she'd already set up in her text messages to Gamgee, when she had found herself searching through Carina Heights for Ella and Everlee. Wracked with insomnia and feeling a little out of sorts, she had gone for a drive. Finding herself in a part of town that was new to her, she'd made a stupid split second decision and had left her car to walk around and explore. Silly her, she had become hopelessly lost in an unfamiliar area. A stumble in the darkness explained away her injuries. She had dropped her phone and keys, had not been able to find them. People had no reason to question it, no reason to not believe her. She was, after all, stalwart and trustworthy to a fault.

Cassidy was fully aware that Gamgee knew that there was more to her story. She could tell by the way he looked at her that he was confused as to why she had not gone to him straight away to tell the whole sordid tale. But he did not press for details. For that she was grateful. Perhaps she would share it with him eventually. She just wasn't ready yet. How could she even explain all that had come to pass while she was away? There were still some things she could not even explain to herself.

She did not have a sample of the water from The Lotus Fountain to turn over to him. Cassidy suspected that, in Gamgee's mind, her mission would ultimately have to be declared a failure. How could she explain her reasoning to Doctor Gamgee? He was a man who dealt with data and cold hard facts; emotion was something that was very rarely a factor used in his rationale. Cassidy hated to disappoint people and she vowed to make it up to him if given the chance. She hoped to have the opportunity again, despite the still underlying anger over the fact that he had not been open and forthright with her about the portal at the agency to begin with.

CHAPTER FOURTEEN

She'd never actually had a need for one before but there was always a first time for everything, especially when you were Cassidy Cane.

As the bank manager left the room to allow her a modicum of privacy, as the door closed softly behind him, Cassidy eyed the safety deposit box on the table in front of her with a mixture of relief and dread. It was an entirely last resort option, but it was the best solution she could come up with in the final moments before she left Plainsfield again. Who knew when she'd be back again this time around.

She gingerly placed her messenger bag on the table next to the box, flipped it open and paused, her fingers tapping against the canvas flap. Well, there *was* one other option. She bit her lip, torn; her thoughts a jumbled jigsaw of pieces she wasn't sure she could ever put back together again. No, it had to be this way. Final decision. She simply could not bring herself to destroy something of such utter significance but she *was* determined to keep it out of the wrong hands.

The book went in first, gently. It's faded viridian cover

nearly blending in with the slate grey of the box. Next she took a small package from the depths of her bag and held it aloft with both hands so that it caught the light. She observed closely as the fluid inside the small, airtight capsule, enclosed inside a vacuum sealed bag, reflected the glare of the overhead florescent bulbs. It sure appeared innocuous enough. Cassidy smirked. She knew the difference though. Oh boy, did she ever.

It was her sample of the Lotus potion.

She placed the parcel inside the box, right next to the book, and locked it up with a decisive turn of the wrist. She slid the coffer back inside its compartment and pocketed the key. Done.

She picked up her bag, turned around and walked out the door.

She did not look back.

CHAPTER FIFTEEN

"Come quick!" Zikix yelled, his cries echoing through the hall of the solitary confinement wing of the Xik'en world penitentiary. He bellowed with such force that it seemed to kick the sawdust up from the floor. His voice was panicked but forceful -- the voice of someone in charge but faced with a new, surprising situation.

His tail flicked with agitation, twitching this way and that as he paced.

Kizix stepped into the shadowed dark of the hall, holding the low ceiling with one hand as he bent and peered in. Kizix was taller than most Xik'en by a foot and a half, and often had to watch his head in this way. He waited for his serpentine eyes to adjust to the light, his scaled skin twitching.

The hallway before Kizix was narrow, with cells on either side. There was a single light hanging from overhead casting strange, oblong shadows on the walls all around.

"What is it?" Kizix called, straightening the collar of his guard uniform. It wasn't made for a Xik'en of his size and was always too tight.

"It's the warm-blood!" Zikix yelled in return. "It's not

breathing!" Before Kizix even had a chance to respond again, Zikix took out his emergency key card and pushed it against the reader of the warm-blood prisoner -- named Tallis' -- cell. A red light turned on in the hall behind Kizix.

Tallis was passed out, face down in the sawdust, which was stuck in his black, shoulder-length hair, and sprawled out, his limbs looking like spider-legs. He was dressed in the same black shirt and jeans he'd worn the day he was brought in, now soiled with mammal stench. The sawdust was everywhere, and Zikix was instantly worried that he'd had a seizure. He grabbed Tallis by the shoulders and pulled him over onto his back. His lips had begun to turn blue.

Kizix ran down the hall, stopping briefly at a hand washing station in the center of the hall and scrubbing. He picked up a portable light from a dispensary beneath and flicked it on, its bright rectangle shimmering out as he made his way towards the action. He lowered it when Zikix held up his hand to block his eyes.

Zikix motioned Kizix to look at the lips. "They're not supposed to do that, are they?"

Kizix shook his head. "No, they aren't." He paused. "Do you know warm-blood CPR?" He got down next to Tallis and placed his head on his chest.

"No I don't know warm-blood CPR! Why would I know that?"

"There's supposed to be someone on every shift that knows it!"

"Take it up with scheduling!" Zikix snapped. "What are you doing?"

"The heartbeat is strong." He placed two hands over Tallis' solar plexus. "I'll push. I think this is where its lungs are. You breathe into it?"

"You expect me to touch its mouth?"

"Just do it!"

Zikix sighed and bent down, hovering over the strange shape that was the mammal's breathing orifice, and mentally prepared himself to place his own over it.

Kizix pushed down on Tallis' chest.

At once, a small, thin stress ball flew up from his mouth and struck Zikix in the eye!

"Aah!" Zikix screamed, the shock affecting him more than the impact. He splayed back from it, wiping the saliva from his eye.

Kizix's head snapped around to Tallis, just in time for Tallis to bring up his fist and knock him to the ground.

Tallis coughed, struggling to his feet. He found his stress ball in the hay, picked it up, then took the keycard from Kizix. He then turned to Zikix and held out his hand. "I'll take your Branch."

Zikix stared at Tallis for a long moment, his mouth twisted in a sneer. Reluctantly, he reached up and removed the Branch of Languages from the side of his face and held it out to Tallis.

The golden nanotech wires cradling slivers of green Vao stones shimmered, reflecting in Tallis' hungry eyes. He took it and placed it along the left side of his face, whereas Zikix had worn it on the right. He felt it become alive. Moving like a snake, it slipped along Tallis' jawline, its peak disappearing into the hair above his left ear. A comfortable warmth replaced the tingle it had started with.

"Thank you," Tallis said with an all-too-polite tone, turning and leaving his cell and shutting the door behind him.

Zikix could only watch as he went, up the stairs and into the main area of the prison. Soon after, alarms sounded.

PLAGUE OF THE DREAMLESS

JENNIFER SHELBY & JD RYOT

CHAPTER ONE

Cassidy lowered her voice to a desperate whisper, her knuckles whitening around her phone. "I'm getting cabin fever in here, Gamgee. It's just a cold."

"I understand your frustration, but I can't have you diving into potentially dangerous worlds if your reflexes are down. Admit it, you feel sluggish."

Cassidy refused to admit it, but she also knew her silence said as much. "At least send me a chaperone so I can go get some cold meds."

"I'll have cold medications sent to your hotel room. I'm not going to unleash an adrenaline junkie like Cassidy Cane into a country as restrictive as Saudi Arabia and hope for the best," said Gamgee. "Jubail isn't a tourist city like Dubai and you aren't a member of a respected archaeological team this trip. I don't mind paying bribes and pulling strings to get you out of a mess, but I'm sure as heck not rich enough to send you out there when you're already on the defensive. You've got to play by the rules in this country if you want to make it to the portal; any arrests and the owners will revoke their permission for you to visit their refinery. I had to throw a lot of dollar signs their way to get you that."

Cassidy didn't like it, but she knew he was right. "Fine."

"When you're feeling better, call the number I gave you. They'll arrange a chaperone to escort you from the hotel to the refinery portal. You have your abaya?"

"Yes." Cassidy glanced at the black polyester gown and head covering hanging over a chair in the hotel room. Local women were required to wear the gowns by law, but it would also serve Cassidy well sneaking through the refinery in the dark to find the portal.

"Good. Don't forget to stash it somewhere safe when you get to the other side of the portal. You'll need to be wearing it when you return. And Cassidy?"

"Yes?"

"I know it doesn't feel right, but for god's sake don't tell off any men while you're there."

Cassidy hung up and tossed her phone onto a nearby chair. It bounced half-heartedly and fell onto the thick carpet. Her sprawling hotel room was papered in a pearlescent Arabian design, the bed swimming in endless pillows. The massive jacuzzi tub was a wonder of bubbles and excess, but after two days of being cooped up with a cold and nothing but the WIFI to distract her, she was itching for something to happen. Anything to get her pulse going.

At last a knock sounded at her door. It must be the cold meds from Gamgee. Cassidy bounded to the door, reaching for the handle. She hesitated, glancing back to the abaya laid across the chair. She should put it on, and had put it on, albeit resentfully, when she accepted her room service meals, but darn it she needed a thrill, even a tiny one. She flung the door open, baring her face and hair to the world.

No one was there to see it. A small paper sack sat on the floor.

Cassidy sighed and snatched it up, closing the door behind her.

An hour later the cold medication cleared the lingering fog of her cold symptoms, but feeling better did little to settle her restlessness. She paced the room, resenting the way her toes sank deep into the luxurious carpet and how it muffled her furious stomps.

Enough of this nonsense. She felt fine. It was time to get to work. She dialled the number Gamgee had given her. A male voice greeted her. "This is Cassidy Cane," she said.

After a pause the voice told her, in English, "Put on the abaya. We'll be there in five minutes."

Cassidy grinned, shoving a few extra cold pills into her pocket just in case, and pulled her long, red hair into a ponytail.

***

Even in darkness the heat of the desert country was stifling, made a hundred times worse buried in swaths of black polyester. Cassidy peered over to the older woman acting as her chaperone. She seemed friendly enough, but had said nothing during the whole of the lengthy car ride. Neither had the driver. It was disconcerting, but Cassidy supposed that neither of them had any regular need to speak English and her broken Arabic did little to inspire lengthy conversation.

Cassidy turned her attention to the strange world coming into view beyond the car windows. A forest of tangled pipes crowded the horizon, broken only by the barrel-like squat of oil reservoirs. Here and there flare stacks belched a burst of flames into the sky. Strange to realize she hadn't left her home world yet.

Cassidy squinted at the map on her phone, a quick schematic of a single refinery marked with an arrow to indicate the position of a portal. It opened on the north side of a large silo, though where on that north side would be up to her to find. Gamgee had arranged for the security lights to be off until Cassidy completed her work, and swathed in the black abaya she should be able to travel unseen into the portal. Getting home would be another matter, but the uncertainty added to Cassidy's fun. Gosh, it was good to be free of that blasted hotel room.

The driver turned off the highway, pulling into the pipe forest. Far in the distance, the reservoirs sat, a scrawl of Arabic she couldn't read delineating one tank from another. Her driver appeared to know the area well, navigating with ease through the maze of repetitive structures.

The car stopped beside a reservoir painted white with a gold strip along the top. Cassidy's driver turned in his seat and nodded to her.

She opened the car door with a quickening pulse and tucked her phone securely into the pocket of the pants she wore beneath her abaya. Slinking into the shadows, she jogged to the reservoir. The structures were much bigger than they appeared from afar. She estimated this one to be at least six stories high and twice as wide around.

She circled the round structure, hunting for the telltale signs of a portal, usually revealed by a shimmer of light, but found nothing. On the north side of the structure there was nothing but darkness and a maintenance ladder. "Nowhere to go but up," Cassidy said to herself, leaping past the locked entry rungs and scrambling upward. The abaya tangled around her feet, tripping her up. Cassidy cursed and considered chucking the thing, but thought better of it. She'd need it to get home, after all. Instead, she pulled it up with one hand and tucked it into the waistband of her pants as best she could.

Six stories should have been an easy climb for her fitness level, but halfway up Cassidy felt sluggish, a slight stuffiness returning to her sinuses. Maybe she should have waited another day. No, dang it, she felt like a bird flapping against its cage, empty of every thought but her desperate need to escape.

She caught her breath and steadied herself on the ladder. Bursts of flames flashed in the distance, and something else, something white, flickered in the air just below her feet. Cassidy focused on the familiar light: the portal.

The portal was positioned a meter out, on the far side of the safety cage surrounding the ladder, and still some three stories high. Cassidy whistled.

It was quick work to climb down and back up along the outside of the cage. The heat pressed down on her, but she trusted her body to take her where she needed to be. She calculated the distance she would need to jump, climbing above the portal to give herself the right trajectory.

Gamgee would disapprove. He'd want her to check the portal, not dive headfirst into the unknown, but she had no tools on her person and she'd be damned if she was going to go back to that hotel room to await whatever Gamgee could scrounge up at the last minute.

Besides, her pulse was climbing already. She needed this. Her abaya and the darkness hid the wide grin splashed across her face, but her loud whoop echoed through the forest of pipes and reverberated against the reservoir walls as she leapt from the ladder and disappeared into the portal.

CHAPTER TWO

Cassidy exhaled slowly as the portal enveloped her body. A sensation of pressure weighed upon her skin. Holding her breath, she opened her eyes to a purple light. A group of burgundy, tentacled creatures the size of a tall building hung in the air. Whether they were giant squid, octopus, jellyfish, or all three, Cassidy couldn't say, though they were definitely some sort of cephalopod. The creatures stared at her with quiet power, their dark, oval pupils milky in the strange light. Cassidy forced herself to look away, dizzied and uncertain if it was the lack of oxygen or something else.

The nearest cephalopod reached out a tentacle lined with suction cups and flexing with lean muscle. Cassidy tried not to gag as it poked inside her mouth, prodding gently down her throat. The tentacle tasted of salt, a strange tingle leaving her mouth momentarily numb. She fought against the instinct to bite down, hoping the creature meant her no harm.

The tingling ceased when the beast removed its tentacle and probed inside her ears instead. Cassidy struggled to hide her annoyance. Were these cephalopods simply curious wild animals or sentient beasts who roamed a liminal space between dimensions? Either way, she'd soon need air ...getting lightheaded; and what did they want, anyway?

A deep fatigue overwhelmed her senses; she'd black out soon. The cephalopods blinked in unison and Cassidy slipped out of the portal.

A sweet burst of oxygen filled her lungs, air whooshing over her skin. Oh crap. She was falling. Cassidy flailed her arms, strange half-glimpses of patchwork skyscrapers and orange vapour filtering past the rush of adrenaline that left her giddy with misplaced glee.

Something scraped at her elbow and slammed into her armpit, jarring her shoulder joint and collar bone but giving her something to cling to. She ignored the pain, wrapping her legs up and around the pipe that caught her. Once secure, she gritted her teeth and, wincing, reached up to a smaller pipe sticking out of the brick to test her shoulder. Sore, but nothing broken or dislocated.

Sitting atop the pipe, she took a proper look at the world she'd entered. Jagged high-rises filled an industrial skyline. Floors the size of warehouses sat stacked on top of each other, chimneys and exhaust pipes sticking out along the sides, puffing orange smoke into the air. The horizon lay cloaked in rust-coloured clouds, the day a perpetual sunset. The air smelled of salt, yet acrid with old grease. Below her, several stories down, the orange smog gave way to a purple mist that hovered above the streets.

Cassidy peered to her right, sucking in her breath to see one of the cephalopods from the portal hanging in midair. In this light, she could make out flecks of burgundy along the soft milky flesh beneath the tentacles, bruising to a dark purple at the tips. She dared not meet the creature's eyes as it stared at her a long moment before closing its eyelids slowly, its body never moving.

"What are you?" Cassidy whispered to herself. She counted seven uneven stories in the building behind it. The cephalopods couldn't have made the buildings, she realized. The common architecture suggested the skyscrapers were the work of fellow humanoids. Did the two live in unison?

Cassidy shrugged off her questions. She needed to find a way off this perch. The portal shimmered above her, but she could see enough space to squeeze past, clinging to the building, if she could find handholds in the brick.

Brick struck her as an odd choice for a high-rise and odder still, each story in the buildings she could see were all built different from the last, as if every floor was unplanned. How could the original foundation support so many afterthoughts? Yet there they stood, reaching into the sky between sleeping sea monsters.

She refocused on the climb ahead. The mortar had crumbled in places, providing hand holds she could take advantage of, and an open window pushed out some ten meters above her perch, past the portal.

Heaving herself around to face the building, the pipe beneath her shifted, likely broken when it caught her. Cassidy hurried to her feet, pressing her body against the wall as she searched for toeholds to relieve the pipe. Her sturdy boots weren't the best footwear for such a task, but the sole at her toe fit snugly into the depression of mortar between the layers of brick. The abaya flapped in the wind around her like a misbehaved shadow, catching on bricks and pipes. Cassidy climbed steadily, holds revealing themselves as she got close to them.

Hot desert air breathed on her skin as she moved past the portal. It wasn't going to be easy getting home, three storeys in the air off an oil reservoir, but there was plenty of time to worry about that later.

She clutched the frame of the open window with her sore shoulder, aching in earnest now, and slipped inside as the first voices of this world reached her ears. Her hands slapped at the cool concrete floor and she somersaulted behind a long stack of palettes.

Cassidy pulled off the abaya and stuffed it into a palette for safekeeping. She strained to listen to what was being said across the room, squinting through the crates to see the speakers better. Their shape suggested humanoids, as she'd suspected. They had gathered near a rectangular machine the size of a minivan.

"Line up here. No talking," said a man in an officer-like uniform, his hand on a weapon he wore on his waist. Probably a handgun or a Taser, given the shape. His use of English irked Cassidy. She didn't expect to find another world which spoke English. That seemed extremely unlikely. Her stomach knotted. Something wasn't right.

Cassidy scowled at the group of people. She didn't like the way they were positioned, either. A handful of youth openly wept while the armed guards looked on, their expressions suggesting annoyance.

The lights overhead cut out and a large television screen flickered to life. A middle to late-aged man, his hair white and tidy, facial hair trimmed just so, gazed out at the room with practiced confidence. He smiled, his unnaturally perfect teeth flashing. "Happy birthday to the newest employee-citizens of Factorytown! I'm Bryce Bezanson, CEO of the Amazing Company and owner of Factorytown. Science has proven again and again that sixteen is the safest and most effective age to extract your imaginations, and today you have come of age. Congratulations!"

"What in the actual heck," murmured Cassidy. She took advantage of the televised distraction to creep closer to the group of huddled teenagers. A boy in a grey jacket turned to look her way, furrowing his brow. He was just a kid, large brown eyes, his face still smooth and feminine, dark hair tumbling across his features.

"By removing your imaginations, all employee-citizens of Factorytown are guaranteed to lead happy and productive lives without the dangerous and criminal distraction of daydreams. Rest assured, your imaginations will be put to good use: fed to the visionary engineers who will use them to create more and more of the Amazing Company's trademark transcendental technologies."

Cassidy cocked an ear. Gamgee would be interested in that kind of tech. This trip might be quicker than she thought.

Bezanson's lips stretched into a thin line, speaking through clenched teeth. "Let me remind you that Factorytown is the wholly owned subsidiary of the Amazing Company and any citizens living without compliance to Company Policy will be removed with extreme prejudice. Safety must be upheld."

The film skipped, Bezanson's position to the camera

shifting to the left. His anger was gone, replaced by the same calculated composure as before. "Since implementing mandatory imagination extractions, workplace accidents have become non-existent, productivity has never been higher, and citizens' quality of life has skyrocketed."

"Liar," said grey-jacket boy, scowling at the screen. One of the officers pulled out a small club and pushed the boy to the front of the line.

Bezanson flashed a smug smile. "With your new, enhanced brains, you will be able to focus completely on the task at hand. Congratulations! You are about to become full-fledged staff members of the Amazing Company. Please approach the Imagination Extraction Device and complete your journey into your career!"

A woman in a pair of blue coveralls pulled a lever and the van-sized metal box, presumably the Imagination Extraction Device, groaned and creaked as the gears hidden behind its metal frame began to turn. "Him first, Rika." One of the officers shoved the boy in grey forward, forcing him toward a ragged chair made tiny by the machine looming around it. Strips of silver tape strained to hold the worn vinyl seat together while thick restraint braces protruded from the arms and legs of the chair. The boy paled as the officer shoved him into it. Rika, the lady in coveralls, fastened a belt brace about the boy's neck while the officers did the same to his hands and feet.

Rika squeezed the boy's hand once and pulled a branched dome down over the boy's head. She flicked a switch and the neural interface lit up as it hugged his skull. Thin yellow tubing ran from the electrodes of the interface to the belly of the machine.

Cassidy struggled with her conscience. She was here to steal tech, not save the world, but she could see the silver sheen of reflected light where the boy's silent tears tracked down his cheeks, disappearing into restraints that had probably absorbed far too many tears already. He hadn't consented to giving up his imagination: that Bezanson fellow had removed all choice from the matter with his 'mandatory compliance' nonsense.

Cassidy's mind made itself up. All eyes were on the boy, drinking in his terror. She took the chance and bounded up to the rear of the machine.

The welds, though crude, were strong along the box's edges. The only weakness Cassidy could see was an access panel the size of a small door with an intimidatingly large padlock barring any further exploration.

Thin, steel tubing ran from the IED to the exterior wall, a gash in the metal revealing a softer tube protected within, filled with a purple fog like she'd seen on the streets below. Cassidy prodded her fingers into the gash and pinched the soft tube closed. The tube jumped and swelled like she'd cut off suction. She saw nothing else connected to the machine; could this be its power supply? Cassidy tugged a length from its protective sheath and tied a quick knot in the tubing.

The IED coughed and wheezed, the knot she'd tied lifting off the floor as it fought for breath or fuel. A long creak sounded from within the metal box, followed by a zinging bang.

There was a small moment of nothing, and then smoke poured out around the access panel. The building's fire alarm went off without hesitation.

The guards and youth on the far side of the machine ran for the exits as the sprinkler systems spat a half-hearted burst of grimy water and fell silent.

Cassidy dashed for the boy still strapped to the extraction device, surprised to find Rika still there, undoing the boy's restraints. "Stay still till I get you out, Merrick," she told the boy. The interface over Merrick's head was still lit up, his eyes wide with fear as smoke slowly filled the room. Cassidy tackled the leg restraints while Rika switched off the buttons on the interface.

He remained still until Rika lifted the halo, then he leapt from the ragged seat and cast a grimace towards the extraction device. Cassidy met his eye and gave him a lopsided grin.

"Run, you idiots!" hissed Rika.

CHAPTER THREE

Merrick grabbed Cassidy's arm, pulling her along as he dashed towards a dark hole in the wall opposite the one she'd come in from. "Trust me, this is the best way out," he told her when she stopped cold. He released her hand and launched himself, feet first, into the tunnel.

Cassidy hesitated, but the steady stomp of footfalls behind her sent her sliding down behind him. The chute twisted and looped, its bottom uneven. Someone far above shouted, the sound bouncing off the dark chute in unison with her body until it deposited her atop a lumpy pile of blue coveralls.

"Grab a pair and come on," said Merrick, his hair falling across his frightened face.

"Who are we running from?" asked Cassidy, reaching for the coveralls.

He threw a pair over his shoulder. "Compliance Officers."

Cassidy followed him down an alley, wisps of purple fog swirling in their wake. The streets were cobblestone and slippery with a mildewed, perpetual damp, the sun long blocked from reaching the ground. The only living

thing Cassidy saw was a few sprigs of orange lichen clinging to the cobbles.

The boy led her through a maze of alleyways and
crumbling ground floors propped up by joists and stacks
of rotten brick. Most of these lower levels were abandoned
for the churning, thumping upper factories. The machines
towering overhead vibrated through the foundation,
small showers of dust and debris falling at regular inter-
vals. Here and there someone crouched or slept within the
dim light of these dubious shelters.

Cassidy struggled to take note of the route they were
taking, as she'd need to find the portal home later, but the
boy dodged through the city with the ease of the familiar
and everything was new to her. Shouts from behind let
her know that someone—had he called them Compliance
Officers?—were still in pursuit.

Cassidy and Merrick ran up a flight of stairs, the bright
lights and industrial rhythm of a working factory blasting
through her senses. Cassidy's adrenaline spiked with a
dizzying euphoria and her thoughts narrowed into strict
details. The tingling scent of the steaming dye vats. The
thump of a loom shuttle. The whir of unspooling thread.
A door slamming behind them. Another shout, running.
The smash of her own footsteps against a metal walkway.
Endless rows of rattling sewing machines spewing out below, workers dressed in the same blue uniform she held
tight against her chest.

The boy ran on, never pausing, though in the foul air
Cassidy's lungs ached. A row of doors appeared ahead,
Merrick peering back at their pursuers before clutching
her hand and pulling her through an opened one.

"Quickly, put the covvies on." He zipped his pair over his clothes. "I'm Merrick," he added, shuffling to a second door on the other side of the closet. He cracked it open, filling the space with light.

"Cassidy."

"Thanks for saving me back there, Cassidy." He pointed to a group of similarly coveralled employees milling around an open break room. "They're heading back to work. If we slip into the group as they go by, we might be able to sneak off this floor without the officers seeing us."

"Okay," Cassidy agreed. "And what exactly happens if they do catch us?"

"They'll turn you over to the Dreamkeeper." He said the word as if it filled him with dread.

He signalled for her to come closer and they slipped into the workers' midst. The employees eyed them with curiosity but said nothing.

Below, the officers from the imagination extraction made their way between the sewing machines. One of the officers looked Cassidy's way, but they didn't recognize her. Cassidy doubted they'd seen much of her at all. Merrick, on the other hand... "What about you? Are they after you, too?"

"I'm not sure," he answered, eyeing the officers himself. "I don't think they saw me leave. If they think my extraction was completed, they won't be interested in me at all."

"Did they complete the extraction?"

"Nope, thanks to you." Merrick grinned, a wide, happy thing. "Where did you come from? You just appeared."

Cassidy shrugged. "A few towns over."

"Shippingsburg?"

"Um, yeah." The moment the words left her mouth, she regretted them.

"It is true that the Underground there has access to dream dust?" His eyes were serious, intent. This meant something to him.

Cassidy swallowed. The employees had quieted their chatter, listening for her answer. Lying had been a bad idea, but the truth wasn't much better. "Maybe. Why?"

"I've got an aunt in the last stages of the plague. If you know of any way I could get dream dust to save her, it would mean a lot."

Plague? A sweat prickled at Cassidy's underarms. What had she just walked into? The factory workers glanced over to her, openly hopeful. "I'm sorry. I'd help if I could, but I don't know."

The air hung heavier than it had before. Merrick's brow creased as the group reached the factory floor and splintered. Cassidy and Merrick moved through an exterior door that opened to a fire escape winding downward, a bulge in the walls of the first floor obvious from their vantage point. Cassidy shuddered. The entire high-rise should have collapsed a long time ago.

On the ground in the now-familiar mist, Cassidy tried to get her bearings, but the city was a hopeless jumble: buildings built haphazard and without any real streets she could make out. She felt a pang of longing for a tree.

Sneaking down another alley, the sky suddenly opened to reveal a cephalopod. Cassidy held back, staring, waiting for it to open its eyes. "What are those things?" she asked.

Merrick followed her gaze. "What, the Engineer? You don't have Engineers in Shippingsburg?"

Cassidy sighed. "I'm sorry, I'm not from Shippingsburg. I shouldn't have lied to you, but it's not easy to explain. Can we just say I'm visiting from afar and leave it at that?"

"For the lady who rescued me from extraction? Absolutely. You get a free pass for life." He gave her a silly wink. "Come on, there's a broken 'scraper up ahead, we'll be safe there. Compliance Officers don't like going inside."

This time he led her toward a high-rise leaning at a severe angle, held up by grace of the two buildings that stopped its fall. The chimneys and exhausts pipes lay idle, it's factories long since abandoned.

To her horror, Merrick scrambled up the leaning building. "Merrick, that isn't safe." She could risk her life, fine, but she didn't like the idea of this kid risking his, not for her.

He winked at her. "Scared?"

"Kid, if you only knew the stuff I've done."

"It's safe. The Engineers keep it from falling."

"Those cephalopods?"

"Yeah." He gestured farther up the building. "There used to be a cannery up there years ago, when I was a kid. We can find something to eat."

"Don't you have a home, a family, someone who makes you dinner?"

His posture sagged as he shook his head. "The plague got them a year ago. Dad didn't last long after Mom died.

They arranged for me to stay with my aunt, but she's..."

"She's the one you mentioned earlier, the one in the last stages of plague." Cassidy studied his face for signs of grief, but youthful skin didn't tell the same stories as older folks.

"That's right." His expression darkened for a moment before he forced a weak smile. "Now come on, it'll be dark soon and I'm hungry."

The orange sky had dimmed some, though Cassidy doubted the night in this industrial place would be much darker than Jubail had been under its myriad of security lights. She climbed the building, the angle steep enough to be challenging and the strange perspective of walking up the side of a Leaning Skyscraper of Pisa worth making a memory of. Insta-worthy, even. She chuckled to herself, working hard to climb steadily, imagining Gamgee's re-action to posting her inter-dimensional exploits on Insta-gram. When Merrick wasn't looking, she pulled the phone Gamgee gave her from inside her coveralls and snapped a few quick shots. Of course, she'd never post them any-where, she just wanted the small thrill of rebellion and its accompanying endorphins.

CHAPTER FOUR

Some dozen storeys later, Merrick slid open a window and showed Cassidy a rope attached to the frame they could climb down. Street kids could be counted on to know all the best places, no matter what dimension you were in, she supposed, wishing she could do more for him.

"If your extraction was successful, would you have a job in the factories?" Cassidy asked him.

"Yeah. I may still, if they think it worked. I'll check in tomorrow and see if I have an assignment."

She waited while he climbed down the rope and found his footing below. "And once you have a job, you'll be able to find a place to live?"

He blew on his hands, hot from friction, and kicked at the debris at his feet. "All workers get assigned barracks and food cards."

"Bezanson provides everything?" Cassidy asked, descending slowly and wishing for a pair of gloves as the rope seared her palms and the ache in her shoulder reawakened.

Merrick dug out a few unlabelled cans from a tangle

of broken crates and tucked them into the pockets of his coveralls. "They don't provide dreams," he muttered, anger in his voice.

Cassidy fished out a can of her own. "Provide for the body, not the mind."

"The companies make it seem like a good thing—the shelter, the food—but I've been out here a few months on my own and I'm fine." He threw a bloated, dented can to the far end of the room. It crashed against a conveyor belt, the sound echoing through the room. "I don't need them."

"Then why show up for extraction at all? Why not run?"

He stared across the cannery, a haunted expression on his face. "Because we get three free dream tokens when we get our first work assignment."

"And you wanted to save your aunt."

Merrick nodded and shifted a crate to the side, revealing a fresh trove of cans. "Sweet!" He handed her one and replaced the crate.

Cassidy gave him a questioning look.

"Any more than two without a backpack and we're not going to be able to climb out of here," he told her. "Besides, the next kid up here will be hungry too."

Cassidy climbed the rope first, helping Merrick crawl over the awkward windowsill. She noticed a small, palm-sized brown flag a few stories above. "What is that?" Cassidy asked.

Merrick hesitated. "Can I trust you?"

She kept her gaze on the flag. "Probably not."

He lifted his head in shock, not recognizing it as a joke

until he met her eyes. "Fair enough, you did save me back there. That," he gestured to the window by the flag, "is Resistance headquarters." He climbed up to the window and pushed it open. "Just popping in before nightfall," he said loudly, and slipped inside.

A makeshift ladder descended into the darkness below. Once inside, Merrick led Cassidy past a blackout curtain and into a room which made her head ache. The floor, monstrously tilted from its collapse, had makeshift scaffolding set up to straighten the severe angle of the original floor. A small laboratory sat atop the scaffolding, its technology recognizable.

"We call this building Nightfall," Merrick told her. "The Resistance works to get dreams to those who need them."

"But undermining the dream economy is the ultimate goal," said a beautiful young woman with a sleek robot suit strapped over her limbs, a similar neural interface to the one used in the imagination extractions hugging her head.

"This is Minseo," said Merrick, "She's fourteen, still has her imagination, and she's also a chemistry genius."

"I'm not a genius." Minseo rolled her eyes, a faint blush on her cheeks as she gave Merrick a shy glance. "I'm trying to reverse engineer the dream dust, so we can bypass the Dispensary altogether. If I was a genius, it would already be done, but I'm not, so here we are."

"It's more than I could do," said Cassidy, trying hard not to stare at the girl's robot suit.

"My parents are both chemists as well," said Minseo, catching Cassidy's confused smile. "That's how they were able to get me a suit before I'm of useful age. I'm one of the lucky ones."

"Useful?" Cassidy glanced at Merrick.

"Cassidy's not from Factorytown," said Merrick.

"Oh?" Minseo's expression turned to one of deep interest. "Where are you from?"

"She's not telling and it's very mysterious, but she saved me from my extraction and if I'm not mistaken…" Merrick raised an eyebrow and winked at Cassidy. "She still has her imagination."

Minseo's eyes grew wide, her robot-supported fingers twitching. "Oh my gosh, how is that possible?"

"She's not telling," Merrick answered for her again. "But I trust her. Is that good enough for you, Min?"

The girl nodded, giving Cassidy a curious look.

Cassidy crossed her arms. "Where do you get the samples of dust to reverse engineer?"

"We had a source close to the Dreamkeeper who smuggled them out to us, but she's been missing for several weeks. We're more than a little worried she got caught, but we're still able to run simulations based on those former samples. The trouble is that there are elements in the dust that we don't recognize and can't source naturally." Minseo sighed. "Which is unfortunately common when the Engineers' technomagic is involved."

A processor behind Minseo beeped and she turned, obviously distracted. "We'll let you get back to work," said Merrick. "I'm just showing Cassidy around. Tell the others if you can, we have a new ally."

Minseo nodded and held up her hand in a half-hearted wave, scarcely looking up from her work.

Cassidy waited until they were back on the outside of the Nightfall building before she asked. "Why was she wearing a robot suit?"

"Why? I don't know, I thought it rude to ask," said Merrick.

"Rude? Is she a cyborg?"

"No," said Merrick slowly. "It's a suit connected to her brain, allowing her to use her body to its full potential."

Cassidy struggled to make sense of what he said. Why would she need that—oh. "Wait, is the suit an accessibility device for someone with disabilities?"

"That's a strange way to say it, but yeah, essentially. The neural interface can replace damaged biological elements, like a severed limb or spinal cord."

Cassidy's mind raced. Gamgee would love to get his hands on something like that. "How does it work?"

"The Engineers make them work," he said, a trace of sadness in his tone. "The more they sleep the more we stand to lose."

She wanted to ask him what that meant, but she didn't want to change the subject yet. "Where could I get one of those suits?"

Merrick shrugged and held up his hands as if in surrender. "It's not that easy. Each one has to be calibrated to the user's brainwaves, which takes a long time, and the cost is astronomical."

Maybe not this trip, then. Cassidy filed the knowledge into the back of her mind in case she ever needed it.

"Let's go," said Merrick. "I don't want to be up here all night. We can stay in the plague room on the lower level for the night. We'll be safe there."

"Plague room? That doesn't sound like it's safe from the plague."

"You can't catch the plague, it's not contagious." He froze, his eyes widening. "You don't have the plague of the dreamless where you're from?"

He whistled when she shook her head. "Wow. Well, don't worry, because if you've still got your imagination, you can't get the plague and neither can I."

CHAPTER FIVE

The shadows were darker near the bottom of Night-fall, creating an atmosphere of secret and mystery. Unseen people shuffled in those shadows as Merrick and Cassidy entered the crumbling first floor, a grim space lit only by a garbage can fire in its centre and the dwindling light of day. The faces Cassidy glimpsed were dirty, hungry, and haunted. Some, perhaps sicker than the others, huddled under ratty blankets, pressed against the walls, noticeably twitching, an air of desperation aching in their eyes.

The scent of unwashed bodies did little to mask the pungent decay of the building itself; mushrooms bloom-ing on wooden shelves, a pool of brackish, oily water seeping mildew in its wake as it gathered up the weeping damp.

Merrick chose a dry-ish bit of empty floor and sat, pulling a can opener from somewhere in his coveralls and attacking one of his cans. "Pasta! You're in luck," he de-clared, handing it to Cassidy.

She peered inside at the canned spaghetti she might have loved if she were still twelve. Still, looking around at the dirty faces past the firelight, she wouldn't waste it. "I think the sick need it more than I do."

Merrick shook his head. "They won't eat, they're tweaking; all they want is a dream. You should eat. We don't have any way to get meal tickets so long as we still have our imaginations. Eat when you can," he said, slurping at a can of peas he'd opened for himself.

Cassidy tried the cold spaghetti. It wasn't awful, and she was hungry. "Can you tell me more about this plague?"

"Will you tell me where you're really from?"

Cassidy thought it over. "Maybe. If you help me."

"Works for me. What you do you want to know?"

"You said the plague is caused by a lack of dreams?"

"Right. You see, after our imaginations are extracted, we're no longer capable of dreaming, but it turns out our brains need dreams to work properly. And without them, our brains slowly break down."

Cassidy slurped at her spaghetti, flecks of sauce splattering onto her coveralls. "And this transcendental tech stuff is worth this kind of sacrifice?"

"Maybe. I've never seen any of the tech Bezanson's always talking about, but I'm the son of factory workers, we were never wealthy."

"But surely you've heard of it, seen it somewhere. Has Minseo ever mentioned it?" Cassidy chewed the cold noodles thoughtfully. Beyond Minseo's suit she hadn't seen anything remotely transcendent in this broken down city.

"Well, the Engineers built the city and they power our factories," Merrick said, faltering.

But the factories looked old, dingy, and worn out.

Cassidy decided not to point that out to him. "Then why do it? If you get nothing from this, why comply?"

"Legend has it," Merrick began.

"Legend?"

He shrugged. "There's no one left alive from back then. The plague gets most people in middle-age." He sighed. "When the extractions first started, the Engineers were active, not dormant like they are now. People adored them and were happy to share. Only now, the Dreamkeeper and the CEOs control the dream dust and every year the price of dreams gets higher. Now everyone is working for dreams. The cities belong to the CEOs who dole out rooms, food, and wages in exchange for absolutely everything we have, and after we're bled dry, we end up here." He gestured around the room. "To die."

"And the Resistance?" Cassidy stared hard at the boy.

He shook his head. "It's not enough. Even if Minseo can reverse engineer the dust, Bezanson still controls the ingredients."

The room grew dark as the sun disappeared from the sky. One by one, the lights shut off across the city. "The CEOs shut the power grid down after the factories close, to save electricity," said Merrick.

Someone in the shadows behind him tossed a pair of coveralls onto the fire, dampening the embers a moment before the fabric whooshed aflame. Cassidy chewed her lip. These people deserved better.

"So, where'd you say you were from again?" asked Merrick.

Cassidy's nose twitched, her sinuses suddenly seizing. The sneeze ripped out of her before she had the chance to tuck her face into her elbow. She shook her head to clear it. "Sorry, that snuck up on me."

"Are you okay?" Merrick's voice sounded concerned.

"I'm fine, just getting over a cold."

"Cold? Let's stand closer to the fire, would you like my coat?" he asked.

"No, no, a cold, not I'm cold. But thank you, that's very sweet." She ignored his confused look. The renewed firelight highlighting the miserable faces tucked into the shadows. "So all anyone in here needs to get better is a single dream?"

A sick man across the room met her eyes and nodded. "And this Dreamkeeper fellow," she continued, "is okay with people dying because they can't afford a dream that they should be entitled to by dint of forced brain surgery?"

"The Dreamkeeper likes to watch people suffer," warned Merrick, his voice low. "It gives him pleasure."

Cassidy rubbed her eyes. Nothing in this bleak dystopia made sense. "Let's go back a bit. How does that machine back there work? How can it extract a person's imagination?"

Merrick gave her a bemused look. "You really don't know anything, do you?"

"Not from around here, remember?"

"I'll say. The Imagination Extraction Device is enhanced with the Engineers' technomagic."

"How?"

Merrick shrugged. "Sorry, I don't know anything about that. All I do know is that the technomagic makes the machines do what they are designed to do. It fixes any flaws, powers it, and repairs the machine when it breaks."

Cassidy glanced around the caved-in room. "And that's what keeps these buildings from crushing each other?"

"Exactly."

Cassidy watched his face, waiting for signs that he knew something was wrong, that these buildings were breaking, that the machines were barely holding on to functionality. Everything here was on the cusp of falling apart. But he was young, she reminded herself, he may not have known it any other way. And if the older people were systematically being killed off, then no one ever would.

"Minseo could explain the science to you in more detail," said Merrick.

"I'll have to ask her," she told him. "Because this place is bewildering."

"Compared to what?"

"Would you believe me if I told you I'm an alien from another dimension?" asked Cassidy.

Merrick looked thoughtful in the firelight. "Fair enough. Any other weird questions you'd like to ask me?"

He was taking this rather well. "What do you call your world?"

"Cephalon."

"Okay. And what do you call yourselves?"

"People."

Huh. His answers irked Cassidy. This wasn't Earth. The odds that they called themselves the same English word were ridiculous. Unless they were a splinter group of humanity with convergent evolution... but even then, the likelihood was less than slim. "How many genders does your species have?"

Merrick considered the question a long moment. "Four? Male, female, neither, and both. I could be missing some. My experience is limited. Anything else?"

Impossible. Unless— "Do you get a lot of visitors from other dimensions and planets here?"

"There's an old story my father liked to tell, one he said he learned from his dad, that sort of thing. In this story, we were refugees without a planet. No home, just lost and drifting in outer space until the Engineers found us and shared their world with us."

"You're the aliens, then."

Merrick nodded. Cassidy gestured to the darkness past the building. "Does the story say what this world was like when you first got here?"

"No factories," Merrick answered, sitting cross-legged, his voice distant. "An endless purple fog unbroken by 'scrapers and a myriad of Engineers active in the sky."

"Are they sick, too?" asked Cassidy. "Is that why they're always asleep?"

"I don't know," said Merrick. "One day they just stopped, hanging there, like they were waiting for something."

"Waiting?"

"Yeah. Don't you think they look like they're waiting?"

"I don't know about that," said Cassidy. She shook her head, struggling to unite this new information of the cephalopods with her impression of the ones she met inside the portal. Neither the cephalopods there nor the one watching when she arrived here had been asleep. She shivered, trying to shake the uncomfortable feeling that they were watching her even now.

The night fell quiet as the fire's fuel ran low. The dreamless shifted into a small heap to sleep, holding hands like children. She noticed Merrick watching, too.

"Comfort," he said quietly. He stretched out on the ground and tucked up his arm for a pillow. "Sorry I can't offer you anywhere nicer on your first visit to Factorytown."

Cassidy smirked, saying nothing. The fire would be out soon, its glow and crackle a comfort. Strange to imagine the Engineers hanging in the darkness somewhere overhead. She wondered if the smog made them sick as it blocked out the stars, or if they breathed at all.

Rats or worse shuffled in the shadows as she shut her eyes. This was a hardscrabble life. If she wanted to get her hands on any tech, she needed richer neighbourhoods, wherever they might be.

The fire snuffed out, the darkness complete. Merrick began to snore lightly, holding her in this world as an anchor while her imagination unspooled with all the worlds she'd visited, and sleep stole away the night.

CHAPTER SIX

Cassidy awoke to a world thick with purple mist, the dreamless already awake and gone, Merrick snoring fitfully. She sat up, stretching out the aches of sleeping rough. From the broken window she spotted long rows of workers heading to their factories, a sea of blue coveralls.

Many wiped sleep from bleary eyes, but no one smiled. The joy had been sucked dry from these people, and it tugged at Cassidy's conscience. There had to be something she could do.

She could start with the Dreamkeeper, learn what she could. Go from there. If nothing else, he was the immediate barrier to these people's happiness.

She leaned past the broken windowsill, flinching as she saw an Engineer's tentacle from the corner of her eye. It must have moved there in the night. Shaking off her discomfort, she stepped outside, hands stuffed in her coveralls. Gosh, she could use some coffee, but all she found in her pockets was her pocketknife, a few tablets of cold medication, and the can of food from last night.

She peered up the half-collapsed high-rise, the early morning shadows tinged purple from the heavy mist that had replenished itself overnight. There was not one, but three massive cephalopods hanging above, shifting in the colour spectrum from blue to purple. Their tentacles appeared to fall downward, but at this vantage Cassidy could see their long muscles flexing. The larger, outer tentacles had undersides dotted with suction cups Cassidy tried not to imagine squeezing around objects or squishing the life from her bones.

"Good morning," Merrick rubbed his forehead as he walked over to her. He froze when noticed the cephalopods overhead. "Whoa. They never move."

Cassidy had been worried about that. First the portal, now here. Were they tracking her? Warning? Or just keeping an eye on her? She looked to Merrick, biting back the questions she knew he couldn't answer. His skin tone was paler than it was yesterday, his eyes puffy.

"My head feels like it's overstuffed," he said.

"You did have a partial, magical brain surgery yesterday," said Cassidy, her tone light, but she didn't like the way he looked. "You okay?"

"I'm sure I can power through, but I feel strange." He straightened his posture as if to prove his words. "What are your interdimensional sight-seeing plans for today?"

Cassidy chuckled. "You really are taking that revelation well."

"I promise, I'm struggling on the inside. There's no shortage of weirdos here on Cephalon. Our imaginations are short, their expiration dates clearly stamped, and we have to make the most of what we've got, before and after."

"Fair enough," said Cassidy. "I'd like to see this

Dreamkeeper fellow today."

Merrick startled, but recovered quickly. "He'll be at the Dispensary."

"Merrick? Is that you?" someone interrupted.

Merrick embraced an older woman who was clearly sick with plague. Her twitching body shivered with it, her expression hollow and desperate. "Aunt Tristine." He broke away and held her hand in his. "Something went wrong with the IED. I can't say for sure if I'll get my tokens today or not."

Tristine's lower lip wobbled, but the woman forced a smile. "You've still got your imagination, though?"

Merrick nodded.

"Maybe you'll be able to keep it," she said in a whisper, glancing around to see if anyone might hear. Her hands shook as she took them back, bulging into fists she pushed into her pockets. Her mouth pressed just enough to reveal the lie in her words and the guilt she felt for her own disappointment.

"I'll find some tokens for you somehow if I don't get any. There's still hope," Merrick told her.

Tristine pushed her lips into a smile. "Of course, and I love you either way." She turned to go, meeting Cassidy's eyes for a brief moment. Cassidy stepped back, overwhelmed by the bitter hopelessness in the woman's eyes.

Merrick watched her go with a furrowed brow before he turned back to Cassidy. "I've got to check and see if my work assignment and tokens have come in. Fingers crossed."

Cassidy nodded. "Be careful, it could still be a trap if the Compliance Officers were onto you. If you notice anything out of the ordinary, get out of there."

"I will. And you be careful, too. Word will have gotten around that a red headed woman blew up the extraction device; the Officers might be checking anyone with that description to make sure they're proper citizens."

"How would I prove I'm a proper citizen?"

"Comply. You would never do anything to risk your next dream."

Merrick stepped out of his coveralls, revealing the grey jacket he'd been wearing when she first saw him in line for extraction. He was a good kid, Cassidy decided. He'd helped her, fed her, and in some small way helped her through her first night here. She'd hate to see anything happen to him because of her. "If you do get your assignment, when would you begin?"

"Tomorrow. I'll be back here tonight either way, because if I get my tokens I'll need to find Aunt Tristine." He paused, unsure of himself. "Any chance we'll run into each other again?"

"I don't want to get you into any trouble," said Cassidy. "And I expect I'll be making some trouble."

Merrick grinned, swiping at his nose. "Come on, I'm heading across the factory district. There are several Dispensary tentacles along the way."

"Tentacles?"

He hadn't exaggerated. On almost every block lay what Merrick called a dream button: a tarnished gold circle embedded into the cobblestones. The Dream Dispensary itself was located in a hot air balloon hovering over the city's high-rises. The balloon proper echoed the shape of an Engineer, painted to match the burgundy tones of their skin and the bruised grey around their ever-sleeping eyes. The style of the artwork reminded Cassidy of comic books back on Earth. Judging by the height and the detail Cassidy could still make out from the street, the balloon must be massive.

A middle-aged, dark haired man stepped onto a dream button as she watched. A flap unrolled from the ship beneath the balloon, a flowing false tentacle that curled around the man's waist and snatched him up into the belly of the air ship.

"You've got to be kidding me," said Cassidy.

Merrick chuckled. "Beats dying of plague. The Engineers are a symbol of peace and friendship, it's meant to put customers at ease."

Cassidy shuddered. The Engineers did anything but put her at ease. "Have you ever been up there?"

"No, dream dust is pretty dangerous if you have an imagination, so be careful. Everyone knows someone who knows a kid who got into their parents' dream stash. Their parents or sibling would find them, brain dead, blood trickling from their nose and ears. People used to be able to take the dust in a cup of tea before bed, but nowadays the Dreamkeeper administers it before anyone can leave the Dispensary to cut down on kids getting hurt. They claim that's why they put the Dispensary in an air ship, too, but I think it's got more to do with security and controlling who goes in and out."

"Controlled substance," murmured Cassidy, staring upward.

"Yeah." Merrick squinted with her. "Be careful up there. I wouldn't know how to send you home again if you end up dead and I owe you that much. And watch out for the Dreamkeeper. He doesn't like loiterers very much.

"I'll keep that in mind."

Merrick sneezed, catching it in his hand at the last moment, a bewildered expression on his face. He stared at his wet hand as Cassidy turned away, to save him any embarrassment.

"If I don't run into you again, thank you for your help," she said, stepping onto the dream button.

The false tentacle whistled as it tumbled downward and wrapped around Cassidy's waist. The moment she felt the small pressure of it coiling tight, her feet left the ground and she went spiralling upward. Cassidy grinned. Though ridiculous, it was an undeniably fun means of travel. The factories below spun around her as she rose through the orange sky that tumbled through her vision. Strong winds buffeted against her face until a dark shadow swallowed her whole and she found herself inside the Dream Dispensary.

CHAPTER SEVEN

The false tentacle fell limp to the floor, coiling itself to wait for its next customer as Cassidy stepped out of it. She gripped the sides of the hatch as the balloon swayed in the fierce winds and peered outside, automatically seeking her only landmarks, Nightfall and the Engineers. More than one collapsed building lay on the ground. Factories spewed endless orange exhaust waste as the morning's purple mist visibly thinned.

She counted no less than eight cephalopods from her vantage point: the cluster of three from that morning, and one just below the Dispensary that hadn't been there when she'd been on the ground. The remaining four clustered around a teetering high-rise swaying in the heavy winds. No exhaust fumes billowed from the building, nor did it hold the strange, too-tall warehouse stories of the others. This looked more like an apartment complex back home. Maybe it was the barracks Merrick had spoken of.

Her stomach churned as the building swayed too far, a puff of dust rising from crumbled bricks, faces suddenly running to the windows, opening them wide, leaning out, their shapes too small to be adults.

Cassidy glanced around the strange entryway for something, anything, she could use to help, finding nothing. She turned back to the building in horror. Another gust of wind heaved the structure and she caught her breath as it leaned at an angle far too extreme to escape gravity, certain it was about to collapse like Nightfall had. Just as it should have fallen, the four cephalopods exuded a vast plume of purple fog that surrounded the building, setting it right. Cassidy could still feel the wind on her face, but the building swayed no more, solidified by whatever the Engineers had done with their strange mist.

She leaned against the wall of the Dispensary's entry hatch. Most adrenaline rushes were fun, but this was not one of them. The burgundy and blue creatures hovering over the city had saved that building, of that she had no doubt. She just wished she knew if it was out of kindness or the necessary maintenance of one's crop of human imagination. The idea unsettled her.

She had a Dreamkeeper to meet, she reminded herself, turning back into the Dispensary. The hatch had smooth, chrome-coated walls, well-polished and worn at the corners. A large, framed drawing of a man in a crimson coat grinned from its place on the chrome wall. The floor had a living quality to it, a three-dimensional glisten that gave the impression of walking on water as she stepped forward. Cassidy tried not to feel agog of it, remembering Merrick's warning of the danger present. She passed through a hallway lined with more comic book style drawings of the same man, up a small set of stairs, and into the Dispensary proper.

At the top of the stairs she found a round room with

shelves and counters piled high with thousands of small, colourful bottles. The walls were painted the red of fresh blood, assaulting Cassidy's senses, now accustomed to industrial gloom. In the centre of the room stood the man from the drawings, the Dreamkeeper himself, adorned with a heavily embroidered, tailed jacket that matched the walls.

He glanced up at Cassidy as she entered the room, his face greasy with sweat, shadowed with stubble, and eyes too quick to wink. In the centre of the ring sat a bespectacled, middle-aged woman, her face lined with worry, her shoulders slumped with the weight of her world, her eyes never leaving the Dreamkeeper's face as he pranced from one shelf of bottles to the next.

"How's about a beach location? And oh, here, a dollop of sunshine. We've got ourselves a bona fide summer romance in the making, no guilt required." He poured a little of the glowing dust from each bottle into a tube he held tight in his fist. The dust inside glowed brighter as it shivered from the bottles to the tube. His fingers, Cassidy noted, were stained with splotches of black ink.

"Do you have anything that might cast off my inhibitions?" asked the woman. "I really need to relax. Let the stress go for a little while."

"Sure, sure," purred the Dreamkeeper. He wriggled his stained fingers over the bottles, making a show of selecting the perfect one from his collection.

Cassidy crossed her arms and watched, his every gesture exaggerated, his movements graceful, his voice booming and singsong as he spoke. The Dreamkeeper hunted for ingredients back and forth across the floor, his coattails taking flight behind him. He mixed the ingredients into a bullet-like tube, working with deft, powerful gestures and licking his lips, clearly salivating with anticipation.

In one deft movement, the Dreamkeeper pulled a large handgun from a hidden holster behind his crimson coat. He shoved the dream tube into its magazine, arced his arm over his head and pressed the barrel against the woman's temple. Cassidy froze.

"Say please," said the Dreamkeeper in his sing-song voice.

The woman giggled, her hands a-flutter. "Please."

The Dreamkeeper squeezed the trigger, the report of the gunshot echoing off the painted walls, the now-empty tube skittering across the floor to Cassidy's feet. The woman rubbed her temple and got to her feet. "Oh, thank you, Dreamkeeper," she babbled as she collected her purse.

Cassidy bent to retrieve the capsule. "I'll take that," said the Dreamkeeper, striding over and snatching it from Cassidy's hand.

Cassidy bristled with sudden loathing. "You like shooting people in the head?"

He laughed, a fake, theatrical thing. "All a part of the experience, my dear. What is sleep but a little death, in the end? After the first few hundred times, it loses its ability to disturb."

Cassidy whistled, walking around to put a table of bottles between them. "That's some over-the-top villainy right there."

The Dreamkeeper ran his fingers along the hot barrel of his gun and pressed his lips in a hard line. "I am not accustomed to being questioned in my methods."

"I suppose not. Head office sent me," lied Cassidy.

"I'm sure. And you have nothing to do with the strange, red-headed woman my Compliance Officers were chasing yesterday?"

Cassidy smiled as wide as her cheeks would allow. "Of course not."

His jaw clenched, but then something behind Cassidy distracted his attention away from her. His manner turned predatory, teeth bared, muscles taut, a growl rising from his throat. "You'd better have a dream token this time."

Cassidy turned to see Merrick's aunt standing behind her, body bent, twisted, the expression in her eyes more desperate than Cassidy remembered. The woman didn't notice Cassidy, intent upon the bottles. She rushed toward them, hands reaching to clutch at any bottle, eyes wide at the wealth of life-saving medicine laid out on the tables.

The Dreamkeeper was on Tristine in an instant, back-handing the woman before Cassidy knew what was happening. Tristine flipped over, landing on her hip, moaning. "How dare you steal from me!" he roared. His left leg rose to kick the older woman's belly when Cassidy threw herself at him, sending him off balance and tumbling into a table of dream dust bottles.

Colourful glass bottles shattered all around him, sending up puffs of blue dust that set him to panic. The Dreamkeeper leapt to his feet, taking off his crimson coat and throwing it to the floor in horror. *Dream dust was a danger to anyone with an imagination*, Merrick had said.

Tristine snatched a half-broken bottle as it rolled her way, spilling a small trail of blue glowing dust. Cassidy flinched as the woman gulped down what dust remained, paying no heed to the glass shards that were surely within.

Cassidy grabbed a few bottles and shoved them into the large pockets of her coveralls. She'd blown whatever small cover of anonymity she'd had; she might as well steal what she could while the Dreamkeeper wasn't looking.

A small gasp pulled her attention back to Tristine. The Dreamkeeper sat on the older woman's chest, gun in hand, his eyes filled with rage. "How dare you play the hero, how dare you steal from me!" he roared, smashing the butt of his gun down into Tristine's temple.

Cassidy grabbed at the largest bottle of dream dust within reach, pulled out its cork, and flung it at the man. It hit his gun, poised for another strike, and rained down a shower of blue. He dropped the weapon and rolled out of the dust, struggling to get to his feet. Spasming with fits of coughing, he threw his arm over his mouth and nose and stumbled down the stairs toward the tentacle hatches.

Tristine lay still. Cassidy lobbed a few more open bottles after the Dreamkeeper, to be sure he'd stay away, but she knew it was too late. She knelt over Tristine's prone body. Her eyes staring up, unseeing, her skull caved in where the Dreamkeeper had struck her.

Cassidy kicked the Dreamkeeper's gun away with her foot and covered her face in her hands. She gave herself a moment before getting to her feet. The Dreamkeeper would be back, and she doubted he'd left her with the means to escape. For all of its outrageousness, this place did have the advantage of a quick lockdown. She grabbed as many bottles as she could fit into her pockets and wrapped Tristine's body in the Dreamkeeper's embroidered coat. Lifting the woman onto her shoulder, she took a look around the room. It glistened with shattered glass and glowed with dream dust, a small pool of blood on the floor where Merrick's aunt had died.

Returning the way she'd come, it came as little surprise that the tentacles were gone, unfurled and anchored somewhere below. A clever way to trap a thief. Cassidy placed Tristine's body gently against the wall and leaned out over an extended Dispensary tentacle, getting a sense of the dizzying height. She wouldn't survive a slide down something so vertical, not unless she had something to slow her descent. No, even then, she couldn't leave Merrick's aunt up here. She deserved better.

Cassidy moved to the rear of the room, throwing open the hatches. Maybe there was a building close by or a way to climb up to the balloon and fly the Dispensary elsewhere, touch down on some distant and teetering roof.

Flinging open the fourth hatch, a massive cephalopod's eyes stared in at her. Cassidy stumbled backward from the shock. "What do you want?" she shouted.

The Engineer continued to stare. Cassidy shook her head, venturing closer and gazing downward. The creature's tentacles led to the rooftop of a half-finished factory scraper. She couldn't jump it and survive, but… probably best not to think about it. Cassidy pulled Tristine's body onto her shoulder, hearing the clink of the dream dust bottles in her pockets. "If Gamgee could see me now," Cassidy said aloud.

With a whoop, she launched herself from the airship and onto the cool, clammy skin of the cephalopod's tentacle.

CHAPTER EIGHT

Gripping the tentacle between her thighs, Cassidy felt the cephalopod's lean muscles flex and rise at an angle, helping to slow her descent. The thick appendage thinned as she neared the bottom, the bulge of the suction cups on its underside rubbing over her knees. The beast was helping her, she knew, but some primal instinct made her physically recoil, even as the beast set her gently on the rooftop. Cassidy stared up into its squidgy face. "Thank you."

The Engineer blinked once and coiled its tentacle around Tristine's body. The Dreamkeeper's coat fell to the ground with a flash of red. The cephalopod lifted the body, staring at Tristine for a long moment before closing its eyes.

"No, don't go into hibernation mode again, I need that body back!" Cassidy shouted. "Her nephew deserves the chance to say goodbye."

The creature's eyelids did not move. "Give it back!" She reached inside her pocket for something to throw at the cephalopod, just hard enough to wake them up, get their attention, but all she could find were the bottles of dream dust. After staring at them, tempted, she shook her head and returned the bottles to her pockets. She couldn't squander something so precious to the dreamless.

Cassidy rifled through the pockets of the Dreamkeeper's coat. A ring of grime ran along the velvet inner collar, the edges beginning to fray. The pockets were worn smooth of their velvet and filled with the nonsense debris of a stranger's life: a pencil nub, a scuffed ring, a note written in an illegible hand. The coat's lining was a shiny black fabric, less obvious than a crimson coat on the arm of a woman walking through a sea of blue coveralls. Cassidy flipped it inside out, tucking the majority of the dream bottles she'd stolen into the pockets. She counted fourteen bottles before a sound from above startled her.

Shots skidded over the roof. Cassidy eyed the Dispensary overhead. The hatch hung open and the Dreamkeeper leaned out, sunlight glinting off of his gun. He must have been hiding up there the whole time. Cassidy wasted no time gathering the coat and escaping through the roof access.

Hugging the coat as she ran down the stairs, a waft of the Dreamkeeper's body odour rose from the lining. He must have worn the coat often. The stairway led on and on, as haphazardly added as the storeys themselves. In a place populated with the singular fashion of coveralls, citizens and Compliance Officers would know exactly where the coat had came from. She could ditch the thing, shove the bottles back into her coveralls, but she didn't.

Her knees grew wobbly as the floors gathered behind her, the echo of unseen machinery bouncing off metal handrails, odd smells growing, lingering, left behind for the next until at last the stairs ended and spilled her onto the now-familiar cobbled streets.

Ahead, a small group of red-headed women were being questioned by a Compliance Officer with a lean frame and a haircut Cassidy could only call a reverse pompadour. She held her breath and shifted down an alley adjacent to the building she'd left.

From the corner of her eye she saw a tentacle flash down from the Dispensary, likely depositing someone on the button to explain to Officer Pompadour how he'd lost their target. She ran, dodging into alleys until her way was barred by the gaping maw of an aqueduct over a dry riverbed.

A seething pile of textile factory trash, snippets of thread, broken bobbins and debris piled up in the riverbed. A lone woman, her hair tied up with a kerchief, used a pitchfork to pitch it all into the open aqueduct.

Cassidy plucked a piece of dark cloth from the pile and wrapped it over her hair to hide the red, wishing she hadn't stashed the abaya so far away. Grabbing a second pitchfork, she busied herself working alongside the woman, who gave her a nervous smile but said nothing. When Cassidy was finally convinced that neither the Dreamkeeper nor his Compliance Officers were following her, she thanked the woman and leaned the pitchfork back against the aqueduct wall, surprised to see a small crowd of dreamless appear in the gloom.

"Cassidy? What are you doing here?"

"Merrick?" She held out her hand to help him out of the garbage pit. "Running from Compliance Officers, of course. I was trying to infiltrate the Dispensary, what about you?"

Taking her hand, he stepped up beside her. His eyes were swollen, his nose running. "Looking for my aunt. Sometimes the dreamless come down here." He held out three coins. "I got my dream tokens and my work assignment. I can save her." His eyes glowed. "And since you know how the extraction went, maybe the Resistance has a better chance moving forward. Things are good."

"And I've got some dream dust for Minseo," she told him, showing him the bottles. She watched the sudden delight in his eyes as he recognized the coat, her heart sinking with the knowledge that delivering news of his aunt's death would destroy whatever victory they'd managed today.

"That's one for the books," he said, eyebrows high. "How did you steal the Dreamkeeper's jacket?"

Cassidy bit her lip. "He was beating a woman in the Dispensary, so I threw open bottles of dream dust at him and it got all over his coat. Apparently your Dreamkeeper has an imagination and didn't want to accidentally dose himself."

"He does. Dreamkeepers always do, it gives them the skills to put together dreams in new combinations." Merrick blew his nose into a handkerchief he pulled from his pocket. "Is the woman okay? Was she dreamless?"

Cassidy nodded. "Yeah." She took Merrick's hand and squeezed. "It was your aunt, Merrick. I'm so sorry, I couldn't stop him. She didn't make it."

Merrick stared at her, quiet, as her words sunk in. He dropped her hand and clenched his fists. "I had the tokens for her, why wouldn't she wait?"

"She was trying to steal dream dust, maybe for herself or for her friends down here. She grabbed a bottle and chugged it down before he got her."

"She did?" He tried to smile. "That's no small feat." He stared off into the darkness of the aqueduct. "Is she still up there?"

"No," answered Cassidy. "Believe it or not, one of the Engineers took her body."

"It did?" The sudden lightening of his tone was unmistakable. He swiped at the tears tracking down his cheeks. "It's considered a great honour to be laid to rest by the Engineers, but it hasn't happened in a long time."

"She must have been someone very special," said Cassidy.

Merrick held his face in his hands and stumbled slightly. "I feel terrible."

"That's understandable."

"I'm really sick. I need to lay down or I think I might fall."

"Okay, where can you do that? Would you like me to take you to Nightfall?"

"I got my barracks assignment this morning, it will be safe there," he said.

Cassidy thought of the building almost-collapse she'd witnessed earlier. "Merrick, do you know if anyone has ever been killed in a 'scraper collapse?"

"No, never. Why do you ask?"

"I think the Engineers are still watching out for you. They're not just sleeping."

Merrick shut his eyes and wobbled on his feet. "Sorry, I'm having trouble keeping up with you. Everything feels so overwhelming."

"Let's get you home." Cassidy tightened the fabric hiding her hair and clutched the dreams again. "You'll have to direct me."

The barracks were a handful of residential high-rises clustered around the one that nearly collapsed earlier that day. The Engineers had drifted away. There remained an unmistakable purple haze to the structure. To Cassidy's chagrin, the damaged structure matched Merrick's assignment, some twenty flights up.

"Your world needs elevators, Mer," she muttered, waiting for him to stop and rest. Twenty flights of stairs were too much for someone as sick as he, but she doubted he'd appreciate it if she tossed him over her shoulder and marched him to his room. They made it eventually, the sway in the building knotting Cassidy's stomach.

His assignment was a tiny room with a bed, desk, lamp, and a single chair. He lay down on the bed with a small moan of comfort. She looked out a small window, sealed shut. The city sprawled along, the purple haze thin this time of day, the orange sky in strict contrast to the endless buildings.

"What do you think you're sick with?" she asked him.

"I don't know, I've never been sick like this before. My head is congested, my nose is stuffy, and my eyes feel hot."

Cassidy chuckled. "Sounds like you've got a man-cold."

"A what?"

"You know, a cold, but when a man has it." It felt

like a jerk thing to say out loud. He shook his head and a shiver ran over Cassidy's spine. "A cold? It's a virus that affects your mucous membranes, causing congestion and a runny nose."

Merrick pulled the blanket over his body and shivered. "I've never heard of a virus like that before."

Cassidy sat down hard. No. No, no, no, that wasn't possible. Oh crap. Did she just bring her cold virus into a civilization with no immunity? Her heart sunk deep into her belly, remembering how such viruses had brought her world to a halt not so long ago.

CHAPTER NINE

Calm down, Cassidy told herself. Look at the facts. One individual sick, that's not a pandemic. Stay calm. But now she was inside a dormitory of people whom she'd just exposed to the virus, including everyone where she and Merrick had been since her arrival. There were at least a dozen dreamless in the bottom of Nightfall with them last night.

Cassidy reached for the bottles of dream dust. At least she could save them from one plague. She reached for an empty bottle from Merrick's desk, opened it, and poured the contents of the stolen bottles into it. When she wrapped the small bottles in the Dreamkeeper's coat again, the scuffed ring fell out of the pocket with a small tink of metal. Cassidy retrieved the ring and tucked it into her pants pocket beneath the coveralls. The bundled jacket and bottles she tucked under Merrick's bed.

His snores filled the room, no doubt worsened by his illness. Cassidy camped out in the chair, unwilling to leave him. Just because a virus is unknown doesn't mean it has to be deadly, she reminded herself, but that didn't make the hours pass by any quicker. She remembered now, too late, learning about dark tourism in her early anthropology courses; of the invisible diseases explorers spread to the people they met in their travels, decimating entire populations. She'd been a fool, gallivanting off to these uncharted worlds, never stopping to think what germs she might carry with her. Her thoughts filled with memories of the measures her world had to take when such virus' had happened there, and the fear and uncertainty that had followed. If Factorytown shut down like the countries of Earth did, how would anyone get their dreams? Her guts ached.

***

An alarm sounded throughout the building before dawn, startling Merrick awake. "Cassidy?" he sat up, groggy, his clothes crumpled and sweaty from fever.

"Yeah. Are you feeling any better?" The alarm went off again. "What is that?"

"Morning wake-up call, it's time for work." He threw his blanket off and struggled to his feet.

"Are you sure you're up for that?"

"No." He put his face into his hands. "I got assigned to work in the Dispensary. The place where she died, under the direct supervision of her murderer."

Cassidy's jaw dropped, her mind racing. "I'll go in your place. It's not safe; you said yourself that it's dangerous to be around the dream dust if you still have your imagination intact."

"The Dreamkeeper manages."

"Mer, let me go. Think about it: inside knowledge of how the dream dust is made, how to fly the damn Dispensary, where it's stored. I could use this information to take them down. Imagine what this could do for the Resistance."

Merrick stared at her. "You're right."

"Perfect. Give me your identification or whatever, let me do this. I owe you in ways you don't know, please let me do this for you."

He shook his head. "You can't, Cassidy. He knows what you look like. They'll be looking for you. The Dreamkeeper isn't going to let you get away with stealing from him."

Cassidy blinked. The lack of sleep must be getting to her. He was right. "I don't want you near him, Merrick. He's dangerous and manipulative. He mesmerizes people, but none of it is real."

"I know," he said. "But I'm doing this. For my aunt, my parents, and everyone else."

The edge in his voice told Cassidy there was no stopping him. "Be careful," she said. "You caught this sickness from me and I am so sorry about that. It's annoying but relatively harmless back home but I can't say for sure that it will be the same here."

His eyes grew wide. "This could be bad, no?"

"I'll take care of you, I promise. This is my fault. For now, just listen: with this virus, sometimes you feel great in the morning, but symptoms come back." She reached for the cold pills she still had in her pocket. "These will help you stay alert if you need them. Don't let your guard down."

Merrick nodded. "And what are your plans for the day, overthrowing the government?"

"Depends. Is there any chance of finding a coffee shop?"

"A what? I'm not sure what that is."

"I know. Don't worry about it." She followed him down the stairs, the bottle of dream dust tucked into her pocket, her red hair hidden inside the cloth again.

A man in a robot suit passed them by, taking the stairs two at a time. Merrick gestured to the dream dust with his hand. "Do you think you can save a little extra for Minseo?"

"Probably. How much do the dreamless need to give them a dream?"

"About a capful. Minseo would only need a fraction of that to run her tests."

The stairwell grew crowded with citizens leaving for work and the pair fell quiet, guarding their plans. Reaching the first floor, Merrick left the building alone while Cassidy held back to make sure they wouldn't be seen together. The steady stream of workers descending the stairs made her worry. She kept her gaze on the floor, a war waging in her conscience, sick with worry that she was exposing these people to a potentially dangerous virus while a bottle filled with life-saving dream dust waited in her pocket. Isolation and avoiding others had been key to surviving the plagues of her world, but the dust could only save lives if she gave it out. There was no obvious right or wrong path to take and it haunted her. She didn't know how the virus would affect anyone long term, but she did know that people were already dying from lack of dreams. *Act on the certainty, Cass,* she told herself.

She joined the flood outside the doors, keeping with

the main flow of traffic until she passed a tight alley she could slip into unnoticed. The damp splash of small puddles between the cobbles gave a rhythm to her steps, the earthy smell reminding her of home with an unexpected pang of longing. She wondered how her family would fare in Factorytown. She hadn't seen anyone past middle age since she arrived. Her parents, like Merrick's, might have died of the plague years ago. She pushed the thought away, quickening her pace.

The alley opened up ahead and she stopped, gazing out carefully, tucking a few loose strands of telltale red into her makeshift kerchief. A lone woman sat in the middle of the square, sneezing and looking mystified by the action.

Cassidy's jaw clenched. Another person with a cold.

***

At last she arrived at Nightfall, ducking inside, hoping to find the Dreamless she'd seen there with Merrick two nights ago. Only two of the sickest among them remained, half-dead and unable to get to their feet, propped against the wall. One had a face so pale he looked blue, a dark hoodie pulled over his head, clutching the hand of a second person in a thick blue sweater, the blinking of their eyes the only indication they were alive.

"I have dreams for you," said Cassidy, falling to her knees before them and reaching into her pocket. When she withdrew the bottle the dust's blue glow chased away the shadows from their faces and their eyes locked on the dust in disbelief. "A capful, right?" She reached for the man's hand and shook as much into his hand. He held it to his friend's lips, who thanked Cassidy with their eyes.

"You, too," said Cassidy, shaking a second dose into his hand and watching him swallow it down. Then she closed his fist around the bottle. "I want you to take the rest and give it to anyone else who is dying. Can you do that?" He nodded. "Thank you. Now sleep, dream."

Cassidy left them to rest and climbed up Nightfall to find Minseo. Cassidy had retained a small bottle for the chemist, though a small part of her just wanted to see the girl to make certain she hadn't caught Cassidy's cold. Cassidy wasn't up for witnessing any deaths today, not from dreams, and definitely not from a freaking virus.

She tried to throw her frustration into the climb, but her fears were no stranger to adrenaline and followed her storey after storey. Had she saved the two Dreamless to watch them die of a cold instead? What about Merrick? Should she have quarantined him at home? Dammit. Gamgee should have sent an epidemiologist instead of her.

She was formulating a plan to take night classes in epidemiology when she reached HQ's window and slipped inside. "Minseo? Are you here?"

"Ah-choo!" was the only answer. Cassidy's hopes fell. "Minseo?"

"I'm here!" Cassidy pushed past the blackout curtain. Minseo sat at her desk, a small pile of tissues collecting at her side. "Cassidy, what brings you back here? Ugh, I'm sorry about this mess." She indicated the tissues. "I've got this virus that's been spreading around the city faster than Engineer fog. I've been watching it replicate here in the lab, and it's wild." She stopped, catching Cassidy's look.

"Sorry, I didn't mean to bore you."

"It's not that. It's the virus—I'm worried it's my fault."

Minseo held a tissue to her nose and raised her eyebrows. "How could that be your fault?"

"It's a long story." Cassidy pulled out a small bottle. "I was able to get you some dream dust, though."

Minseo's eyes lit up. "Excellent!" She took the bottle from Cassidy and scooped a tiny measure into a glass tube that she slipped inside a magnification device with a click. Minseo blew her nose into a tissue before peering into her microscope. "Hmm. This is strange. The dust was physically changed since the last sample I received."

"Changed how?"

Minseo flipped slides, connected the microscope to a viewing device, and handed the device to Cassidy. "This is what the dust looked like on my last sample, and all samples before that, actually. See how it sits stationary in a crystalline structure on the slide?" She flicked to another slide. "This is what it looks like now. The crystalline structure is not just moving, it's dividing."

"What is this shadowy stuff attached to the crystal?" asked Cassidy.

"I'm not sure," said Minseo. "Oh, this is very exciting. I need to make some notes." She reached for a writing instrument but froze midway.

"Everything all right?"

Minseo sat back into her chair, her robot suit clinking against the metal frame. "That pattern of division is familiar." Her brow knitted lightly as she stared into space, a small blush creeping across her cheeks. "I saw this before.

I saw it today." The crease between her eyes deepened for a moment before she leapt to her feet and flicked back several more slides, settling on a new one, with tiny blue globules shifting around the slide. "This is a cell sample I took from myself earlier today; watch the pattern of the division."

Cassidy straightened. "It's the same."

"Yeah. I fluoresced this sample and magnified it higher than the dust. I wonder what we'll see if I do the same with the dust." Minseo busied herself with the tools of her science, fingers moving with robotic reflexes faster than Cassidy could follow. Little time passed before the second sample was prepared and Minseo studied it through her lens.

"Is the shadowy stuff a virus parasite?"

"I think so," said Minseo. She tapped the device. "Look, you can see actually see the hole inside the crystal where the virus burrowed itself inside. This is impossible, this is a living parasite infecting what is essentially a solid object and giving it life. The Engineers must have something to do with this." Her voice trailed off, lost in her theories and calculations.

"So, my virus infected the dreams? What does that mean for people who need them?" It came out whinier than Cassidy would have liked, but her guts were sloshing with guilt and worry and oh god what had she just done to that poor couple at the bottom of Nightfall? She blanched. She'd handed them an entire bottle of dreams to give away, and she'd tossed the stuff all over the dispensary yesterday.

"I don't know," answered Minseo, her voice sounding

far away. Cassidy may as well of not existed for how deep inside her thoughts she'd withdrawn. "But I'm going to find out."

"I'll see myself out," said Cassidy and headed for the ladder outside. Maybe the couple at the bottom of Nightfall were still asleep and she could get the bottle of dreams back from them: start there, worry about the Dispensary itself later. She needed to think. She needed a plan. She needed not to be the Typhoid Mary of this universe.

Her descent of Nightfall eschewed all local records, but it wasn't enough. The room where the two dreamless had slept was empty, nothing but the steady drip of moisture, the relentless clang of the nearby factories, and the endless purple fog to greet her.

Cassidy pounded her fists against the wall until she was spent and fell sagging to the floor, her head between her knees and her face hid from view.

CHAPTER TEN

"Cassidy! Wake up." Merrick's voice pierced through the fog of her sleep, his hand shaking her shoulder doing the rest.

She sat up and rubbed her eyes, disoriented in the gloom of the collapsed room. "Sorry. I didn't mean to fall asleep."

"I'm glad I found you. I'm on my lunch break." He chewed on the words like the phrase felt strange in his mouth. "There's a shipment of dream dust going to Shippingsburg this afternoon and I think I can get you on it. Compliance Officers are everywhere, Cass, and the Dreamkeeper has been threatening them that if they don't find you, he'll go after their dreams. You'd be safer in Shippingsburg." He smirked. "Unless you manage to anger their Dreamkeeper too."

Cassidy shook her head. "I can't, Merrick. I brought some dream dust to Minseo and she says the dust is infected with my cold virus."

Merrick sat down on his haunches beside her. "Almost the whole city is sick with it now. They had to shut down factories; I've never heard of that before."

Cassidy felt sick. This was like the plagues of her planet, all over again. "How are you feeling?"

"I felt pretty bad a few hours ago, but those pills you gave me worked wonders," he told her.

"That will only last a few hours. My god, Merrick, I'm so sorry. I never meant for this to happen."

"It's okay, Cassidy, honest. The Engineers won't let anything terrible happen to us." His eyes were full of concern.

God, he was a good kid. A swell of sisterly affection rose in Cassidy's chest. "The Engineers allowed the plague of the dreamless to happen, Mer; forgive me if I don't trust them to stop another."

He dropped his gaze. "I guess, but you can't just give up and hide out in this broken basement. Do something."

Cassidy's pride burned at the idea that she needed to hear those words, but here she was. "Yeah, but do what?" She thought over what he had said about the shipment. "The dust on the new shipment is probably contaminated, which means we can't send it to Shippingsburg. Maybe if we're lucky, we can contain the outbreak to Factorytown. You said you could get me onto the shipment?"

He nodded, looking unsure now.

She licked her lips, a plan forming. "How many guards are on a ship?"

"None, just the pilot. It takes imagination to plan a heist, and as far as they know, nobody here has one but kids."

Cassidy smiled. "Except for us."

"Come on, then." Merrick reached for her hand and

got to his feet. "I've spent the morning training in the shipping department. It's not on the Dispensary ship, but it is at the top of the building where we met."

It would be some relief to find the building with the portal home again, if she didn't accidentally wipe out this population first. "Is the extraction device still broken?"

"Yeah." He grinned. "Come on, the cargo ship is sitting in the warehouse dock, getting loaded."

Cassidy scrambled to her feet, her calf muscles stiff from Factorytown's stairs. "So different cities share dream dust?"

"It was news to me too. I guess the CEOs trade them."

"I take it Shippingsburg is owned by a different CEO, then?"

"Exactly. My trainer's been trying to explain it to me, but it doesn't make any sense. Doesn't Shippingsburg have their own Engineers?"

"Wait, you're saying the dream dust is traded like a commodity?" She waited for Merrick's nod. "No wonder the Dreamkeeper won't give the dreamless any for free, it's what is making the CEOs rich." At the least the virus she'd brought into this world was accidental; these monsters were intentionally letting people die of the plague to make money.

She kept her makeshift kerchief tight over her hair and her head low as Merrick led her through the maze of Factorytown and into the high-rise where they'd met. Cassidy groaned internally at the idea of another dizzying staircase. "Does the Dreamkeeper have his own elevator or does he take the stairs like everyone else?"

"Apparently, the Dispensary ship drops him off at his penthouse apartment before it docks at the warehouse for the night."

Cassidy slowed her pace on the stairs. "This airship hijacking, can it be tied back to you?"

"Nah, I'm the new guy. I can't even drive the things yet."

Cassidy swallowed back a statement that she couldn't fly one either. She'd figure it out. "Here's my plan: I can't risk infecting another city, and I know this dream dust has been contaminated with my virus. Instead of taking it to Shippingsburg, I'm going to unload it into Nightfall. There's plenty of room in there, and Minseo can study it to her heart's content. If somehow it ends up being safe, we can distribute it freely to everyone in Factorytown from there. But first we need to make sure the Dispensary doesn't come anywhere near Nightfall until I'm gone."

Merrick's expression cheered. "One of the Dispensary pilots is a Resistance member, he could help."

She put her hand on his arm. "Is there any way you could be there too, just in case something comes up that needs some creative problem solving, like a lie? It'll take an imagination to think fast in that situation."

"I still have my tokens. I could duck out of the warehouse early and head to the Dispensary, pretend I'm shopping for my first dream."

"Good, that'll work," said Cassidy, thinking quickly. Everything was falling into place, so long as she could figure out the airship.

"How do we get rid of the cargo pilot?"

Cassidy shrugged. "We'll figure that out when we get

up these damn stairs. Factorytown citizens must have calves of steel." She fell silent, thinking, her head full of problems needing solving. She knew from experience that worrying about them wouldn't do any good, their solutions would come when their full details were fleshed out in the moment, but Merrick was with her and the fun of risk was dampened significantly by the thought of something bad happening to him. Even now he wheezed slightly, working away at the stairs, the symptoms of his cold breaking through despite the medication.

Sweat trickled freely down her back before they reached the warehouse at the top of the skyscraper, the sway in the building giving Cassidy the sensation of mild seasickness. It was hard to forget that these buildings had an unsettling tendency to collapse. She'd be happy to climb aboard the airship she couldn't fly and leave it behind.

Merrick pushed open a door atop the final staircase, the sound echoing downward behind them and forward through the shining, vast, and empty room. If dream dust was indeed a commodity, it was either all inside the ship already, or Bezanson was broke. Either way, he was about to be once she had the dust in her hands. Her resolve strengthened, worry giving way to the clear, clean mental precision of her beloved adrenaline, her pulse climbing quickly higher in her fingertips.

Stepping out into the smoggy orange air of an outdoor hangar, Cassidy caught her first glimpse of a cargo ship. Unlike the cephalopod-shaped balloon of the Dispensary, this looked like an Earth Zeppelin, complete with a vast gas envelope hugging a long shipping container below its belly. A walkway and safety rails lined the container's roof, an engine room sitting tidily up front and four strong, pivoting propellers below that, protected by a series of steel cages attached to the container itself.

Merrick strolled over to a group of workers standing around, their work complete, waiting for the ship to take off. Cassidy ducked along the far side of the dock, waiting until she was out of sight to jump up and grab hold of the container's upper safety rail. Pulling herself onto the ship, she found a clear line of sight into the engine room, with no pilot present. Peering back towards Merrick, she saw a woman with a headset chatting with the group. Cassidy shrugged; couldn't beat that kind of easy.

She turned to the airship's controls, a mess of toggle switches, dials, and levers. The symbols were unfamiliar and non-intuitive. Did the damn thing have any pedals like a proper plane? She checked; it did. Pulling the chair closer, she pressed a pedal cautiously and the airship started to rise, slowly at first, then faster, ropes skittering off the ship as the shouts of the pilot and warehouse crew fell behind her.

Her sense of victory faded as a maze of skyscrapers she'd have to manoeuvre through loomed ahead. Cassidy swallowed hard, flicking each toggle and dial, trying to determine which one controlled the propellers she'd seen below so she could steer the damn ship. She depressed the only button on the beast and a half-moon steering wheel popped up from a compartment amid the toggles.

"How is that efficient?" she muttered in disgust, clutching the wheel with both hands and working to get a feel for piloting the zeppelin. Now all she had to do was find Nightfall.

Her breath calmed for the first time that day; the view beyond the airship too stunning to ignore, dark monoliths piercing an orange sky with layers of smog and purple haze. Here and there a cephalopod hung stark in the distance, lending the landscape such an otherworldly vibe that she fumbled for her phone again, taking one more photo. Hopefully it would remind her of something more than killing a dimension of humanoids. Hopefully, she still had a chance to redeem herself here.

CHAPTER ELEVEN

Cassidy flew the airship low and slow, keeping close to the worker's barracks and an eye out for the Dispensary. Finally, she lowered the airship onto Nightfall, the caged propellers striking the broken skyscraper rougher than she would have liked, shaking a few bricks loose in the crumbling sections leaning against the nearby buildings.

After several minutes of attempting to shut the ship down, she gave up and left it idling as she lowered herself into the cargo hold and pushed open the big bay doors. Inside lay half a palette of dream dust in cloth sacks. Cassidy stared at it, questioning. Only half a palette? As commodities went, that was very little dust. Compared to Earth, she reminded herself. Comparisons need not apply on a strange world in a strange dimension. Still, an entire airship to ship a cargo so small seemed like overkill. Surely a smaller ship would have been more efficient, unless the show of pomp mattered more than the actual dust.

Cassidy shook her head and hoisted a sack onto her shoulder, carrying it out of the airship and tossing it gently into a vacant room on the other side of a window several stories short of Minseo and HQ. If by chance she was seen, she'd prefer not to incriminate them. Scanning the sky, she saw nothing out of the ordinary, just buildings and orange. She ducked inside the hold and hoisted two sacks this time, testing the weight and finding her footing secure. This time, when she stepped out into the daylight, her view was blocked by a sudden quartet of Engineers closing in around her. Cassidy's first instinct was one of fright, but when she pushed past her fear she realized the cephalopods had significantly concealed her from the sight of any airships which might happen upon them.

She nodded at them from between the sacks of dust on either shoulder. "Thanks." The creatures did not respond, but she liked it best that way and carried on her work. Her half palette she estimated to hold untold thousands worth of dreams, but they fit into a mere twenty-one sacks. She finished shifting the dust in a lather, small bits of glowing dust clinging to her sweaty skin where it had seeped through the weave of the sacks. She'd take her chances with what small danger that might put her in, she decided, certain it was less than she'd thrown at the Dreamkeeper in the Dispensary.

When she returned to the airship's engine room, the Engineers drifted quietly away, their tentacles shifting slightly and their bodies gliding through the air like water.

The air ship followed them with significantly less grace, Cassidy eager to put some distance between herself and Nightfall but unsure of her next move. The ship wasn't something she could park and hope it went unnoticed. She couldn't return it to the dock where surely

Compliance Officers would be waiting. She rose above the 'scrapers, looking down over the city for somewhere to park the beast, her breath catching to see how it sprawled on and on and on, in every direction, without breaking.

In the far distance, a half-heartedly built wall wove in and out of the taller buildings, giving Cassidy the distinct impression that this was the border of Factorytown. The humanoids had used up every available space and had started climbing into the cephalopod's sky. Cassidy wondered how the cephs felt about that, and if this was something that they could have suspected when they brought the humans to this place. But then again, looking up into the unfathomable free space above it all, maybe this was nothing to them.

The fuel gauges on the zeppelin still read half full, so she pushed the throttle forward, making slow progress. She supposed a big enough roof would work, though all the stacked factories below appeared too rickety to handle much extra weight. Turning the ship carefully around, it puttered in the opposite direction as three birds rose to join her on the horizon.

The orange of the sky deepened, warning Cassidy that she had little time to find a safe place to land and somewhere to spend the night before the grid shut everything into darkness. She squinted downwards, half her mind on the horizon and the other half searching for a decent structure. Another fallen scraper, far from Nightfall, would work.

A new engine joined the sound of the zeppelin, setting Cassidy at full attention, throbs of adrenaline pulsing in her ears. The birds were much larger. "Crud, those aren't birds," she said aloud. "Crap, Cass. You need to pay more attention, you haven't seen a damn bird since you popped into this world."

Smaller airships, clearly built for speed and manoeuvrability, no doubt belonging to the Compliance Officers, zoomed towards her. She wasn't going to be able to outrun them in this monstrous rig, but she might be able to lose them long enough to land the beast and make a run for it. Steering downward, into the thick of the skyscraper forest where it was already getting dark, she manoeuvred her ship past emptying factories, their constant spew of exhaust easing, making it easier to see but also to be seen.

A sharp metallic clink rang sudden in Cassidy's ears: bullets ricocheting off the container beneath her. Dang it. One wrong spark and the gas bag above her head would ignite and she'd Hindenburg all over Factorytown, sending a heavy metal box careening down on top of who knows how many innocent people. Cassidy set her jaw, furious and refusing to allow any of it to happen.

Steering the ship dangerously low, she skimmed along the second stories of the factories, tornadoes of purple fog swirling away from her propellers. At least down here the container wouldn't have far to fall, and the streets were emptying fast, escaping the approaching dark. Cassidy tapped the controls with her fingers. She didn't want to get stuck down here in the thick dark of a Factorytown night either, bump steering off of rickety skyscrapers.

She had no choice but to go higher and find somewhere safe to land, hunching her head as more bullets clinked against the ship. The Dreamkeeper obviously didn't want his ship back, she decided, throwing whatever caution Cassidy Cane was capable of to the winds and pushing the throttle full bore, yanking the kerchief from her hair, stuffing it into her pocket and shaking her red hair into the wind.

A large cephalopod floated ahead. She flinched as the whiz of a bullet left a breath of wind on her cheek, hoping the officers wouldn't shoot at the Engineers, but neither trusting them not to. Banking left around a leaning 'scraper, she bypassed the cephalopod before it came within shooting range of the idiots tailing her, only to find another pair of cephalopods dead ahead. She swore under her breath, banking right this time, squinting to see by the meagre lights of the factories as the last light of the sun winked out. The cephalopods were only shadows in the distance now as her hand automatically slowed the ship to a crawl and the grid went off with a hush, leaving her in darkness.

Her breath and the sound of the zeppelin's engines seemed the only thing that existed in the universe. She closed the throttle, feeling the airship lurch. Her mind searched for her next move while her fingers probed the controls, forcing herself to remember where everything was located. Her foot tapped on the pedals. Those, at least, were easy.

Her only reassurance was the knowledge that the ships giving chase were in the same situation. Did she wait here, in stasis, until the ship ran out of fuel? She was kilometres above the ground; she'd never survive the fall. Her mind groped for the next solution. Every problem solved as it came, in order, no hesitation. That is how to survive. First problem: she needed light. She hunted through her pockets. A forgotten bottle of dream dust, the Dreamkeeper's scuffed ring, her pocketknife, and a bit of paper, the nonsense scribbles from the crimson coat. Could she use the pocketknife and the ring to create some sort of spark and ignite the paper? Maybe, if the paper only needed to burn for a minute or less. Crud. She was in some real trouble here. Wait, the dust. It had glowed before. She shook the bottle, the blue glow of the dust igniting, bright enough to see the controls of the airship. It wasn't much, but it was a start.

Cassidy held up the bottle, hoping it might reflect off the windows of the nearby buildings, giving her something to steer by. Instead, a soft rose light responded to the dreams, growing brighter, longer, rippling. Another light rose to her left, and another. Cassidy watched in awe as the light grew strong enough to frame the cephalopod tentacles it was fluorescing from. "Phosphorescence, that's amazing," said Cassidy under her breath, kicking the zeppelin into action again.

But if she had enough light to fly by, so did the Compliance Officers. Rounding another building, a smattering of cephalopods in the distance lit up in response to the others. Cassidy couldn't help but smile, until one of the small black ships pulled into position in front of her, close enough for Cassidy to spit on.

The pilot got to his feet, standing tall and bathed in the Engineers' glow: the Dreamkeeper himself. A sneer split his face and he fell into a dramatic bow before raising his gun and aiming it at Cassidy's head. "You have something that belongs to me!" he hollered over the roar of the engines.

He seemed to expect an answer before he fired his weapon, but Cassidy wasn't interesting in playing his game. She pushed the throttle hard and fast, ramming the small ship, sending the Dreamkeeper off his feet, and the ship scuttling downward.

The ships behind her opened fire, whatever they'd been holding back before abandoned as they saw the Dreamkeeper's ship fall. The soft light of the cephalopods' phosphorescence was broken by a thick sheet of sparks flying behind the bullets as Cassidy steered the ship in a zigzag pattern, knowing she was running out of time and ideas.

A cephalopod in her path moved suddenly toward her. "No, no," cursed Cassidy, "I need you to get out of my way."

A whoosh of heat and the world around her erupted in fire, the force of her ship's gas envelope igniting throwing her from her feet. She closed her eyes as something squeezed around her waist and drew her from the heat and into the cool, sweet air beyond.

CHAPTER TWELVE

Cassidy forced herself to smile at the cephalopod who had rescued her, unnerved by the squeeze of its tentacle around her waist. The creature had another tentacle wrapped around the container pod of her wrecked ship. She breathed a small sigh of relief that it wouldn't be crashing down atop of anyone.

The cephalopod pulled her, still coiled in their limb, up to their face. "Hello human," the creature spoke into her mind, its face never moving save a slow and steady blinking. "We sense you are afraid of us."

"Yeah, well, you're very large and I don't fully understand what your relationship with the local humans is," Cassidy said aloud, hoping the ceph would understand.

"Then I will tell you," said the cephalopod, its voice shifting to more soothing tones. "When we first encountered humanoids, the presence of imagination in their brainwaves gave us a wonderful gift, and my people dreamed for the first time. These dreams pushed out our stress and our worries for a short time, and we delighted in them. When we learned the human colony was adrift without a home, we invited them to join us here on our world. The resources the humans needed to live did not overlap with our needs and their population's imaginations granted us our dreaming."

Cassidy closed her eyes, trying to make sense of the mismatched pieces of information she'd gleaned from this strange world. "Then why are you collecting their imaginations to make new technologies?"

The massive eyes wobbled with reflections of wavering phosphorescence as a great tear gathered. "We have never done what we stand accused of."

"Okay," said Cassidy, worried the creature's massive tear might flood the street below. "I believe you, but I don't understand."

"Before the human colonies arrived here, the humans sent five engineers to create the human cities to house them. One of these engineers, Dr. Chimi, became a great friend to my people. It was she who first discovered that she could use our night fog in combination with human engineering to manufacture human food and materials. She shared her discovery with the other engineers and prepared for the arrival of their families. Many times the other engineers wanted to set up an economic system, but Dr. Chimi thought it best to keep all humans equal. For many years the human lived peacefully, the original engineers held in high esteem and seen as leaders."

"As they aged, Dr. Chimi's wife fell ill with a rare disease that removed her ability to differentiate between reality and fantasy. They came to us for help. Together, we determined that if we removed Tarryn Chimi's imagination, her life could be spared. Dr. Chimi knew her beloved would not be able to dream properly following the extraction of her imagination, so she found a way to turn the imagination into a dream dust that could be administered over her wife's lifetime."

Cassidy's heart sank. "Oh, no." A breeze blew up from the city below, its skyline a soft silhouette in the glow of cephalopod phosphorescence, but that wasn't what made her shiver.

"The other engineers had grown jealous of Chimi's success. They wanted her inventions under their own control, and in her Imagination Extraction Device they saw a terrible potential. When Dr. Chimi refused to turn over the device for widespread usage, the engineers murdered the Chimis, copied the device, and split the human civilization amongst themselves. When the humans resisted, the engineers told them that the directive to remove their imaginations came from us, that we now required their imaginations to make the technologies that made our world habitable for humans. We did not discover this until it was far too late."

"Why didn't you tell the humans the truth?"

The cephalopod closed its eyes a moment, its own glow dimming below. Cassidy glanced downward when she noticed, awarded with a strange view of sleek tentacles shivering into darkness below.

"We were too late. Our brains are well suited to long, deep ruminations, rather than the quick wit and reflex of a human. We discovered that our communication with humans requires both an intact and fully matured brain. By the time we knew to speak up, the only humans left who could understand us were also the ones responsible for our silence."

Cassidy wondered if the engineers knew that or if they'd gotten lucky with a side effect they didn't know to look for. She had a hunch it was the former. "You could have destroyed the IEDs."

"We considered this, but we feared that without a renewing source of dream dust, the CEOs would hoard what remained and the humans would die in horrific numbers. Instead, we formed a new plan. We dug wormholes and placed portals in other human worlds, leaving members of our kind as sentinel within them, and waited. Now, here you are."

"But it's been *generations* of suffering. You helped create that device; you have some responsibility here. Maybe you prefer meditation or whatever, but you're capable of saving entire buildings from collapse; you need to step up and help these people. They are broken, yet they still look up to you."

"You are here now."

"Yeah, and I brought a virus with me that's causing a pandemic. Can you do anything about that?"

"We are aware of your virus," said the cephalopod.

"You knew?" Cassidy asked. "Do you have any idea how dangerous this is? My friend down there is sick, and I may have infected the entire city with a novel virus. I've seen this happen on my own world; a lot of people died. *A lot.*"

"We altered the virus to our will when we reconfigured the language centre of your brain. The virus will not cause lasting harm."

Cassidy rubbed her forehead. "What are you talking about?"

"Before we allowed you to enter our world, we altered your brain to act as a universal translator. Without it you would not be able to understand the human's dialect nor ours."

She remembered the cephalopods inside the portal, both the discomfort and the personal invasion of the tentacle that probed her mouth and ears. "That was... brain surgery?"

"Yes. We altered you to give you the ability to understand and speak all languages you may encounter. It is both a skill needed to serve our purpose and a gift for your efforts."

She was speechless. On the one hand, she was furious that her consent had not been obtained before messing around in her brain, but on the other, she'd been given an incredible gift. More importantly, the cephalopod said no harm would come from her virus. The cephs had saved the people in the collapsing building; Cassidy knew they had the human's best interests at heart. Her shoulders sagged with relief. Maybe she hadn't killed everyone after all.

"Will you speak to the humans for us and tell them the truth of their stolen imaginations?" asked the cephalopod.

"I will." She furrowed her brow, thinking. "You said human imaginations helped you dream. Does that mean you haven't been dreaming either?"

"We have not."

She nodded. "Then, if it comes to it, you'll help the citizens fight the CEOs?"

"We will." Its tentacles wiggled with seeming discomfort. "Though we may need direction to act as quickly as the humans."

"Okay, I can do that." Cassidy took a deep breath. All she had to do was to stage a coup, no big deal. She stared over the city, dark and alien with glowing tentacles spaced out across the horizon, whatever stars shone above cloaked behind thick and smoggy clouds. Her misgivings faded into a giddy sense of abandon. Why the heck not add coup to her growing resume, after all?

"We will take you to your friend Merrick, if you would like," the cephalopod offered.

Her giddiness faded, replaced with worry. She hoped her friend was okay. "I'd appreciate that."

The cephalopod placed the container it was still holding gently atop a nearby building as the group of cephalopods' glowing phosphorescence faded and went out. The tentacle around Cassidy's waist was reassuring in the dark as air moved against her skin, but she saw nothing of their journey. Her feet touched ground and the tentacle loosened gently from her waist, leaving her unanchored in the darkness.

CHAPTER THIRTEEN

Cassidy reached for the bottle of dream dust in her pocket and shook it alight. "Merrick?" The blue in the bottle shimmered and grew stronger. Cassidy expected to find herself in Merrick's barrack, but instead it was a much larger space with half a dozen wide-eyed faces looking her way.

"Cassidy? Where did you come from?" It was Merrick's voice. "It's all right, everybody, she's one of us."

Someone lit a lantern, a strange-looking contraption Cassidy had no doubt ran on cephalopod fog. Another lantern lit up, and another, faces unfamiliar until she met Minseo's eyes. "Merrick called an emergency meeting of the Resistance," she said.

"At first it was to find out what happened to you," Merrick told her. "But you need to hear this. Paul?"

A man in a hoodie with a long face stepped into the light. Cassidy recognized him as one of the two Dreamless she'd given dust to earlier that day. The change in him was tremendous; his eyes twinkled, his skin vibrant.

"The dream dust you gave me this morning restored my imagination. I can imagine again, great epic flights of fancy, stories of things I've never seen, people I've never met. It's wonderful! And it's the same with my friend, the one who took the dust with me."

"The same happened to me," said a woman Cassidy didn't recognize. "Except I got my dust from the Dispensary."

"We think that somehow the virus-infected dream dust is regenerating people's imaginations," said Minseo, clasping her hands to contain her glee.

Cassidy chuckled. "That's what the cephalopods meant." Met with a dozen puzzled glances, she went on. "They told me that they altered the virus, though I didn't understand how."

"You're saying the Engineers are awake? They're speaking to you?" Merrick's eyes were wide.

"Yes, they are, they did, and they want you to know that they never wanted your imaginations. The extractions had nothing to do with them, it was all the CEOs. Apparently, you need to have an un-extracted, mature brain to be able to understand the cephalopods. Once you lost your imaginations, they couldn't communicate with you anymore, so they couldn't tell you themselves."

The rebels exchanged glances, their expressions a gallery of confusion. Paul spoke first. "If our imaginations weren't extracted for the Engineers, why do the CEOs want it?" His voice sounded tight, his fists clenched at his sides.

"Has anyone here actually seen any new tech in the past decade?" asked Merrick, his tone quiet. "Or have we always been too poor, too focused on getting that next dream, to see it?"

"The CEOs have been extracting your imaginations to make you dependent on dream dust. It allows them to control you and brings them unlimited wealth and power." Cassidy took a deep breath. This wouldn't be easy for them to hear. "The dream dust is made from your extracted imaginations. The CEOs are taking it out of you to sell it back to you."

No one said anything for a long moment. A sob rose from the rebels. "Monsters," whispered someone.

Merrick met Cassidy's eyes and nodded, stepping forward and taking one of the lanterns. Holding it up high, he looked into the eyes of everyone in the room one at a time before he spoke. "What they did to us is terrible and we have every right to be angry and rage over the loved ones that we have lost to this unthinkable greed, and we will, but right now we have a chance to change everything. We have a virus that can restore to us the very power they stole. Now is not the time to withdraw and come to terms with what has happened, now is the time to get out there and get this infected dust into every citizen of Factorytown who has been wronged."

The energy in the room shifted as his words ignited a spark in the darkness. His listeners stood taller, their shoulders straightened, jaws firm.

"We take back what they have stolen and we destroy the means to take it again," he told them.

"How are we going to get dust to everyone who needs it?" asked Paul.

Merrick gestured to Cassidy with the lantern. "Cassidy stole a shipment of dream dust this afternoon; we'll start with that."

The expressions that turned to her now were ones of surprise and respect. "I stashed the stolen dust in Nightfall, just a few storeys down from HQ," she told them.

Minseo gave her an odd look. "We're in HQ right now."

Cassidy considered explaining how she'd travelled by a cephalopod to get here, and apparently magicked through a wall, but thought better of it. They'd had enough shocks for one evening. "Will there be enough dust in there for everyone?" she asked Merrick.

"Probably not," he said, "but it would have to be close."

"It's possible that since the virus is restoring the imagination, we may be able to give a smaller dose," said Minseo. "I could run some tests, figure out the best dose with minimal waste. I'll need a few volunteers, but the only side effect would be an imagination. We'd best get started right away."

"I'll volunteer," a few people spoke up at once.

Merrick nodded. Cassidy watched him from afar, wondering when he'd become the leader of the Resistance. The others seemed happy to defer to him, but she had a strange sad feeling like he'd just grown up in front of her.

The group fell into a murmur, small conversations working out different methods of transferring dust over the town, how to ensure no one was missed, and staying hidden from Compliance Officers.

"There's plenty more dust in the Dispensary," said Cassidy, loud enough to make sure she'd been heard. Merrick levelled his gaze at her and nodded. "I'll go with you."

"So will I," said Paul.

"I'll come too," said a woman wearing a kerchief over her dark hair. Cassidy recognized her as the woman who'd been pitching trash into the aqueduct yesterday. "I'm Esmerelda."

Cassidy gave her a warm smile. "Esmerelda, I want you dosed before we go. If we get into trouble, we'll need creative problem-solving and heaps of lying, so let's make sure we have the best advantage of that. Merrick, what are the odds the Dreamkeeper actually parked the Dispensary at the warehouse after it was robbed?"

Merrick shook his head. "I don't know, but I do know they set up guards to watch the warehouse overnight. They were buzzing around in small black ships when I left."

Cassidy knew just what ships he meant. "Oh good, maybe we can hijack one. Can anyone fly those things?"

"I used to pilot the Dispensary before I got sick," said Paul.

Cassidy eyed him with a new respect. "The Dreamkeeper didn't provide his own Dispensary staff with dreams to keep them from stealing?"

"No," said Paul, crossing his arms. "He used fear instead."

"His wife was actually one of us," said Merrick quietly. "She's the one who smuggled dream dust out for Minseo for study. I'm worried he found out and did something terrible to her."

Cassidy pulled her hair back into a tight ponytail. "We might find her yet, Mer, but we've got to make it to the Dispensary before daybreak if we want to steal that dust."

Paul held back, reaching for one of the fog-powered lanterns. The light was dim and Cassidy wondered how they were all going to scale down Nightfall safely, but Paul led the quartet through a hatch in the makeshift floor instead, sliding along the tilted floor until they reached a window at the bottom of the building. He flipped it open, reached for a length of rope attached to a heavy beam nearby, and threw it down.

"This way is safer after dark," Merrick told her, catching her eye. Reaching for a metal figure eight hanging on a nail, he wrapped the rope around it. "I'll go first." Holding on to the eight, he jumped through the window, the rope hissing the long way to the ground.

Paul and Esmerelda pulled the rope back, retrieving the figure eight and releasing the rope again. Esmerelda wrapped the rope around the eight a second time. "You hold on here and here," she showed Cassidy. "Would you like to go this time?"

"Sure, I love zip lining into certain doom." She regretted her snark when she noticed Esmerelda's surprised look. "Sorry, my sense of humour is an acquired taste. I'll go." She grabbed the device as she'd been directed and stepped through the window.

The hiss of the rope against the metal filled her ears, pushing out her other senses even as they desperately probed the humid, inky darkness for clues. The acrid smell of the city eased this late at night, the smog rising away or swept along by a breath of wind winding through the cobblestoned streets, giants hushing in the darkness overhead. Instead, a smell of mildew and warm stone hung in the air, with the soft and ever-present ocean smell she'd come to associate with the cephalo-fog.

Cassidy jerked to a stop. She fumbled with the device in her hands to no avail. She listened, hearing not a single breath in the pitch black of the night. Cassidy swung her feet, stretching, but touched nothing. Was she close to the ground? She felt for the rope with her feet, finding nothing. Next, with one hand, finding the end of the rope in a knot just past her figure-eight. Where the hell was Merrick? Had he fallen to his death? "Dammit," she cursed, furious.

"Cassidy?" It was Merrick's voice. "The rope's a few feet short; you'll have to drop the rest of the way, but—"

Cassidy let go, tucking in and ready to roll if she needed to, but she landed well. "Got it. Could have warned me about the rope, though."

"If I'd known about it, I would have," said Merrick, his voice magnified in the darkness.

Cassidy wanted to scold him for jumping without knowing, but she bit her tongue; she'd been about to do the same. Esmerelda came next, then Paul with the lantern.

They crept along the dark street, the soft light of the lantern little more than a single Christmas light against the dark. Alone she would have been helplessly lost, but the others knew the streets of Factorytown well and guided their small group from one block to the next, until they reached an all too familiar stairwell and Cassidy's calves reminded her how long it had been since she'd had a good sleep.

When the group reached the warehouse and peered

outside to the docking structure, the Dispensary was not there. "Where else could it be?" asked Esmerelda.

A lump of crimson fabric in the centre of the warehouse caught Cassidy's eye. She left the group, walking over to it, hoping she was wrong. The texture of velvet brushed against her fingertips, the familiar weight heavy in her hands. She opened it to be sure, hiding it from the others' view with her body: the Dreamkeeper's jacket she'd stolen from the Dispensary. She rubbed her thumb over the stained velvet. Cassidy had left the jacket rolled and stowed beneath Merrick's bed. The Dreamkeeper must have discovered Merrick's role in all of this. A chill ran over her skin.

CHAPTER FOURTEEN

"Cassidy?" asked Merrick. "Where should we go next?"

She rolled up the coat. "The Dreamkeeper's house. Paul, can you get us there?"

He held up his hands in apology. "I've only ever gone there by ship."

"Then we go by ship," said Cassidy, flinging open the doors and stepping out into the open.

"Cassidy, wait! There are Compliance Officers out there!"

"That's what I'm counting on," she said, never breaking her gaze into the darkness.

The sound of engines firing up and the click of the dock's spotlights coming on, aiming for her eyes, sent her pulse to ecstatic levels. Oh yes, she had been getting a little stale, hadn't she? She couldn't see, but she recognized the engine sound of the bird ship that had chased her earlier that night. There was at least one still intact, and if she was correct, the pilot would be under orders to find her and come in for a closer look.

Cassidy held back against the now-closed doors, making the officers come past the spotlights if they wanted to be sure in their reports to the Dreamkeeper. After a long moment, the ship moved ahead. She waited. A little closer and she could almost see the officer's face. He moved forward again, leaning ahead, close enough that she could see him squint. Now. She charged toward him, legs pumping. He wouldn't be able to shift the ship around in such a tight space before she reached him. Reaching for the railing around his cockpit, Cassidy swung herself into the small gondola, the ship rocking as the bird-shaped gas balloon above worked to balance out the sudden weight.

"Hi!" she said to the pilot, pulling back and punching him in the jaw. Her knuckles erupted with fire, but the pilot didn't go down. Grabbing him around the back, she brought up her knee at the same time she pushed him into it, knocking the wind from his lungs. As he gasped for air, she made short work of tying his hands behind his back.

She gestured to the others to come outside and climb aboard as she hauled the Compliance Officer into the warehouse.

"You don't have to be so rough," said the officer. "I get assigned my job the same as everyone," he muttered.

Cassidy stopped. She hadn't considered that. "Do you have an imagination?"

"No, of course not."

Cassidy gave him a crooked grin and pulled the bottle of dream dust from her pocket. She pinched a bit between her fingers. "Open up." The officer complied and she sprinkled it on his tongue. "Long story short: it's the CEOs who take your imaginations to sell them back to you. This dose is going to give you your imagination back, so don't squander it and maybe look the other way if you see anyone giving it out, okay?"

The shock on his face could not have been faked. Cassidy nodded and turned to go. "I hate to leave you like this but I can't have you squealing until you believe me, so have a good night, I guess." She swung out the door and ran to the ship where Paul was already taking control, rising from the dock. Merrick and Esmerelda had pulled one of the spotlights onto the ship for light.

Cassidy looked on, marvelling. "All this cool tech, but no one thought of headlights?"

Esmerelda shook her head. "The Engineers need the darkness for their courtship rituals, it was part of the agreements when we were allowed to populate this planet."

Merrick chuckled. "I never knew that, that's kind of…" his face fell into an uncomfortable grimace and suddenly he looked sixteen again.

Cassidy laughed. "Well, here's hoping we don't accidentally peep on any mating cephalopods."

The ship banked heavily around a building and hovered before a glass house built into the side of a high-rise. Not a clever penthouse, but certainly Factorytown's brand of risky architecture. To its side, tucked into scaffolding, waited the Dispensary.

The spotlight reflected back from the Dreamkeeper's glassy walls like a myriad of shattered diamonds. Staring at the building with her jaw clenched, Cassidy slipped her arms into the Dreamkeeper's coat to keep her arms free and ready to fight if need be. Ink stains at the bottom of the right cuff caught her eye and she turned her palm up to see them better. The fabric showed extra wearing there.

She looked up, catching Merrick's questioning expression and shrugging in response.

Pulling alongside the Dispensary, Esmerelda, Cassidy, and Merrick, holding the lantern, leapt from the small ship onto the upper deck of the Dispensary. A vast burner and gas tubes took up most of the surface space, with a small railing encircling the area and probably the best view in the city when the sun was high. The hatch in the floor leading to the Dispensary was locked.

Cassidy leaned over the railing, spying a window below. Pulling out her pocketknife, she opened it and slammed the point into the glass. As she pulled her arm back, the window shattered, tinkling to the deck below. She grinned at Merrick and swung herself into the window, unlocked the hatch from within, and let the others inside.

Creeping through the Dispensary, a faint illumination glowed from the walls, enough to see by. Cassidy ran her hand along the wall. Was this the accumulation of so many particles of dream dust? She stopped when she got to one of the framed artist's renderings of the Dreamkeeper as a comic book character. She touched the red coat's stained cuff with her fingertips, wondering if the two were related.

Paul, having parked the ship, leapt in behind them. He strode to a small cupboard she hadn't noticed by the window, pulled out a handgun, and checked for bullets. "The Dreamkeeper always kept it loaded in case the dreamless attacked," he told Cassidy when he caught her watching.

They entered the dispensary proper, Paul and Esmerelda stuffing bottles of dream dust into cloth sacks while Merrick slipped from the room, returning to the landing platform.

"Where are you going?" Cassidy asked him.

She didn't like his guilty expression. "I need to check on Aislyn."

"Aislyn?"

"The Dreamkeeper's wife, the woman who smuggled the dream dust out to Minseo. I'm worried he's done something terrible to her."

Cassidy glanced through the door he'd opened into the Dreamkeeper's house. It hadn't been locked. She lifted her arms and pulled her hair back into a snug ponytail. "I don't like that he left the door unlocked, Merrick." *Especially after leaving the coat to lure me here.* "I'll go instead; I've dealt with this sort of thing before and I'm already on his hit list. You help Ez and Paul gather the dust. You need to save your people."

For a moment she thought he was going to argue with her, but he didn't. Instead, he nodded and turned back the way he'd come.

Cassidy stepped over the threshold of the house and crept down a poorly lit hallway. Lights were on at random inside; the man was likely home. Comic panels, more elaborate than the ones hanging in the Dispensary, lined the walls. Together they displayed multiple pages of the same story, involving the Dreamkeeper and a woman called the Heroine Avenger. Although he was clearly the villain, the other was a hero. The woman had dark, flowing hair, her coveralls more than realistically provocative as she blended in with the citizens, seducing the Dreamkeeper for access to dream dust but falling in love along the way. Cassidy paused, piecing together reality versus the story depicted. Was the Heroine Avenger also Aislyn?

The Dreamkeeper was the same caricatured villain Cassidy had met that first day in the Dispensary, but the comic revealed that he, too, fell in love with his rival in a complicated dance of role play and burning sexual tension. The writer played with the concept of balance between good and evil, personified between the two.

In the climax panel, the Heroine Avenger revealed her name: Aislyn, while the Dreamkeeper refuses to acknowledge he has a name to put to his title. His lover is hurt and angry, breaking him down until he confesses that he abandoned his birth name when his parents sold him to the factories for a handful of dream dust. Small children came in handy for darting between moving gears. His only solace was his art, a nobody child scribbling pictures onto cobblestones between shifts. One day another boy stole his chalk. The Dreamkeeper beat the boy badly for it, his ruthlessness catching the eye of Bezanson who gave him both the title of Dreamkeeper and the chance to keep his imagination, and thus his art, indefinitely.

The story panels had led Cassidy into a wrecked studio. The smell of paint and ink hung thick, papers scattered, each of them a sketch of the Heroine Avenger with the Dreamkeeper, speech bubbles drawn but left empty. Cassidy crouched to pick one of the papers up, noticing the wedding rings and the initials DK in the corner.

"We are all of us a little disappointed in reality, aren't we?" asked the Dreamkeeper, revealing his location on the floor, dishevelled, an open flask in his hand. "That's why we like our dreams. After all, if you could recreate yourself into everything you ever wanted to be—more powerful, more invincible—why wouldn't you?"

Cassidy frowned at the Dreamkeeper in the picture she held. "But you're not just the villain, are you? You're also the artist and the husband."

He didn't answer right away, gazing drearily ahead. "I've lost my partner. She's the one that comes up with our stories. She's the one who figures out our story when it's broken. I'm lost without her."

Cassidy tried to piece together Aislyn's character. "How did she manage to keep her imagination into adulthood?"

"She had no family, nobody watching out for her when she was a kid. Rather than turning her imagination in for security when she came of age, she became the Heroine Avenger, evading Compliance Officers by dint of skill and a street kid's knowledge of the city's secrets."

Cassidy clenched her jaw. The cephalopods had sat by a wormhole and waited while the hero they needed was there all along. She frowned at the woman's picture. Someone who clearly wanted to be a hero, at that.

The Dreamkeeper struggled, drunkenly, to his feet. "That's my coat you're wearing."

Cassidy took it off and tossed it to him. He caught it with ease, she noticed. Not drunk then, or just accustomed to the disorientation. "The kid had nothing to do with it."

The Dreamkeeper checked his pockets, finding nothing. "Merrick? Oh, I doubt that. Aislyn told me all about him and his adorable HQ."

Cassidy held up the drawing. "This is you and her, I

take it?"

"It is." His face filled with sorrow. "We were a dream team. We plotted everything: her daring escapes, my foils. A game of careful balance under the eyes of our unseeing CEOs."

Cassidy struggled to grasp his worldview. "Did the two of you really consider yourselves hero and villain?"

The Dreamkeeper sneered at her. "The nature of our relationship is none of your business. We were two halves of a whole, the opposite sides to the same coin."

"You knew she was stealing dust."

"Of course. We respected each other's work. She didn't steal more than I could cover for, and the chemist kid was never going to figure out the formula, anyway."

"So what? Did you guys get off on being each other's nemesis?" She tried not to make a face.

His expression turned sad, his mouth down-turned, his gaze falling to the pictures on the floor. "No. I was her true love, not her nemesis."

Cassidy arched an eyebrow. "You're not the reason she's missing?"

The Dreamkeeper shook his head and took a swig from his flask. "It was Bezanson, after all. A cruel stroke, don't you think? The symbolic father betrayed me worse than my real father."

Cassidy let the sketch in her hand flutter to the floor. "What did Bezanson do to her?"

Tears streamed freely down his cheeks. "He found out what she was doing. She got overly confident and tried to break into one of his bigger warehouses, where he caught her."

"Is she alive?" Cassidy wasn't sure she wanted to know.

The Dreamkeeper sighed, pressing a trembling hand to the crease between his brows. "He imprisoned her and ripped out her imagination." He kicked at the sketches scattered over the floor. "Our creative dream has ended, our partnership destroyed. No more stories, no more adventures, and no more Heroine Avenger."

"No, you've still got a chance. There's a virus infecting the citizens that's restoring their imaginations."

The Dreamkeeper threw back his head and laughed, a gob of spittle flying from his mouth. "Nice one. But even if it was true, Bezanson would never let anyone keep their imagination." He straightened his coat sleeves and buttoned the front of his scarlet coat, sliding his fingers into his pockets again as his jaw tightened. His arm relaxed, his right hand falling into his trouser pocket where he pulled out a loaded dream pistol and pressed against Cassidy's temple. "But I will be the Dreamkeeper she wrote me to be forever, and you have something that belongs to me."

Cassidy heard a scuffle of papers from behind her and silently cursed Merrick for following her. She reached into her pocket and pulled out the wedding ring she'd found inside the Dreamkeeper's coat as the Dreamkeeper cocked the pistol's trigger. She offered him the ring. "It's not too late, you can have everything back: Aislyn, the stories, the roleplay, everything."

"She made a better heroine than you," he said, snatching the ring. "She would have convinced me." He ground the barrel into Cassidy's temple, the cold metal warming from her body temperature. "Did they tell you what happens if you get a dream dose when you already have an imagination? Because I know you have one, it's the only way you could have gotten this far." He crept in close to whisper into her ear. "They say there's no more painful way to die." Cassidy closed her eyes.

A shot rang out, but it was the Dreamkeeper's body that slumped to the floor, not hers. The wedding ring skittered out of his hand and rolled out of his reach. Cassidy looked up in time to see Merrick lean against the doorframe at the far end of the studio, his eyes locked in horror on the ever-widening pool of blood spilling from the Dreamkeeper's head.

Cassidy ran to Merrick, flinging the gun from his hand. "You saved me, Mer, you really did."

He nodded, swallowing hard, pushing through the shock. "I killed someone, Cass." He winced. "I killed my friend's husband."

"You saved a lot of people today." She pulled him to his feet. "Come on, Merrick. There's more we have to save, focus on them."

He glanced back at the body, guilt oozing from his every movement.

CHAPTER FIFTEEN

If Paul and Esmerelda noticed Merrick's unusual quiet on the flight back to Nightfall, they said nothing. He stared ahead, unseeing, while Cassidy tried to give him space. Dammit. This was exactly what she didn't want to happen to him.

The sun peeked up over a bruised morning, lines of grey feathering the horizon. The sunrise should have felt like a brave new dawn with the Dreamkeeper gone, but instead something ominous hung in the air. Cassidy wondered if a person ever got used to watching the sun come up on an alien world.

A large crowd had gathered at the base of Nightfall and Paul landed the ship a few storeys up. When Cassidy stepped outside of the ship, she could see Minseo dispensing dream dust below. The chemist smiled cheerily and waved when she saw them. It troubled Cassidy that Aislyn had told the Dreamkeeper about Minseo and Merrick's work with the rebellion.

Esmerelda hauled a large sack of Dispensary dust onto her back, bottles tinkling, and she made her way to the crowd with Paul and Merrick beside her, clutching small sacks of their own. The light returned to Merrick's eyes when he saw the people waiting for their cure.

Cassidy hung back, unable to shake the feeling that something wasn't right. The factories sat quiet, everyone amassing here instead of work, but a steady burr echoed off the buildings. She climbed high up the side of Nightfall to get a better view.

A cephalopod hung nearby. It opened its eyes and watched her as she waved in greeting. She wished she knew if it was the same ceph she had spoken with, but it was dark then and her perspective from the ground was wildly different.

By the fifteenth floor, the burr clarified into the sound of an engine. She turned towards it, not surprised to see a larger airship flanked by two of the same black ships she had flown in moments ago. Cassidy hesitated, looking down at the crowd, their laughter and cheer rising into the morning cephalo-fog on the breeze. Maybe the ships were friendly.

Cassidy waited as the ships got closer. The airship had something large and rectangular strapped to its belly. She squinted to make out the details. It looked familiar. An IED, she realized, her heart sinking. She glanced down again, loathe to end the citizens' newfound joy. She turned to the cephalopod, whose eyes were open wide now, watching the ship come in. Cassidy crouched into the building below what might have been an air conditioning if she were back on Earth. Maybe if there was only a few Officers she could stop them or bribe them with the promise of their own imagination.

The airship appeared ready to pass over Nightfall, but

slowed when the crowd in the broken square came into view. The smaller ships circled around while the airship landed on Nightfall, the building rumbling as the weight of the new IED settled onto the brick, its pilot clumsier than Paul and struggling with the angle. The two small ships landed softly at its side.

The laughter of the citizens below died as they noticed the new IED. For a long moment there was silence until it erupted into angry yells. Cassidy smiled, glad to hear them fighting back.

A man leaned over the edge of the airship's gondola. Bezanson himself. Cassidy recognized him from the film at Merrick's extraction. The man sneered at the crowd and signalled for his team to exit the small ships. Four soldiers trooped out of each, large guns in hand. "Kill as many as you need to frighten them into submission again," Bezanson ordered.

Cassidy's adrenaline spiked, sending her to her feet and leaping over windows and stacks as she ran toward the cephalopod. "You need to help them right now!" she shouted, willing the creature to understand her.

The cephalopod's eyes opened wide, its tentacles swimming through the air like water, moving faster than Cassidy could ever have expected, and positioned the considerable bulk of its body between Bezanson's goons and the citizens of Factorytown.

"Shoot the damn thing!" hollered Bezanson, his voice vibrating with rage.

The soldiers looked back at him, clearly shocked. When they met each other's eyes, their postures relaxed, their weapons clattering to the ground. Bezanson stomped his foot and stormed from the gondola to the side of the Nightfall. He grabbed one of the guns with a sneer on his face and spat bullets from the weapon into the cephalopod's eye.

Cassidy froze, the creature's ruined eye splashing down upon Bezanson and his goons. The cephalopod screamed, a vibrating, high-pitched squeal Cassidy felt in the bottom of her stomach. The creature emitted a cloud of red fog so dense that Cassidy could not see her hands in front of her. She crouched, looking around at the odd red cloud that smelled sharp and pungent, like a vinegar. *This is a distress signal*, she marvelled. Bezanson shouted in frustration further inside the cloud, Nightfall too dangerous to navigate without sight or foreknowledge.

When at last the fog dissipated, some two dozen cephalopods circled their wounded friend and Bezanson. Some coiled comforting tentacles around their friend, while another reached for the IED, rolling it up in its tentacles and squeezing, small parts crushing out and pinging as they fell against Nightfall.

A small cheer rose from the crowd below. Bezanson's soldiers abandoned him, heading for the ground as the remaining cephalopods crowded in around the CEO. Her view blocked, Cassidy followed the soldiers. Bezanson had sealed his own fate. She flinched at the garbled sounds he made as he met his end.

The soldiers held up their hands as they approached the citizens. "Is it true the dust restores your imaginations?" one of them asked.

Merrick grinned and clapped the speaker on the back, offering him a dose.

"The CEOs are getting reports like this from all over. First everyone gets sick and then something happens to the dust," said another soldier.

Cassidy smiled to herself, looking back at the cephalopods gathered above. These people would be okay. It was time to go back to her own world. She smiled, turning from the scene and heading in her own direction. Through an alley, up one last flight of stairs, and into a familiar warehouse. The broken IED loomed in the centre, its seat still cracked with all the lives it destroyed, the space still tinged with fear and pain. She lingered over it, wondering if there was anything Gamgee could salvage from it. Then again, she didn't want that thing anywhere near Earth.

"Were you going to leave without saying goodbye?" asked Merrick from the doorway, out of breath from running up the stairs to catch her.

Cassidy grinned. "Yes, as a matter of fact. Important things are happening; you should be there. You're going to be an excellent leader, Mer, and the cephalopods want to help, but you're going to need to tell them when and how to do so," she said. "You'll be fine."

"Not if I don't watch out for my friends, I won't be," he countered. "Come on, let me help you. What do you have to do, jump out the window?"

Cassidy sighed, fishing around in the palette and pulling out her abaya. She flourished it in the air and pulled it over head, letting the cloth drape over her everything.

"What is that? Some sort of shroud?"

She laughed despite herself. "Not exactly."

"You never told me what happened to Aislyn."

Cassidy sighed, wishing she could lie and say the

woman was dead. "The Dreamkeeper said she's still alive. Bezanson caught her breaking into a warehouse, extracted her imagination, and put her in prison."

"She had an imagination?" He shook his head. "She never said anything about that."

"Aislyn was a complicated woman. I wouldn't go looking for her, Mer. I know it's hard to understand, but the Dreamkeeper and Aislyn did love each other. She might not be happy to see you, considering, and I'm not convinced she's entirely stable."

His brow creased. She reached over and squeezed his hand. "You okay?"

He nodded. "I will be, we all will be, thanks to you."

"No, thanks to you, and to the cephs." She reached for a long coil of rope, tying one end to a metal pole and tossing the other out the window. "All right, friend, can you pull this up after you can feel my weight is off of it and promise me you'll never go down there?"

"You still haven't said goodbye," he told her.

"Listen, Mer. I'm not going to. Okay?"

He nodded, his eyes soft. She held his gaze for a long moment, before tucking through the window and out of his world.

Cassidy felt a wave of dry heat coming through that let her know the portal was close. A moment later, she slipped inside the strange inbetween space again. A cephalopod waited, staring, as ominous as they had been in the beginning. After a long pause, her lungs heavy with holding her breath, it spoke into her mind. "Thank you."

Then she was home. Well, Saudi Arabia, all dry heat and daytime this time around. Cassidy struggled as the rope got caught up in her abaya, falling the last meter to the ground and slipping out of the lengthy fabric as she did so. Merrick immediately pulled the rope back up again, her abaya attached. "No wait!" But he couldn't hear her.

"Crud," Cassidy cursed, her head bare, her covvies still on. Digging through her pockets, she found the old kerchief near the bottle of dream dust and tied it over her hair. It was better than nothing. Reaching for her phone, she crouched against the barrel and called Gamgee. "I'm going to need an abaya and a rescue ASAP."

Gamgee sighed. "Cassidy."

"Hey, on the bright side I can speak every language in the universe now. That's got to be worth something, right?"

CASSIDY CANE AND THE QUEST
FOR THE DIGITAL HEART

JON DOBBIN & JD RYOT

CHAPTER ONE

Shouts echoed through the cavern as Cassidy Cane ran for her life.

It wasn't the first cave she'd navigated blindly – far from it. A knife-edge of a smile danced about her face, her sharp mind recalling her recent escapades thanks to Dr. Gamgee.

"Intruder, halt!" The rough voices slid behind her as she skidded around a corner, a plume of dust rising from her feet.

***

"I know little of this reality," the doctor had said to her as they navigated the crowded station just under Times Square. "I fear that it may be too much like your previous life."

"How do you mean?" Cassidy sidestepped a burly construction worker who had his nose in his phone and rejoined Gamgee. It wasn't like him to attempt to reduce her desire to slipstream. Cautious, yes, he was always cautious, but never this down-putting. She stifled an aggravated sigh.

"Oh... erm... I suppose a word I'd use to describe it is cavernous." Gamgee navigated around an elderly lady who was busy digging into her purse. "I just fear that it may be too much like your spelunking adventures in search of ancient artifacts and trinkets." He hesitated and cleared his throat.

"What's your point, Herbert?"

"Well... I don't want you to become bored with my... with our work," Dr. Gamgee said and lead them on further into the station.

***

Cassidy pushed herself forward. She'd known as soon as she'd stepped foot through the portal that Dr. Gamgee's worries were unfounded. For one, despite its overt appearances, the cavernous place in which she found herself was not a cave. It wasn't a tomb, the bowels of a pyramid, or a viking burial ground. All of which she'd seen firsthand. The place she ran through now, though not a cave, was still quite familiar to her.

A crash sounded beside her as she ran, the sound of a plate breaking, and she chanced a quick flash of her phone's flashlight. An arrow. A snort of a laugh bubbled up, but she forced it back into submission. They can't actually be using bows, could they? A derisive, "ha" was her mind's answer.

Another crash sounded to her left, closer this time. She pushed on.

***

"What train are we waiting for, Doc?" Cassidy had

said and rocked back and forth on her heels. Gamgee was acting strange. They'd walked through the stations of New York for most of the afternoon, Gamgee bent slightly at the hips, his hands behind his back, as if he were following breadcrumbs.

"Wait, you're *not* following breadcrumbs… are you?"

The doctor straightened, a strained smile on his face. "Will you keep it down?" he mumbled through a barely open mouth, his eyes darting to his right. "I'm waiting for him to go on his break."

Cassidy followed his line of sight and saw a large, bald man wrapped in a snug reflective vest over a blue jacket. The subway worker was looking the opposite direction and yawned.

"Herbert, is… is that a security guard?" Cassidy found herself mumbling through a nearly closed mouth as well.

Gamgee nodded and furrowed his ample eyebrows in a manner which told Cassidy to be quiet.

"Good, he's gone," he said after a short silence. "Come, we must be quick." With that he jumped off the platform and onto the tracks. Cassidy could hear him scurrying along in the darkness. With a shrug of her shoulders, she followed.

***

Subway tile exploded next to her head, her already moving arms shot up around her face to keep the shrapnel and dust out of her eyes. She cursed under her breath and scanned the narrow tunnel ahead of her for the next platform. It was her stop.

Another volley of arrows pitched forward around her.

Their aim was terrible, she thought, but the more they practice the better they'll get. She felt an arrow slip by her ear, the violent breeze tickling her skin as it passed. More curses spilled from her mouth.

***

The doctor had lead them to the abandoned station under 18th street. A crumbling, graffitied husk of what had once been one of the first stations open in New York City and possibly America. A thick layer of brown dirt and dust covered the station, scrubbed clean in some places where graffiti artists plied their trade, and adventurous teens sat on a dare. Even those hallowed tenements of usage had a healthy layer of dust as Cassidy and Gamgee crept through the abandoned station.

"Ahh, yes. Here it is," Gamgee said and pointed to a cement wall that was opposite to the once crowded stairs that led from the street above. "It took me some time to figure it out, really." Gamgee ran a thin hand through his hair. "Perhaps it was just too obvious?"

"So, you want me to run through this wall?" Cassidy smiled at the doctor. "This wall. This wall that is located in a train station. Isn't that a little too Harr…"

"Don't," Gamgee held up his hand, cutting her off. "Don't get distracted by that nonsense. What we are doing here is for science, and for the betterment of mankind."

"Okay, okay. So, tell me what you know," Cassidy said through a sly smile.

"As I said, I don't know much. I did a quick inspection, but all I saw was a cave. I suppose the other reality didn't need to rely on subway trains for transport. Funny though, I did see some graffiti, not unlike what we see around us now. It was jumbled and painted over many, many times, but one phrase did stand out. Repeated over and over again: the Digital Heart."

"Sounds made up," Cassidy said, looking around at the myriad of images and words that surrounded them.

"Yes, well, nevertheless. When you explore, take note of this digital heart. See if you can decipher its meaning."

"Will do," Cassidy said and readied herself.

"I don't believe you'll be there very long, but let's say three days tops, eh?"

"Sure, doc. What happens if I'm not back?"

"You know the protocol. We block the entrance and I notify your family."

"Cheery thought," Cassidy patted her satchel and nodded. "Good luck getting something down here to block up this one," Cassidy said and patted the doctor on his shoulder.

"Leave that to me," the doctor smiled and watched her disappear into the solid concrete wall.

***

"It's got to be here somewhere," Cassidy cursed and plunged forward. Light was a commodity in these tunnels. Where were the emergency lights and the sounds of passengers going about their day? Where was the functional bloody station?

Cassidy's shoulder slammed into a column and spun her around; more arrows sped through the air. She fell to her knees, the debris and rock cutting into her pants and legs.

"Damn it," she said and struggled to her feet.

"There they are," the rough voice rose from the shadows at her heels.

Anger washed over her. She grit her teeth and clenched her fists. She wouldn't be captured again. Not this time. She removed her collapsible shovel from her bag. A quick flick of her wrist and it was fully extended. Not long by shovel standards, but plenty long for a club or an axe.

"Psst," a small voice to her left made her jump. "This way." It was the voice of a child. She'd been around two younger sisters for too long to not recognize the playful lilt in a child's voice.

"Who…"

"Hurry, this way," a small hand gripped her wrist and tugged at her.

Cassidy turned back towards her pursuers. It was dark, but she didn't think they had caught up yet. If she had a chance, it was this. She let out a low sigh and allowed herself to be led away, hopefully to safety.

CHAPTER TWO

The child dragged Cassidy to a grate that had been dislodged from the ground between tracks – sewer access maybe or some sort of electrical maintenance shaft. Cassidy couldn't say for sure. They crawled down amongst the shadows; their feet on the access ladder made a metallic echo in the tunnel below them that Cassidy feared would draw her pursuers. The child didn't share her worry.

He was a small boy. Skinny, maybe ten if Cassidy was being generous. His skin was a honey brown under smears of dirt and dust. He had large, kind eyes that were a dazzling golden hazel. He put a finger to his full lips and guided her away from the ladder and deeper into the tunnel.

Time stretched on as they watched the entrance to this access tunnel. Cassidy's adrenaline still thundered through her veins, her fists clenched and ready for a fight. Any minute now the dark shadows holding crossbows would descend and she'd have to fight her way free. But that didn't happen. Instead the whispered voices of those that pursued her passed on, without hesitation.

Cassidy could feel her body relax. It was an aching, restless feeling as the adrenaline subsided. It left her limbs weak, her muscles like jelly and all she wanted to do was sit and eat, or do it all over again.

The boy grasped her hand and she flinched away from him. Her heart raced once more, her hands curled into tight fists, but it faded as quick as it had come on when she stared into the boy's gentle eyes. Cassidy forced a smile and held out her hand, and the boy led her further into the tunnel.

It was dark and Cassidy was having a hard time getting her bearings as she allowed herself to be pulled through the strange underpass. And yet, she had the feeling that they were going in a completely different direction from whence she had initially started her escape. Not that it mattered much to her, she was thankful for finding an escape at all before an arrow had made a pin cushion out of her.

"Hey, kid," she said once she was sure they were a sufficient distance away from the open grate. "What's your name?" Cassidy bent forward, hoping to catch a whisper from the young boy, but her only answer was another tug on her arm to signal her to go faster.

"Come on, kid," she said and gave him some resistance; not enough to stop them completely, but enough to make her point known. "I just want to give you a proper thanks, kid."

The boy shot her an annoyed look and pulled her forward with renewed gusto. Cassidy rolled her eyes in return and kept moving, though she dragged her feet some to let the kid know she wasn't too much of a pushover.

It wasn't long before the kid halted their progress all together. His head swiveled from side to side. The hair on the back of Cassidy's neck stood up, her heart picked up speed again. At this rate, she thought, I might just have a heart attack before even putting up a fight. The thought didn't hit her as funny as she had hoped.

A soft clicking noise came from just beyond a bend in the tunnel. A squeaking noise that was akin to a mouse or rat. Cassidy had had to deal with her share of rodents in her life, and while this new sound was similar, it certainly wasn't any sort of rodent she'd ever heard. *Crap*, she thought, and made to put herself in front of the boy.

As Cassidy moved, the boy made his own set of squeaking noises done with subtle lip movements on the boy's part while he sucked his teeth. *Clever*, she thought.

A solitary figure stepped out of the shadows and beckoned them to continue on. Tall and lean, though broad around the shoulders, the man in the shadows had a crossbow laid across the crook in his arm. He cocked his head upon locking eyes with Cassidy, froze for but a moment, and waved them on. The kid gave her a smile and pulled her forward.

Well, this has been an interesting turn of events, Cassidy thought and reached into her satchel to grasp her shovel – just in case.

***

"My name is Daniel Fletcher," the man who had beckoned them on said with a quick look over his shoulder. Fletcher was an average looking man who had the look of a boy that had to age into a man too quickly. He wore a beard that was in need of a trim, but it was obvious he regularly took care with it and, Cassidy had to admit, it suited him. On top of his head was an ill-fitting stocking cap that he had unnecessarily folded so that it seemed to only perch on his scalp like a strange kippah.

He led them through a large steel door and into a tunnel that was lit by oil lamps and torches. Cassidy had become so accustomed to the darkness of the subway tunnels that she had to keep her eyes lowered to avoid the feeling of being blinded. In the meantime, she had to force her eyes not to squint and they were watering profusely for her troubles. She cursed under her breath, she didn't want her first impression to come across as a weepy damsel in distress. She renewed her grip on her shovel.

"I was surprised that Arturo had brought along a... guest."

"Cassidy Cane," she said, "I'm just glad Arturo here came along when he did." She turned the kid around and squat down to his level. "Thanks Arturo," she said and gave his hand a mighty shake.

"No problem," the boy said, his cheeks darkening some.

"It's a pleasure to meet you, Cassidy, and forgive me for cutting to the point, but what the hell are you doing here?" Fletcher stopped and put himself between Arturo and Cassidy, his crossbow held up and at the ready.

Fletcher's glacial blue eyes were fixed directly on Cassidy, his stare unwavering as he waited for her response. It wasn't an easy question for Cassidy to answer. On one hand, she could go ahead and tell him that she was from another dimension or reality and confuse the man, or she could make up some elaborate lie and hope it made sense for this reality. It wasn't an easy choice. Maybe something more in the middle.

"I'm in search of the Digital Heart, and I only have three days to find it."

CHAPTER THREE

Fletcher and Arturo shared an uneasy glance.

"You're looking for the Digital Heart?" Fletcher's trigger finger twitched on his crossbow.

"Yes, I believe it may be of use in my di– home. My hometown."

"Hometown," Fletcher drew out the word, let it play on his tongue for a moment. "And where might that be?"

"Plainsfield," Cassidy said without hesitation, but upon seeing the beginnings of another question form on Fletcher's lips, added, "Massachusetts. Plainsfield, Massachusetts."

"Massachusetts," Fletcher paused and gave a curt nod to Arturo. The boy backed away into the darkness. Fletcher aimed his crossbow at Cassidy, "Now I know you're lying."

"W-what?" Cassidy took a step back.

"No more of that," Fletcher gestured his weapon at her. "So, what did Beckett intend when he hired you, hmm? I must admit, your performance up to this point was remarkable. That 'I'm-not-a-damsel-in-distress,' but 'I-really-am-a-damsel-in-distress' act really sold the authenticity." A smile curled on one side of his mouth.

Cassidy's fists clenched.

"Then you went ahead and mentioned Massachu-setts," he shook his head, a low chuckle escaped from his chest. "You must be a special kind of stupid."

"First of all," Cassidy said, and tossed her phone at Fletcher's head. He ducked and fired his crossbow, the bolt shooting straight for Cassidy's chest, but Cassidy was already moving. She ran in a diagonal line to cross the short distance to the tunnel's wall. At the last second she jumped feet first toward the wall and kicked off of it to launch herself toward Fletcher. As she did she lashed out with a punch.

Fletcher was about to slip another bolt into his bow when Cassidy's fist landed on his jaw. He sprawled backwards on the dirt floor, his crossbow landing just out of his reach.

"As I was saying," Cassidy said, her breathing still steady, her heart rate average at best. She frowned. "I'm no one's damsel in distress. Second, what's wrong with Massachusetts?"

Fletcher rubbed his chin. "You can't be serious," he said and let his tongue explore the inside of his cheek.

"Humour me."

"Massachusetts doesn't exist anymore. It's part of the Greater State of Quebec," Fletcher said and rolled his eyes.

"The greater state of…" She'd been to some strange places since she started working with Dr. Gamgee, but the Greater State of Quebec? That was just too much. "But this is New York?"

Fletcher's eyebrows furrowed. "Yes."

"Just New York, or did we become statewide room-mates with some other states?"

Fletcher eased himself up to sitting. "All the way down to North Carolina, including parts of Ohio, Kentucky, and Tennessee."

"Why?" Cassidy said, intending the question more for herself than Fletcher.

"How do you not know this?"

"I'm asking the questions," Cassidy turned her attention back to the man at her feet and sighed. She didn't know much about him, but Fletcher (and young Arturo) were the only people she'd met so far in this new dimension (reality) that hadn't wanted to capture her or shoot her, right away anyhow. Not only that, but they knew this world, and they wanted to help her, until their paranoia got the better of them. If she wanted to find out what the Digital Heart was and get back to her world, she'd need to trust someone. It might as well be this guy.

"How about we start over?" Cassidy said after a moment and crouched down to look Fletcher in the eyes. He gave her a quizzical look and then nodded.

Oh boy, what have I gotten myself into this time? Cassidy thought and helped Fletcher to his feet.

***

They had started walking again, Fletcher leading the way. Cassidy kept the crossbow, just in case. Fletcher had brought them to a halt after about ten minutes of walking and Cassidy heard a continuation of the rodent sounds that she heard earlier. Once they started walking again,

Arturo joined their ranks. He paused once he saw Cassidy with the crossbow, but only shrugged and moved along next to Fletcher.

"So," Cassidy started once they had settled into a good pace. "Tell me all about these new jumbo states."

Arturo shot her a quick glance and then another at Fletcher. The older man just shrugged his shoulders.

"Pretend I've got amnesia," she said to the boy, who gave her a blank look and another shrug.

Fletcher sighed. "It all started on the Night the Lights Went Out. That must've been, oh, thirty years ago, I guess. One minute we were all watching the war unfold on the television; the next it went dark. Everything went dark. It wasn't just the lights either. No, everything electrical seemed to give out. You don't look old enough to remember any of this anyway, but there was a fair bit of panic. I'm sure you can imagine that. One minute there was light, heat, entertainment, power. The next there was none of that. People got scared.

"Well, we all did our own things then. It's amazing to me that we didn't crumble as a people. Instead we pulled it all together. People actually helped one another. Communities came together, towns, cities. Eventually we managed to get word across the entire continent. The lights had gone out everywhere. Still, that didn't stop us. We came together, worked things out and rebuilt. Of course, because there was no electricity, we had to revisit some of our history books for those ideas."

Cassidy hefted the crossbow to have another look at it. She'd studied ancient crossbows in her travels, even one made with cast bronze fittings from seventh century China, and she'd handled her fair share of modern crossbows. With a closer look, Cassidy could tell that the crossbow she now carried was much closer to the ancient design than the modern. For one, the bow string wasn't some synthetic super fibre, but from hand woven hemp.

"We couldn't reach the world outside of America, but we assumed that if it happened here, it happened everywhere, and took some solace that a second attack wouldn't be coming."

"It was an attack then?"

"Oh yes, very much so. I was only a youngster myself back then, but there was a lot of talk around nuclear weapons during the war, but that wasn't what was used in the end. No, in the end it was an…"

"EMP," Cassidy finished his thought for him.

"Yes, that's what it was. Something that took out our technology. I can only assume that it did its job well, probably too well."

Cassidy fingered the phone in her pocket and thought of all of her devices waiting in her satchel. Hadn't she used her phone's flashlight? *I wonder what these guys will say if I start playing some Eminem*, she thought and removed her hand from her pocket. Probably not a good idea to find out.

"So, who is this Beckett you mentioned earlier? The guy you thought I was working for?"

"Well, these 'super states' as you put it–"

"Jumbo states."

"Huh…er…yes. These 'jumbo states' as you put it were created in a way to keep a form of government. It would have been too hard to communicate with all the states and provinces without the use of technology, or I suppose that's what we thought around thirty years ago. So, instead of a Governor or Premier (as I think they were called in Canada) taking one small area, we gave them control over a larger chunk of real estate and they parsed out responsibility to others, usually landowners or the rich. They're usually the same thing."

"So, Beckett is some sort of Feudal Governor?"

"If you say so. He'd rather be called Lord than Governor though," Fletcher said.

"And why would Beckett hire someone like me to interfere with you? Are you a criminal of some sort?"

Fletcher stopped and turned. His face flushed red and his nostrils flared. "Beckett is an oaf and a bully. He has perverted his position in the government," Fletcher said slowly, picking his words carefully.

"And you're what? A rebel, a revolutionary?"

"I'm just someone who believes in what we have built out of this hardship. I can't continue to watch someone pervert all the hard work we've put in to making this state, this continent, seem good again."

A little of both then, Cassidy thought.

"You, or someone like you, would probably be used as a spy. Someone who could infiltrate the inner circle and shut it down or, at the very least, disrupt it and delay operations."

Cassidy let the silence stand for a few minutes. This was certainly the first dimension of its kind. A world that was almost exactly the same as hers, and yet very different. She started to wonder if the people of this world were still able to go out to dinner; would they go dancing?

She also thought about what it would be like for her to be stuck in this reality. Could she survive without Twitter and her podcasts? No automatically heated water in the shower, no pizza delivery during her late nights correcting. No driving, at all. Would she have to get a horse? She thought with no ounce of irony or foolishness.

"Do you mind if I ask you some questions now, Ms. Cane?" Fletcher had cast a quick glance over his shoulder. Cassidy shrugged.

"What do you want with the Digital Heart?"

"That, my friend, is not an easy question to answer. However, to make it a little more easy to understand, I intend to study it. I hope to review the Digital Heart and learn if it can help people from the knowledge I'm able to glean from it."

"You don't even know what the Digital Heart is, do you?" She could see the lopsided smirk he had given her earlier.

"No. No, I don't. Maybe you could fill me in?"

"Well, not much is known about the Digital Heart. Some believe that it is the key to unlocking all the secrets kept by this newly founded government, as unlikely as that is. Others say it is just a computer file that may be a key to restoring the electricity. To be honest, I think they are a load of hogwash."

"I tend to agree. You can't very well run a computer program without any power."

Fletcher shrugged. "Beckett can."

"But didn't you already say that all the power is gone? That we were effectively plunged into a new dark age?"

"I did and we most certainly are, but that doesn't

change what Beckett can do."

"I'm sorry. I don't understand," Cassidy said and shrugged.

"Listen, I may be willing to believe that you aren't an agent of Beckett, but there's only so much I can do to suspend my disbelief. You must know about the chosen ones."

"Amnesia," Cassidy said and pointed to her head. She crossed her eyes at Arturo eliciting a blush and a smile from the boy. "Continue," Cassidy waved her hand at Fletcher.

"Fine," Fletcher said with a deep sigh. "It was about a decade after the lights went out that stories started to circulate. Rumours that the machines were coming back to life, but that rumour soon changed. It was people. Some special people were able to use machines again. Nothing big at first, a pocket calculator, a watch. That was easy to explain away though, because the batteries were not affected by the EMP. Then a blender started running in someone's hands. Next there was a car roaring down the road."

"And Beckett can do that sort of thing?"

"That and more. People like Beckett, able to raise technology from the dead, were able to place themselves in some strategic positions in the new society. Beckett, for instance, as you know, is Lord of the Greater New York State. Though we wish he wasn't. Many believe he became obsessed with power. His power to use technology, and his power over people. He flaunts it, uses it for control. Absolute control." Fletcher led them on.

"Absolute power corrupts absolutely," Cassidy said quietly to herself.

CHAPTER FOUR

The tunnel narrowed as they walked and they were forced to walk single file. Conversation had halted, and Cassidy was fine with that – she had a lot to process. At the end of the tunnel was an iron ladder bolted into the concrete. Graffiti cluttered the walls around it, aged and ugly, the art was chipped in places that obscured its meaning. Nothing denoted the presence of the Digital Heart.

The climb up the ladder was arduous. Cassidy's legs burned from the chase, and her adrenaline had started to dump. She could feel her limbs shake as her energy began to wane. Cassidy silently cursed Dr. Gamgee and his promise of an uneventful journey. He'd bestowed in her a false sense of security. Worse, a false sense of banality. It's not that she wanted the trip to be boring, far from it, it's that she hadn't properly prepared herself.

Cassidy sighed. Excuses, excuses.

***

They emerged onto a basketball court – or what remained of one. Grass crept up through cracks in the concrete, fighting with the broken glass and debris for existence. A rusted out truck was parked over a collapsed chain link fence to one side, and one basketball net was strewn across the centre of the court.

New York City sprawled around her, buildings reached like fingers toward the sky, pointing to something that could not or would not be seen. Though she had never been to this park before, the sight hit home and Cassidy felt more comfortable. New York City was one of a kind. And yet it was different. Her initial elation at being able to recognize something, or being within her own element again, shrivelled and cowered once she was able to firmly plant herself in her current reality. It was the noise – or the lack thereof. No sounds of cars idling, horns honking, or people chatting as they walked. No music blared from an apartment window, no fire sirens screamed by, there wasn't even the sound of footsteps. New York was many things, but quiet was not amongst them. This New York was a ghost. Cassidy shivered.

"Come on," Fletcher said and motioned they go west.

"Where are we going?" Cassidy said once she had caught up.

"Home," Arturo said, and his young voice cracked some. Cassidy gave him a smile.

"In a manner of speaking," Fletcher cut in. "It's more a base of operations, where some like-minded people are able to meet and discuss things candidly. Where we can prepare."

"Sharpen your knives?" Cassidy said, but was only met with a grunt of a response. "So, are all these buildings empty, does anyone live here anymore?"

"Beckett and his cronies live around here," Fletcher waved his hand vaguely. "Not in this area though, if you're worried."

Cassidy shrugged. "Where is everyone else?"

"Most people were moved closer to fields. Easier to provide for yourselves that way. Food is like currency. If you have nothing else to offer, you can at least offer that."

'Don't you find it strange,' was Cassidy's next question, but it died on her tongue. Fletcher had grown accustomed to the dead city and Arturo hadn't known it to be any different. Cassidy had just this morning been travelling the streets and subway tunnels of New York. The real New York. New York as it should be, not some hollowed chrysalis that paraded itself around as New York.

Then again, she had to wonder, was this really her New York? It was a different reality; could that mean that certain things were already different in this city, even before the EMP hit? Cassidy made a mental note; if she had time she'd investigate further. For now, she needed to focus on the Digital Heart.

"So, the Digital Heart is something that Beckett would have in his possession?" Cassidy said.

"I assume so. If the stories are true, then all Governors should have some version of it." Fletcher's head moved from side to side, scanning.

"And where could I find Mr. Beckett?" Cassidy tried to keep up with Fletcher's sight lines, to try and get a glimpse of what he might be looking out for, but he moved too quickly. Too randomly.

"Listen, Ms. Cane, I would love to continue to tell you the very well-known recent history of New York State, but

I've had a long day. I've been punched in the face, and, frankly, I don't feel like talking much anymore. Perhaps you could save your questions until we reach our destination?"

Cassidy shrugged and muttered something about amnesia.

***

The city was as empty as Cassidy had feared. The silence pushed in on her, echoed within her mind. Loneliness also seemed to creep in, a feeling that accompanied the thought of being deserted. Cassidy had been on some digs in the past, some self-appointed missions where she would have begged for time to herself. A moment to allow her to cultivate even a slim thread of clarity. After being present in this spectre of New York, she doubted she would feel that way again.

Life had been drained from this city. Without people living within it, it just became an exercise in monotony. Buildings began to bleed together until New York became a series of stone walls that guarded a maze of streets and alleyways.

Even the vegetation had refused to live there. Cassidy always assumed that in the result of some sort of catastrophic event, that even if humanity were completely wiped out, Mother Nature would make her presence known, that the earth would reclaim what had once been its own. That didn't happen in this New York. Sure, grass grew where the concrete had split. Roots of trees had gone unchecked over the last decade or more and began to jostle some walkways and fences, but nothing like she had imagined. Where were the vines snaking into every crevice, choking buildings with their presence? Where were the wild animals at ease in the formerly oppressive human city? Not here, Cassidy thought.

The base of operations Fletcher had spoken of turned out to be a hollowed out school gym that sat in the middle of a large, chain link enclosed parking lot. The exterior of the building was a mixture of brick and concrete with windows that lined the flat top ceiling and decidedly fewer that were spread out on the lower level. These latter windows were boarded up. That notwithstanding, the building appeared to be in good shape, with obvious repair work done to the roof.

"Arturo, let everyone know that we have a visitor with us, will you?" Fletcher said and patted the boy on the back as he guided him through one of the large metal doors that guarded the entrance to the building. "I'd like to have a word or two with Ms. Cane, please."

They both watched Arturo scramble inside, an obvious excitement growing on his face and manifested in his jittery, hopping steps within the old gymnasium.

"He seems like a good kid," Cassidy said and she smiled after Arturo, but her sentiment was cut short.

Fletcher grabbed her. One of his deceptively strong, thin hands latched on to her bicep, the other dug into her shoulder close to her collarbone, and he pushed her up against the outer wall of the gym.

"Let me set something straight," Fletcher's voice came in whispers hissed through clenched teeth. "While I believe you don't work for Beckett, nothing else you have said since we have discovered you has made a lick of sense. You're hiding something, and I don't care what it is as long as it doesn't get in my way. Remember that." He pushed her back against the wall and took two small steps backwards and held out his hand. "Now if you could hand over my crossbow, I think we understand one another."

Cassidy could feel the rage trying to explode through her fists and into Fletcher's face, but forced herself to let it go. This time. She wasn't sure how many of his people were around, and she wasn't sure that taking her frustrations out on one of their number would endear her to them. She'd have to settle this particular score later, once she discovered the location of the Digital Heart. She nodded to Fletcher and followed him into the gymnasium.

The space had been converted from what was once an undoubtedly large open room into a division of cubicles, makeshift rooms created with dividers, and a lot of chairs with colourful, plastic seats. Cassidy even noted that the pool had been taken over as a classroom of sorts. A chalkboard had been bolted to the centre of the rounding lip of the pool and more plastic-backed desks had been placed arbitrarily around it.

The gym was a hive of activity. At least thirty people bounced from one side of the gym to the other, sharing little tidbits of information as they went, passing on what needed to be done or doing it themselves. Cassidy never thought she would feel so happy as she did when she was stuck in a room with dozens of strangers. It wasn't a friendly welcome for Cassidy though. She was sure that Arturo hadn't spoken ill of her, and Fletcher didn't have much chance to do that if he was so inclined. Still, for whatever reason, she was given the harsh, murderous stares of people who were made paranoid by having to survive in a wasteland that had once been a prosperous city.

"Not a very friendly bunch," Cassidy said as Fletcher brought her to a large stage that stood near the rear of the gym. Subdued red curtains, faded by lack of use, clung to the walls on either side. Arturo had retreated here and was laughing and playing with other children who were kicking a ball around the stage.

"They're focused. We are close to reaching our goal." Fletcher tossed his backpack onto the stage, the ghost of a smile crossed his face as he watched the children playing. He turned and furrowed his brows to Cassidy once more. "They don't need any distractions right now."

"Point taken," Cassidy said, perhaps a little too quickly. "So, tell me where to find the Digital Heart and I'll be out of your hair."

Fletcher frowned. "Not so easily done, I'm afraid."

"You don't know where he is, do you?"

"No. He has many different buildings that he resides in, or is rumoured to reside in. We had been hoping that he was in the train station where we… encountered you, but it seems to have been just another distraction."

"And what will you do when you find him?"

"Whatever it takes to remove him from power." Fletcher weaved his way through the gym, checking in on people, updating them on what had happened on his mission. Cassidy noted that he left out the part where she had to punch him.

"So, what is this? Some sort of rebellion?" Cassidy cast a dubious glance at the burly gentlemen who were repairing crossbow bolts.

"That's as good a name as any," Fletcher said and took a moment to hug an elderly woman who was weaving clothes.

"And what do you plan to do to remove Beckett from power? Are you planning on killing him?" Cassidy heard the strain in her own voice. Part of it was in fear of what this mindless killing would do to Arturo and the children like him. Innocence was a thing to be cultivated, not dashed away. The other part was undoubtedly her own reservations. People had died in her life, and Cassidy wouldn't wish that kind of pain on anyone.

Fletcher hesitated. Those gathered in the gym were waiting for his answer. They didn't make it obvious; no one stopped what they were doing or lifted their eyes to the conversation. But there was tension in the air, something that had settled suddenly, a pressure that needed to be released.

"Only if we have to," Fletcher said with measured words. "Only if he gives us no other choice. As much of a dictator as he is, Beckett is useful, even if only for his ability to use technology. It would be a shame to have to kill him outright."

The tension lifted, people went back to their work. Still, Cassidy stared at Fletcher and tried to read his intentions. Dealing with plagiarizing students and lowballing museum curators gave her a fair bit of experience in identifying a liar. Fletcher was hard to read. He was like a politician, always trying to find the most pleasing answer for the masses; the answer that would get him the most votes on election day. His answer was fine, she thought, but could it be trusted? That she couldn't judge.

"I think we may be able to help one another, Mr. Fletcher," Cassidy said after some time studying the apparent leader of the rebellion.

Fletcher snorted, "Oh really?"

Cassidy's smile broadened. "Yes, sir. I think we can."

***

Cassidy didn't think she would be able to fall asleep. The cot they scrounged up for her was nothing more than a green piece of tarp stretched between metal poles, and the pillow she received was just a rolled-up towel. She'd slept in worse places, on worse things, but that wasn't what kept her awake. It was the worry. The fear that the doctor would close the door before she could return. What if she couldn't find this Digital Heart in three days, what if she couldn't find her way back to the portal in time?

Despite the negative thoughts and worries that flowed through her mind, Cassidy fell asleep and was joined by dreams of dancing arrows, flashing digital numbers, and Dr. Gamgee's face just before rocks fell before the portal and she was stuck in the husk of New York City. Forever.

CHAPTER FIVE

Cassidy woke up with the sun casting a warm sliver of light on her forehead. The gym was quiet. Many of the people who she'd seen the previous day had left during the night. Scuttling away to their own homes, Cassidy supposed. Still, she could hear the distant sound of breathing somewhere around her.

She chanced a look at her phone. A picture of a ragged goat appeared, its head turned to the side and its dark tongue hanging from its mouth. Cassidy smiled. Cans, the goat, always made her feel better.

6:40am. 10% battery.

Cassidy powered down the phone. "See ya later, Cans."

"What cans?" Fletcher said, coming around one of the many dividers that was used to break the gym into sections. His hooded eyes fell on her, bloodshot.

Cassidy pushed her phone into her pocket. "Nothing. Just thinking out loud."

Fletcher shrugged and zipped up his coat. His crossbow was hanging across his back and flattening his backpack. A quiver of bolts hung from the belt at his waist, and

Cassidy noticed that he added what looked like a buck knife to his ensemble, strapped to his left boot in a worn leather sheath.

"Time to go," he said and started off towards the door.

Cassidy groaned, slid out of bed and gathered her things. She placed the strap of her satchel across her chest and held it tight with one hand before she walked after Fletcher. Her other hand dug through the contents, pushing aside her shovel, a flare, and a hand brush; she felt the cool, smooth plastic shell of what she needed. With any luck she'd be home later today, tomorrow at the latest. A smile grew on her face.

They set out into the quiet streets of the dead New York, the sun lighting their way. Fletcher was quiet, his broad shoulders straight as he strode forward, his head scanning for any movement. Cassidy tried to follow his lead, but it didn't suit her.

"You really don't want to find this place, do you?" Cassidy said, trying to distract from the lonely sound of their footsteps on the cracked asphalt.

"How do you mean?" Fletcher glanced over his shoulder at her, a sneer on his thin face.

"Just the two of us..." Cassidy gestured around and shrugged.

Fletcher allowed himself a short chuckle. "The others left earlier. We spread out in teams of two, hoping to find some sign of Beckett."

"Where are we heading?" Cassidy said, now walking alongside of him. Fletcher was taller and had longer strides than her, but she was accustomed to having to keep up with taller people. To surpass them. It was a little more effort, but nothing that'd make her wheeze.

"Not too far from the subway station where we found you, actually."

"Thought there was nothing there?"

"Well, maybe not. He'd stationed some guards there, as you know, so perhaps he is nearby. It isn't entirely outside the realm of possibility…"

"But it's slim," Cassidy said, nodding her head.

Fletcher shrugged. "We'll see."

They continued on through the surreal empty streets of New York. Signs that Cassidy didn't recognize still hung from their buildings, rotting. Signs that featured a sale on CDs and cassette tapes, comic books, designer jeans. The designer names didn't sound familiar, but then again, Cassidy hadn't been one for anything too fancy. Too expensive meant more guilt when she got them dirty, and Cassidy always got her clothes dirty. Mud, dirt, blood. Cuts, scrapes, tears. Cassidy's clothes didn't last long, so she bought cheap. It worked for her.

"Not many clunkers around here," Cassidy said to keep away the sound of their feet slapping and its echo. It was true, however. The last broken down car she had seen was the old rust bucket of a truck she saw in the basketball court.

"When the lights went out, we tried to keep the roads clear. At first it was just to push them to the side of the road, enough so that people could drag their belongings behind them without having to contend with the obstacles. I remember my dad had me help move our car. He sat me behind the wheel. Allowed me to steer. That was the closest I ever got to driving."

"What happened to them since then?"

"We try to push them into more open spaces. The parks, the stadiums. We move them there to rot and hope none of the garbagemancers come around and decide to use one."

"Garbagemancers?"

"Heh, yes. It was a name we came up with for those still able to use technology. They bring garbage back from the dead, get it?"

Cassidy gave herself a moment to process the reference. "Oh," she said, excited. "Like a Necromancer. Lord of the Rings?"

Fletcher tapped the side of his nose and chuckled. Cassidy joined him. Soon the decrepit alleys and side streets filled with their laughter, echoing it back at them. It sounded as though there were hundreds of people laughing around those buildings.

A stone fell and it all stopped.

Fletcher had his crossbow in front of him in a split second; Cassidy had her shovel in her grip, following his lead.

"What?" she said, her eyes narrowed, looking around with him. "What was it?"

"I don't know. Not much falls around here anymore," Fletcher said lamely. "It's just a feeling."

Cassidy nodded. She knew about gut feelings. Any archaeologist worth their salt knew about those feelings. Down in the desert, or the jungle, or a mountainside, where the only option is to take that leap of faith and find your quarry, or pack it in and go home, you learned to trust your gut. Cassidy couldn't feel it this time, but that meant little to her. As her father used to say, "not my pig, not my problem". She was in a different reality, a different place. Her gut wasn't as accustomed to it as Fletcher's was.

"It must have been a rat," Fletcher said and stowed his crossbow, his eyes still peering into the darkened windows of the buildings around them. With a sigh, he lead them on.

They moved away from the commercial district and stumbled into the suburbs. It wasn't a particularly posh part of New York, the buildings old and without the charm of the brownstones that Cassidy associated with New York suburbs. Eventually apartment buildings turned into more traditional houses, but the last thirty years had been even harder on them than their stone counterparts. Few remained unscathed, many had fallen in on themselves, and even those left standing sustained holes with both their doors and windows missing.

"Do you really think Beckett would set up shop around here?" Cassidy said, eyeing a trio of houses that had fallen in on each other.

"No, but this way is clear. The train station where we found you is just over there," Fletcher pointed west. "We're heading that way," he pointed towards some tall buildings in the distance.

"We're circling around?"

"More or less. It's my belief that Beckett isn't hiding, as much as he is enjoying opulence. Tall buildings, penthouse suites. He wants to be a king in his castle. His decoys are more so he will be left alone than anything else."

Cassidy nodded. It was a fair assessment. She didn't know this Beckett, but from what Fletcher said, he was likely a narcissist and power hungry. Having his own personal hotel and penthouse suite might be the closest he could get to a castle in New York. If they asked Cassidy, who'd been in dozens of old castles, she'd have told him he was better off in a skyscraper anyway.

***

Fletcher suggested a break on a section of freeway just before re-entering the city proper. The freeway was still littered with vehicles, though most had been burned out or destroyed in some other way. Fletcher guided them to the broadside of an old tractor trailer, the shipping container that it had been carrying hung askew with one edge on the pavement. The rest made an awkward stretch into the sky.

"Not your first time here," Cassidy pointed out the remnants of small fires and garbage that was discarded under the shadow of the container.

Fletcher shrugged, "I'm sure many people have used this place. The trailer provides some shelter from the wind and weather, and if anyone was looking from the city they wouldn't have a clear view."

"And you could have a clear view of whatever was coming the other way," Cassidy muttered and leaned against one of the nearly deflated tires of the truck.

"Just so," Fletcher nodded and squat down in front of the pile of ash that remained from a previous fire. He arranged his things around him and took two clear bottles from his pack and tossed one to Cassidy.

Cassidy drank deeply, and sighed.

"Now that we're alone, do you want to elaborate about where you're from and what you're doing here?" Fletcher said after his own long draw of water.

"Does it matter?" Cassidy tried to avoid Fletcher's gaze and studied the bombed out cars that surrounded them. Fire bombs, maybe even Molotov cocktails.

"Would it matter if you told me?"

Cassidy flashed a smile, but it faded fast. She could still feel the bruises where he'd grabbed her the day before. "I think so," she said after a brief silence.

"Call it a professional curiosity," Fletcher paused and drained his bottle.

"I think, for now, it's enough to say that I'm not from around these parts. You help me get that Digital Heart, and I'll tell you more. Deal?"

"If you help me find Beckett, the Digital Heart is yours. Still, I'm not sure why you're so confident you can find him."

"What can I say," Cassidy shrugged, "I'm feeling lucky."

***

They scoured two hotels and half of a swanky apartment building. Each of the hotels were deserted, picked clean more like. The only things left were those that were nailed down. The apartment building had the opposite problem. It had too many things. Shopping carts (for some reason) were piled in the entrance way, more cluttered the stairs. So much so that it forced them to turn back, much to Fletcher's chagrin.

As they moved on, Cassidy had the sudden realization that this wasn't her New York. She'd never spent much time in her reality's New York; did the tourist thing from time to time and took in the big sights. She didn't think much of the strange layout she'd witnessed up to this point. She'd never been to the outer edges of New York, never cared to see them. But this stretch of the city, the big buildings, the tall skyscrapers, she'd been there, and this wasn't it. The Woolworth Building, the Chrysler Building, they weren't there. She couldn't even see them from the skyline. This wasn't her New York.

"We'll try here," Fletcher said and pointed to a high-rise that reminded Cassidy of a certain president elect in her reality. She shivered and suppressed an involuntary gagging.

As they made their way to the multi-door entrance, Fletcher did a poor job of fighting off his dejection. Despite his faults, Fletcher was dedicated to his cause. And from what Cassidy could tell, it was a good one. Liberty, justice, rights – they were all worth a fight. She focused a lot on her own crap back at home. Focused on her career, on the next artifact, the next adventure, the next thrill. Sure, she signed petitions for her students, she donated when she could, but did she ever have to fight like this? She wasn't so sure. Now, here she was, helping a cause, albeit in an indirect way. It felt good.

No worries, Fletch, Cassidy thought, *I haven't brought out my secret weapon yet.* She patted her satchel.

Fletcher moved in on the doors but stopped himself so suddenly that Cassidy almost came up solid against his back. She wanted to ask him what was up, but he hissed her to silence.

Cassidy stepped back and took a long look at their surroundings. Nothing stood out, but something was off. She could feel it now, her gut signalled something was amiss. The air was thick with an apprehensive silence that promised trouble and violence. Cassidy reached in her bag and pulled out her shovel.

"You feel that?" Fletcher whispered, his crossbow loaded, its sight up to his eye as he panned the deserted streets.

"Yeah, I feel it," Cassidy said. She felt it and she didn't like it.

An arrow arched through the sky, dull sunlight glistening off its metal head. With a curse Cassidy jumped headfirst and rolled to her feet, leaving the arrow to snap on the pavement where she had just been.

"Cover," Fletcher said. "Get to cover!"

Cassidy was already running. Arrows started to fall from the sky, black dots that might have been a hard rain. They crashed with harsh crunches that reminded Cassidy of the ugly hail they sometimes got in Plainsfield. With sudden inspiration, she put her shovel blade over her head, and choked back a laugh. *Some rain cap you have there*, Cass, she thought and dove into the alley beside the hotel.

Fletcher dove in behind her, his bolt still notched in his bow.

"Can you see them?" Cassidy chanced and strained to look over Fletcher's shoulder.

Through a stream of curses Fletcher answered in the

negative.

"Well, I guess we know we're in the right place," Cassidy said and started to look around. Fletcher shrugged and tried to get a better look at their assailants.

Arrows still pelted the street at the entrance of the alley. The alley itself was narrow, but it was empty. Long gone were the dumpsters and garbage cans that may have housed themselves there in the past. All that remained of that long-ago time was a high chain link fence that guarded the rear exit. Not a huge inconvenience, but Cassidy figured that whoever was firing arrows would be working to surround them. The longer they stayed there, the easier it would be to hold them up; to encircle them.

"We have to go," she tugged on Fletcher's sleeve and jerked a thumb towards the fence.

Fletcher shook his head. "I need to know if this is another decoy or if Beckett is here." Fletcher took a blind shot around the corner and nocked another bolt in his crossbow.

Cassidy turned to let loose another stream of curses and stopped herself midway. On the fence, one leg over the top and two hands gripped for purchase on the crossbar was a young man. He'd frozen when she turned his way, just as she'd frozen. He had on a grey cap, almost like an old aviator's hat with ear flaps and goggles. The rest of his outfit matched his hat and was a muted grey right down to his boots. His face was soft and warm with two rosy cheeks and a trimmed beard in the style of those old pictures of Shakespeare. He wore an expression of a child being caught stealing a cookie from the cookie jar. Cassidy had a moment to wonder how Beckett managed to accomplish outfitting his men in a matching wardrobe before their stalemate was broken.

"Jones, get your ass over that fence. Now!" It was a series of harsh whispers. Whispers that Cassidy was sure she wouldn't have heard if she wasn't looking at poor Jones with his mouth squirming into a sheepish grin.

"Sorry Jonesy," Cassidy said and rushed the young man. Shaking his head, Jones put out his hands in surrender. *Too late*, she thought, and slugged him a good one with her shovel, sending him back over the fence.

She barked a laugh like a challenge at anyone else who attempted to crawl over the fence and saw two more men (both in grey) pick up Jones and drag him out of the alley on the opposite side.

Cassidy turned back to Fletcher. She wanted to draw him over, to reiterate their need to escape, but he was distracted firing his crossbow and cursing into his messy beard. Smile faltering some, she realized that the men she'd just driven from the alley were likely waiting in the opposite street for them to emerge in escape, only to capture them or fill them with arrows.

"Damn it," she said and turned in a circle fuelled by frustration. Her satchel swung out from her side and came down hard on her hip.

"Damn it!" she said again, rubbing where the satchel had landed.

Her satchel.

She looked back at Fletcher, his attention still on the arrows that were now only imitating a pitter-patter of rain. She shrugged.

"No time like the present," she said to herself and

pulled out the EMF detector.

The device she held in her hand, the electromagnetic field detector, wasn't high-tech. Just bigger than the size of her palm, encased in a thick black plastic, with four simple buttons and one screen that was now blank, the EMF didn't look impressive. It wasn't even something that she had intended on taking with her. It was a joke gift given to her by one of her students. EMF detectors were supposed to pick up on ghosts. The theory was that if a ghost was trying to manifest in the area it would draw on the electromagnetic energies around it in order to get the power to do that. Like gathering its chi, Cassidy supposed. Of course, it was all bullpatookey. Her students knew she didn't believe in ghosts, or goblins, or curses for that matter. What kind of archaeologist would roam around in old tombs if they believed in that sort of thing? So, it was a joke. Ha-ha, very funny. She'd shoved it in her bag and forgot all about it.

In a world where there was absolutely no electricity, and no possibility of electromagnetic fields, it could sure as hell detect anyone who could control (was controlling) that energy. In a way, this dead world was the perfect testing ground for an EMF detector. At least that was what she was hoping for. She just had to get close enough, and hope that ghosts didn't really exist.

Cassidy switched on the EMF and saw its dull, green display screen come to life. Numbers began to fluctuate, up and down, but she wasn't worried about that. The device needed to get itself accustomed to its environment – she hoped.

Keeping her back to Fletcher she manoeuvred herself

closer to the building they'd meant to explore. 0.0 blinked at her. She held it to the beige PVC-like pipe that stood out on the wall and got the same result. She bent down and held the EMF toward the ground. It was a long shot, she knew, but she wanted to give it try. Nothing, again.

She looked over her shoulder at Fletcher, who returned her stare with a curious look. He seemed about ready to tell her the coast was clear when another arrow crashed against the wall closest to him. A curse filtered through his moustache and he went back to loading his crossbow.

Not here, she wanted to tell him, but how could she begin? *Not here Fletch, I used my doodad to check electric fields and it said nadda. Oh, what's that? Yeah, I have some pieces of tech that still work. No, I'm not a garbagemancer, thanks for asking though.*

Cassidy turned to walk towards him, a sigh cascading out from her chest, when a flicker of movement in her peripheral vision caught her attention. The EMF lit up.

She brought the device up and looked at it. 2.5 flickered there for a split second. 2.6 replaced it briefly and then 2.5 again. She cast her eyes to the building on the other side of the plaza. Another hotel, smaller than those they'd already scoured perhaps, and certainly smaller than the obelisk beside them, but pleasant to look at all the same. There was something going on in there though. Beckett was putting his abilities to good use.

"Hey," Cassidy said after she had stowed her EMF away in her satchel. "I think I found him."

Fletcher's head snapped toward her so quickly that she thought he may have given himself whiplash. He was on his feet just as fast.

"What do you mean?"

Cassidy nodded her head to the other building. "He's in there."

Fletcher's mouth hung open, not unlike a surprised Mr. Jones when he was found trying to ambush them just a few minutes before. "How…how can you be sure?"

Crap, Cassidy thought. She hadn't really decided on a plausible story. Chalk poor planning up to excitement. She looked around, and her story fell into place.

"See there," she said and pointed to an old grey security camera. They had gone out of fashion a long time ago on her world, replaced by much smaller, much rounder cameras. Thankfully this big, square model was still in non-use in this world; and still so apparent.

"I saw it move. Like it was trying to get a bead on us." Sure it was a lie, Cassidy thought, but it was a white lie. It saved her and Fletcher some trouble, and it solved their problems.

"He's using cameras?" Fletcher said, his brow bent in a scowl as he watched the camera. He brought his crossbow to his shoulder, took careful aim, and put a bolt in the eye of the unmoving camera.

"Good job," Cassidy heard herself mutter, but what she really wanted was to bust in and get the Digital Heart and get back to her world. Fletcher was ahead of the game now, there wasn't much more help she could offer.

"We have to get back to base. We have to plan our attack."

Cassidy's stomach sank. Plan an attack?

"Can't we just sneak in and grab the Digital Heart?" she said in a near whisper.

"No, we need a plan. If we are going to overthrow Beckett, we need a plan and we need people."

Cassidy shrugged. It made sense, but she would still rather just grab the Heart now while they were here.

"Come on," Fletcher turned to her, his face a maniacal mask of joy and excitement. "I think I can find us a way. Stay close and run fast." He laughed as he launched himself out of the alleyway. Arrows flew, but they were few and far between. Cassidy followed but looked back at the modest hotel, hoping to see it again soon. She only had two days left.

CHAPTER SIX

They ran out of the alley, the number of arrows now crashing around them amounted to a light drizzle. Cassidy smiled. They didn't need much room, they just had to get amongst the buildings, play a game of hide and seek, and hopefully wait out Jones and his buddies. After all, they seemed easy enough to trick in the subway tunnels.

Despite the dwindled number of arrows flying, Fletcher took to zigzagging through the street to make himself a harder target to get a bead on. Cassidy followed suit. When in Rome, she thought. She hadn't seen Fletcher book it before. Her times with him up to this point were long, disciplined and slow hikes through the decimated urban landscape. Just like everything else about him, his movement had been reserved; calculated. Now, with reason behind him, Fletcher ran like a gazelle. His long legs pumped with precision and training, something that she'd only seen in the star athletes at her university. Those athletes that were bound for the Worlds', maybe even the Olympics.

Fletcher could run, but Cassidy wasn't about to let him show her up.

Where Fletcher bounded over obstacles, Cassidy either pushed through them or slid atop of them, letting her momentum push her along. When Fletcher gave small spaces a wide berth, Cassidy moved through them. They each played to their advantages, and it kept them at a fairly even keel. Until they discovered the real reason the arrows had almost stopped.

Almost three blocks away from where they were attacked, a dozen men dressed in grey from head to toe stepped into their path. They both skidded into a stop, nearly toppling into one another. They all wore the same outfit that Jones had worn when Cassidy had clocked him with her shovel; grey hats, grey double-breasted coats buttoned to the throat, and grey gloves. The only one that stood out amongst them was a hatless man that stood in the centre of all the others. He was bald, his face bare to match his head, but he had a pair of old Ray Ban Aviators resting on the tip of his nose. Blue eyes blazed from behind them in measured aggression.

Most of these men had bows, two had crossbows to match Fletcher, but the man in the centre had a gun. It was a silver Glock, if Cassidy wasn't mistaken. She was thankful that it wasn't an AK-47 or a M-16, but really, a Glock was more than enough.

Guns, Cassidy thought. Why hadn't she seen more guns? More importantly, why hadn't she thought to question it earlier? *You were too busy avoiding arrows*, she consoled herself, but she didn't think that excuse held a lot of water.

"It is the will of his Lordship, Quinne Beckett, of the Greater New York State, that you are to be placed under arrest," the bald man said. The gun was still pointed to the ground, but that didn't give Cassidy any sort of ease. "Toss your weapons to the ground and surrender peacefully. Failure to do so will end in your death."

Baldy's gun wasn't raised, but the bows and crossbows of his companions were as they moved forward. Cassidy tightened her grip on her shovel, but she was brought around by the clatter of Fletcher's crossbow to her left.

"What the hell are you doing?" Cassidy said gaping at Fletcher.

"Not dying." Fletcher stripped his backpack off and threw it next to his discarded crossbow; his bolts came next.

"I thought you said he was a tyrant, a dictator?" Cassidy could feel her face flush. "Where I come from, men like that, they wouldn't hesitate to kill."

"Well, I'll just have to make sure that we are worth more to him alive than dead," Fletcher said with a subtle grin. "Besides, we're supposed to be back at the base tonight. If we don't check in someone will be along." He said this in a whisper, his eyes on the grey coats walking towards them.

"Rescue party?" Cassidy said, thinking of the number of children and senior citizens she'd seen just the day before.

Fletcher shrugged. "More likely to pick up our bodies, but when they get here…"

"You know what, I'll handle this myself." Cassidy took her cellphone out of her pocket and prayed that it hadn't died since this morning.

The phone flicked to life with the white startup screen,

the startup jingle rose above the muted footsteps of the grey jackets. They paused. Each one coming to a stop, their heads raised in confusion as they tried to understand and pinpoint where the music was coming from.

"Behold, peasants," Cassidy said and switched on her phone's flashlight. "I am a garbagemancer, here to raise technology from the dead and rule over you!"

The grey jackets fell back a step, even Baldy, with his Glock and his Ray Bans, stopped in his tracks. Cassidy would have smirked if she couldn't feel the intensity of Fletcher's gaze on the side of her face.

"Another garbagemancer?"

"Does Beckett know about this?"

"Where did she come from?"

The muttering echoed through the streets as each grey coat turned to Baldy for guidance. For his part, Baldy seemed to be maintaining his cool, and that worried Cassidy. He stared straight ahead at her (not her, her flashlight) and pushed his sunglasses up on his nose. At his side, he thumbed back the hammer of the Glock.

Cassidy's upraised hand wavered. *That's not good,* she thought.

"She only has a flashlight," he said with a southern drawl, which was somehow more surprising than anything else she'd encountered over the last couple of days.

"Run," Cassidy said and threw her phone at the grey coats.

It may have only been a flashlight, but it still sent those big burly men on the back peddle. Cassidy bolted into the building closest to her, and dove into the darkness.

She ran down the length of a hallway, not realizing

that Fletcher wasn't with her until she came to an abrupt stop, her face introduced to a wall.

Tasting the blood that ran from her nose, Cassidy groped her way to standing once more, and turned back towards the entrance. Pale light pierced the dirty windows, dust filled rays of light zigzagged the room, but none reached the back of the room where Cassidy stood in gloom and shadow. Fletcher hadn't come with her.

Cassidy's mind raced. Was he shot? No, she didn't hear the gun go off. Pierced by an arrow then? No, the grey coats had been spooked and scattered, they wouldn't have had time to nock an arrow. *Was it me? Maybe,* she thought. *Maybe he thinks I'm exactly what I said out there. A liar, a traitor.* Maybe he thought it would be better dealing with the devil he knew.

The door swung open and the daylight spilled in. The silhouette of a man darkened the opening.

"Fletcher?"

The gunshot was deafening in the enclosed space. Cassidy brought her hands to her ears and ran to her left, hoping another wall wouldn't impede her escape.

Another shot rang out, muted by the effects of its predecessor. Cassidy ducked down and flailed into a hallway with a bank of elevators to the right and a set of stairs to her left. There was a small window at the end of the hallway that allowed scraps of light in, but it seemed so far away, and Baldy was right behind her. Cassidy took the stairs.

Running up the stairs two at a time, Cassidy pulled herself along with one arm, taking the corner of the twisting stairwell with the agility of a lazy cat. She threw herself into the opposite wall, her shoulder impacted and aided in her rebound as she headed up the stairs to the next level.

Light filtered in through the many windows that were broken open, their glass glittered the floor. A fire exit glared at her from the end of a hallway on the opposite side of that level and she ran to it, the thudding footsteps of the gun-toting bald man echoed up the stairs behind her.

Cassidy thundered across the empty floor; each footfall made her wince; she knew she was giving away her position. Her only other option was to duck into one of the empty rooms and hope Baldy wasn't patient nor thorough enough to check every room. Cassidy didn't want to take that chance. Not only wasn't it smart, but it gave the other grey coats time to recover from the slight shock they may have had.

Where the hell was Fletcher?

A grey clad arm shot out of a room to her right, its thick fingers wrapping around her bicep with ease. Cassidy was pulled back in mid-run so viciously that her legs flailed into the air.

"Where are you going, girl?" The grey coat's voice was gruff. It bristled like his beard, under green eyes. In his other hand he held a thick bow made from a bone white wood, shellacked and obviously cared for. He pulled her in close, his breath warm on her face. She could hear the stairwell door swing open somewhere behind her. Baldy had arrived.

"Just trying to get some fresh air," Cassidy said and drove her knee into the large man's groin. The effect was immediate. With nothing more than a whimper and some deep breaths, he fell to his knees and released his grip on her arm to console himself, rolling on the floor in the fetal position.

"Stop!" The southern twang of Baldy rose up behind her, the distinct click-clack of his Glock's slide being made ready for fire.

Cassidy blew through the fire exit, the bang of the handle on the wall drowned out by another gunshot from behind. The bullet impacted in the wall next to her, dust and wood particles spraying her right side.

Her thighs hit the railing of the metal fire escape and she almost fell headfirst into the alley below. The door swung shut behind her, but Baldy was on his way. She could go down, but the rest of the grey coats were down there (perhaps Fletcher too?).

Cassidy took a deep breath and ran up the fire escape, the clanging of the metal steps rang into the air, and she thought she heard the frenzied shouts of the grey coats coming from the front of the building. She couldn't look back to see if they were coming. The fire escape door slammed open behind her.

She made the top of the brick building in a few minutes, the hurried steps of Baldy behind her. Instead of taking to the roof on her feet, Cassidy rolled over the edge and turned herself to face the stairway. Her hand dipped into her satchel and pulled out her shovel once more, another flick of her wrist and it popped open.

Baldy came up the stairs with reckless abandon, his bald head caught the sunlight as it breached the edge of the roof. He came so fast that he didn't notice Cassidy there until he was half way up the stairs, and by then it was too late.

Cassidy lashed out with the blade of her shovel. She had been aiming for his gun, but at the last second he moved his hand, defending his weapon. Instead, the shovel's blade swung wide, the force dragged Cassidy forward, off-balance.

A curse flew from Baldy's mouth, himself off balance, as he brought his gun back around in a panic. The gun fired twice, dust flew just wide of Cassidy and she pushed herself to the side, lashing out with her shovel once more. The shovel glanced off Baldy's gun hand, scraping off the muzzle of the silver Glock. Again he pulled his hand back, but he was steady.

He didn't fire again, instead he made a grab at the shovel. His long, thin fingers reached out, their tips scraping the handle as Cassidy pulled it out of his reach.

Baldy, his eyebrows furrowed behind his aviators, brought his Glock back up. He gripped it in two hands to steady himself and took aim. Cassidy read his movements and brought the shovel up like an uppercut. The shovel hit the butt of the gun and sent it, and Baldy's hands, into the air. Another shot rang out as a bullet cut through the sky. Baldy refused to let go. Cassidy spun herself around and slammed the flat end of her shovel into Baldy's stomach.

He bent forward, his breath pushed out of him in a wheeze. Cassidy could see his grip loosen on the Glock, but he refused to let it go. His Ray Bans, however, had escaped his face in the scuffle, lost somewhere between the roof and the ground below.

With a frustrated grunt, Cassidy pushed the already off kilter grey jacket over, sending him over the small flight of stairs. He landed with a groan at the junction between the stairs up and stairs down, gun still in his hand, but squirming in pain.

"That'll have to be good enough," Cassidy said through gulping breaths.

More shouting came from below, the angry voices of the regrouped grey coats trying to decide what to do next.

They'll be coming up through the building, she thought. They'd come up the dark stairs see the big man on the floor and he'd guide them to the fire escape. They'd find her, and soon.

Cassidy cast a quick glance at the neighbouring buildings. She flirted with the idea of making the jump to one of them, but the space was too much, the alleyway too large.

"I've jumped farther," she muttered as she turned to take in her surroundings.

It was a flat, empty roof, save for one large metal compartment that probably housed air conditioning or venting of some sort. Cassidy checked around the metal box, her hand sliding over the cracked and scaly rust that plagued its corners and edges. A PVC pipe crawled along the ground away from it and disappeared over the edge of the roof.

Cassidy looked over the edge following the PVC pipe to its end. There were some hard angles in the pipe's descent, but it looked to go all the way to the bottom. With a sigh and a shrug, Cassidy started the climb downward, cursing to herself for not packing a length of rope.

Sweat coated her forehead, she could feel it roll down her back and her t-shirt clung to her ribs and stomach when she finally hit the ground. The grey coats were shouting from the rooftop, blame of her disappearance shifted back and forth. With a smile she stole off into the shadowy alleys and side streets. As she made her way into the unfamiliar, abandoned city the raspy voice of Baldy wormed its way through the buildings, followed her and tried to grip her with thin, wormy fingers. It was followed by the loud bang of a gunshot, silencing everything.

CHAPTER SEVEN

Cassidy moved quickly. She dipped behind cover when she could, but there was precious little of that going around. It was obvious that in the years since the EMP blast there had been a massive clean-up. There was really no other choice. It wasn't the end of the world, after all. Life went on, people needed to live and work and build and grow. The apocalypse was never going to be like it was portrayed in movies and books. Humans were survivors, and more than that, they thrived on community, no matter how splintered that instinct had become over the years.

Cassidy had read about different parts of her own world, when things got downright apocalyptic, people joined together and solved the problem. They took care of each other. She bet that was what happened here. Whether it was Fletcher's handful of rebels moving vehicles out of the road, or some other group clearing the dumpsters to melt down or for some other use. The people here made it easier and safer for each other.

So, what happened after that?

Government was reinstated. Granted it was a crude

feudal type government, but it put one person over another and that's when everything started to break down. As much as humans were great together in a pinch, when power was evoked and given, when one man or woman was placed on a pedestal above others, it caused tension. Oh, it probably gave some a feeling of comfort. Those people would accept their place in the world, but there would always be those 'what if' thoughts.

What if I was in charge?

What if I didn't have to pay my taxes?

What if I had more land?

It was the 'what ifs' of the commoner and the gluttony for power of the powerful that caused tension. That tension caused arguments. It caused fighting. It caused wars.

Then the garbagemancers came along and that added another level of power and 'what if'. Theirs was a natural power that most couldn't overcome or match. Didn't mean that people wouldn't try.

The government leaders were quick with the appearance of sharing power. The garbagemancers were made into landholding lords, given freedom to do what they wanted and the authority to back it up. Though Fletcher never told her as much, Cassidy was willing to bet that even with lordly power, they still owed a monthly tithe to the President of America (or whatever he was called in this world).

They tossed power to their subordinates like candy to children, but the candy was from a bargain bin at the dollar store. The powerful didn't like it and wouldn't miss it.

Cassidy was willing to bet that Fletcher and his band of revolutionaries were just one of many across the country, maybe the world. They didn't know eachother existed, but they all played by the same rule. A rule based on that instinct they experienced when the world first went to squalor: help each other, build, live. Hope, too. Maybe Fletcher and his group could actually pull it off.

Fletcher. Part of her thought that he may have been the recipient of that one gunshot she heard as she fled, and another thought it was just Baldy airing his tension. Then again, it could have been meant to draw her back to see if Fletcher had been shot. Or maybe….

"Stop it," she said and put her focus back on her escape.

Cassidy moved down another dark alley, her legs and arms screamed in protest, and she forced herself to sit in the shadows where one building joined the next. She regretted it immediately. Her back ached between her shoulder blades, her shoulders quivered, even her buttcheeks screamed in pain.

"I need to get back to the gym," she said and ran a hand through her hair, pushing it back and out of her face. "Maybe a haircut too."

To hell with it, when you get out of here treat yourself to a spa day. Gamgee can pay for the extra long massage.

Gamgee. She needed to get moving. This was the second day and the light was already falling from the sky. Cassidy had to get the Heart. Get the Heart and get back to her world or she might be stuck in this dead world forever. She heaved a heavy sigh. *You'd think you'd get better at this over time?*

"So," she said, "how are you going to do that?"

Don't forget about Fletcher.

"No, I won't." Cassidy struggled to her feet (which now burned and flared with a sharp pain).

What are you going to do?

"Get Fletcher. Get the Heart. Get home." Cassidy limped out of the alley and forced herself to keep moving in the general direction of Fletcher's base. She stopped, leaning one hand on the rough brick of the building to her right, and she nodded to herself.

"Wait. First, I'll get reinforcements."

And not the kind that are only looking for your dead body.

"Then, with their help, I'll get Fletcher. Help Fletcher dispose of Beckett. Get the heart. Then, get back home. How's that?" Cassidy said and stumbled forward.

***

She was lost. The night had fallen sooner than she had anticipated (was that another quirk of this New York that wasn't her New York?). Cassidy was sure that she was headed in the right direction and moving toward the freeway they'd entered this part of the city through. Even so, she couldn't find a freeway, or anything that looked like it. There were no ramps, no openings, nothing. Just block after block of abandoned buildings.

Cassidy's muscles were begging her to give them a break. They rippled unbidden and seemed on the verge of giving up the game whether Cassidy allowed them to do so or not. She cursed. She had to find shelter. She needed the rest, though she certainly didn't want to imagine what her muscles would feel like in the morning. Another curse was spat into the open air.

Eventually she came across an old building, not quite a brownstone, but close enough. Three in a row actually, but the one she eyed didn't have the door beat in, and the door handle and lock were where they were supposed to be.

Cassidy opened the door with as much caution as her shaking muscles would allow her and poked her head in. It was dark. The interior was completely shielded from the dull light of the moon and stars. The air was dry and had the sour odour of dust and neglect. If someone had been using this place as a shelter it was a long time ago.

Her muscles gave her enough leeway to drag herself in through the entrance and close the door before she collapsed to her knees. It was a bittersweet relief that washed over her. She wanted to just lie where she'd fallen. She wanted to lie there and sleep and forget about her weary muscles and guns and dead worlds and no cellphones.

Mustering all her will and remaining strength, she managed to crawl into the living area of the little house and into a corner that faced the entrance way. She couldn't be sure that no one followed her, or that they couldn't track her stumbling, erratic trek into a strange part of this unknown New York. Cassidy needed to be prepared in case someone tried to surprise her in the middle of the night.

With her head leaning against the wall behind her she stared at the door, her mind racing despite the exhaustion of her body. How could she be certain there weren't other factions roaming the deserted city? Fletcher mentioned that most people had been moved to farmland to make a living, but his group was able to escape that life.

Who's to say that another group didn't as well?

Could there be another group of freedom fighters, or a band of thieves looking to survive off the suffering of other people?

And what would they do with a bone-tired archaeologist from another world with nothing more than a cheap EMF and a collapsible shovel?

"Doesn't matter, I'll make them eat it if they aren't friendly," she said with a weak swat towards her satchel.

She nodded to herself then and fought back an unbidden laugh. All she needed to do was sit in the dark. They'd miss her at a cursory glance, and by the time they got around to really studying the space, she'd be awake and ready for them. She'd done it before, she'd be able to do it again.

Were you this tired back then?

"Yes, I was exhausted." She cleared her throat. Anyway, there was nothing more that she could do about it now. She needed to sleep, she needed to rest. When the daylight reappeared, she'd find the freeway, get her backup, and finish all this. She'd be back home before supper time.

This time she did laugh as her eyelids closed over her dry, strained eyes and she crossed over into a deep, uninterrupted sleep. Never aware that she was being watched, and watched closely.

CHAPTER EIGHT

When Cassidy woke, the reality of her night came back to her in bits and pieces. She took a minute and confirmed that she felt fine, all things considered, and, with great effort, stretched. The aches and pains of the previous day's activity fell on her like a leaden weight. She cried out as her limbs fought against her attempts to move and pulled back, tight. Cassidy could feel her calf muscles dance on the verge of a cramp.

"No, no, no…" she said through gritted teeth and somehow managed to pull her legs back and massage them into a semblance of relaxation.

"That's it. Gym. As soon as I'm done this, I'm signing up for the gym," she said with a sigh and fell back against the wall again.

"Jim? No, I'm Argyle," the voice came from another room.

Cassidy watched as a shadow of a figure crept around the doorway from the next room over. Its legs were long and spindly, bunched up as it crawled into her room. Its hands were flat on the floor and pulled it forward. Its long fingernails scraped over the laminate flooring as it went.

She reached for her shovel, but her satchel wasn't by her side.

Did I take it off, she thought as she fixed herself to be squared up with the creature that had just made its way into her space.

Despite her still sleep addled mind protesting against it, the creature was most certainly a human. She didn't have to push far past her initial fright to see it. Legs, arms, head – all where they were supposed to be. And then there were the creature's eyes. Bright white, save the small brown iris that wouldn't move from her.

"Some call me the Rat," the creature said and pulled out a football helmet to place in the centre of the room. "But I'm Argyle. Always have been, always will be." He shambled over and sat on the helmet, Green Bay Packers judging by the colours. He drew his knees to his chest and crossed his arms over them, still studying her.

"Where..."

"Argyle owns the house. Owns this street, this block, this city." He gestured with both hands, "It's Argyle's."

"Were you here when I showed up last night?" Cassidy said and fought to keep the anger from her voice.

"Oh yes, Argyle watched you come in. He watched you crawl to that corner and watched you fall asleep. You slept well, yes?"

Not if I knew some creep was watching me, Cassidy thought. She could feel the ache in her back and legs begin anew, her shock subsiding. She wanted to sit down again, to give herself a minute to get used to the idea of stretching out her tensed muscles. The thought of sliding down the corner to sit again crossed her mind, but it was soon overridden with another darker image. A premonition of Argyle, as quick and agile as a spider, scuttling across the space between them and on her – all limbs and teeth. Cassidy shot a quick glance at the man's mouth, it was a red slash in the early morning darkness. She shuddered.

"Argyle, where is my bag?" Cassidy tried to ignore the pain and stood away from the wall with her shoulders squared and back; ready.

Argyle squinted at her, his eyes suspicious. He turned his torso to the side and tried to keep it out of sight. "Argyle doesn't know anything about a bag," he said, yellowed teeth bared some.

Cassidy wanted to curse and pounce on him, beat him until he admitted he had her satchel, but she held herself steady. There was something in Argyle's eyes that told her there was another way. Something in the way he looked at her.

"Argyle," she said and put her fists on her hips, "are you lying to me?"

One of his lips curled back over his yellowed teeth in a sneer, "No."

"Argyle, this isn't how you treat guests, is it?"

His stance faltered some and he turned back towards Cassidy, sulking.

"Taking someone's things is an awful lot like something a rat would do. You're not a rat are you?"

"I'm Argyle. I always have been, always will be," he said and puffed out his chest.

"That's right," Cassidy said through a forced smile, "so where are my things Argyle?"

He pouted some, but he pulled her satchel out of his

long, grey coat and handed it to her. His eyes finally left her face. They turned to the ground.

"Thanks, I appreciate that," Cassidy fought the urge to check inside the bag to make sure everything was there.

That might be pushing my luck a bit, she thought and slung the pack over her shoulder.

"You have good tech in there," Argyle said. His eyes fluttering between her face and the ground. "I bet Beckett really likes you. Do you work for Beckett?"

"No," she said cautiously. Perhaps this was the grey coat's version of a bloodhound. Cassidy fought a sneer from appearing on her own face.

"Good," Argyle said with a sigh. "Argyle doesn't either. I just," he shifted his eyes to the left and right, "I just borrowed this coat." He opened the coat as if it relieved him of all implications.

"Do they like you much, Argyle?" Cassidy had the feeling that she already knew the answer to this, but wanted to keep him talking.

"Oh no, Beckett does not like Argyle. His men try to hurt me, to take my things. Beckett is just jealous. He thinks he's the Lord of this city, but it is Argyle's city. Argyle is… Argyle is king!"

"Well, Argyle, Beckett doesn't like me much right now either. But he has something of mine, and I need to get it back."

"Yes? Yes, what is it Beckett has of yours?" Argyle skittered a little closer to her, leaving the helmet behind. Cassidy stepped back into the wall.

"Well... he has something called the Digital Heart, have you ever heard of that?"

Argyle rubbed his chin and scratched his head. "No, Argyle hasn't heard of a Digital Heart. A heart," he thumped his chest, "but not a Digital Heart. What is it?"

"Oh it's just this little thing, but it's important to me. Very important."

Argyle nodded his head.

"He also has a friend of mine. I need to save him."

"A friend?" Argyle shook his head. "Beckett doesn't like friends. He doesn't like keeping them for long."

"Do you know where he would be?" Cassidy heard the panic slip into her voice, but that couldn't be helped. Not now.

"Beckett keeps them close, do you know where Beckett lives?"

"The squat hotel with the cameras."

"Yes, yes. Your friend will be there. Argyle is sure of it."

Cassidy held her breath for a long moment. She had wanted to get back-up, to get Fletcher's small rebellion to come to her aid, storm Beckett's so-called castle, and rescue Fletcher. Argyle could probably point her in the right direction, and get her started on the trek back to Fletcher's home base. That would take most of the day, and even then would anyone even be there? They had daily scouting trips planned, and Fletcher wouldn't be missed for another day. There'd be no reason to halt their original plans. Even if everything went perfectly and they were all there, ready to go when she arrived, would they believe her? They didn't know her, and Fletcher had treated her like an enemy the minute he met her. Would they be any different, especially if she returned saying that Fletcher was captured? They'd probably blame her for it. By the time she could convince them otherwise, her three days would be up and Fletcher would be dead. There just wasn't enough time.

"Argyle," Cassidy spoke slowly, "could you show me where Beckett lives? I've forgotten the way."

*****

Before noon they left the house. Argyle wanted some assurances and some of her tech. After a brief discussion, he settled for the EMF reader and the promise that he didn't have to set foot inside Beckett's building.

The skittering creature Cassidy had associated with Argyle transformed as they exited onto the street. In the open space, Argyle stretched out his legs, a series of pops and cracks sounded in opposition. Arms stretched toward the sky, he stood almost seven feet tall. It took Cassidy a moment to adjust to the sudden, and unexpected, change. She had students in her class, basketball players mostly, who were six foot seven, six foot eight, but Argyle put them to shame. His fingers were long and lean and highlighted by long, often curved, fingernails. Through the initial shock of Argyle at his full forbearance, Cassidy could only focus on how glad she was that she didn't choose to tangle with him.

"Come," Argyle's voice was hushed, his restless eyes constant as they roamed the buildings that surrounded them.

Cassidy could vaguely remember her surroundings from the night before, but the path Argyle was leading her over seemed more familiar than not. The brownstones they had left were an oddity of that neighbourhood, surrounded by large grey concrete monoliths that parted only in their middle for doors and spotted with windows. When Cassidy looked up to the sky, a lone curtain seemed to blow out into the wind like a flag at half mast. It was that image, the lone curtain, that made her thankful for choosing Argyle's brownstone. Images of creatures far worse than Argyle crawling through that building floated up from her imagination. Creatures with unseeing red eyes, stripped to the waist, and foam dripping from their fang-like teeth. She shuddered and hurried after Argyle.

Their pace was slow, but constant. Argyle sniffed at the air, cocked his ear to some distant sound Cassidy had no hope of hearing, and poked through debris as if it were some sort of treasure trove – or a dead body he was ensuring was properly deceased. He halted their advance many times, and scurried off on all fours, often reappearing from a high ledge or window, his face grim and mouth set in a frown. Cassidy had spent more than her fair share of time dealing with paranoid sherpas, self-conscious trackers, and overzealous hunters, so she was aware of what Argyle was doing – at least she thought so. The poor fear-addled man was checking for traps, for spies, and for anything that would give away their position. He was cautious, but perhaps that was what living the life of a scavenger in this world was painted with: caution. Cassidy shrugged, he knew the way and she didn't, she had little choice but to allow him his extended rituals.

It was well after midday before they entered an area of the city that Cassidy had some recollection of. It was the freeway Fletcher had led her through.

"That's where I came from," Cassidy said pointing out the freeway exit to Argyle. She didn't quite know why she said it and certainly didn't understand why she had to say it to Argyle.

You don't want him to think you're stupid. That you're a stupid, lost little girl that needs his help.

That could be, she thought and felt a frown deepen on her face. For Argyle's part, he just shrugged and went back to sniffing the air.

***

The first arrow struck the ground in front of them. Cassidy's recollection had been growing the further they ventured into the city, and she felt a wave of relief when they reached the buildings that she and Fletcher had explored before the ambush. She was about to mention this to Argyle when he yelped and skittered backwards into the shade of an alleyway. The arrow struck a moment after and sent Cassidy backpedalling into the alley with Argyle.

"That was sooner than expected," Cassidy said, trying to look around the edge of the building to see where the archer was.

"Beckett moves positions. Especially when he's suspicious." Argyle growled and studied the building they were leaning against.

"Makes sense. I was only here yesterday," Cassidy massaged her sore tricep muscles.

Argyle grunted and stretched up, grabbing the ledge of a window that Cassidy hadn't noticed until she heard Argyle's fingernails scratch across it. With one quick pull he was up, his long legs hanging briefly in midair over her head.

"Come," he said, his wild face appeared and he slithered one long arm down for her.

An arrow cracked against the asphalt road and Cassidy could hear the shouts of men getting closer and closer. She jumped up and grasped Argyle's wrist, his long fingers wrapped around hers in return. The feel of his thin fingers and their too long nails caused a ripple of disgust to walk up and down her spine.

Argyle dragged her into another dark room. She wasn't surprised. The gloomy light from the overcast sky tried to pierce the darkness in that room, but it was of little use. Cassidy pulled her hand away from Argyle, his bright white eyes seemed to be the only thing she could see in the gloom and moved further away from the window. She tripped over something and fell on her ass. The sudden jolt of pain set all her muscles to aching again as if her body was one big cramp. Cassidy stifled a scream. She was really starting to hate this world and its lack of electricity.

She reached around and pulled up what she had tripped over. A wooden baseball bat. She ran her hand over its length, feeling the smooth surface spotted with dry spots where the lacquer had been worn away.

"Wait, they're…," she started, but was cut off by a sudden howl that came from the door as it was kicked open.

A lone silhouette burst into the room with a metal bar or baton raised above its head. Cassidy couldn't make out the minute details, but they had on a grey jacket.

Cassidy started to rise to meet the man, the baseball

bat in her hands and ready to club him about the knees, but, again, she was cut off -- this time by Argyle. A loud, screech went up from her spindly guide and he threw himself upon the attacker, not giving him enough time to bring down his weapon.

She faltered. Argyle had his arms and legs wrapped around the man, his face was at his neck and just under the screams of the attacker, Cassidy thought she could hear a chewing or slurping sound. Her stomach wavered and she leaned on the open window, the fresh air suddenly very welcome.

There was yelling outside and a sudden crash from somewhere not too far below her. *The door,* she thought. *They're coming.*

Cassidy didn't spare a glance at Argyle and the fallen grey coat; she wasn't sure that her stomach could've handled it anyway. She pushed passed them into a stairwell, even darker than the room she had just left. Noises drifted up from the floor below: muffled conversations, stomping of feet.

"They don't know we're here," Argyle poked his head through the doorway and Cassidy nearly screamed. What little light there was reflected from Argyle's too white eyes, and she was glad for it. There was a slick sheen on his face and chin, black in the near dark, that she knew she didn't want a clearer image of. "They're just looking. More are in the street."

Yes, Cassidy thought, that had some sense to it. They couldn't find them in the alley, so they'd check the buildings. They hadn't expected Argyle to be so tall, so they didn't figure anyone would be on the second floor, only on the first. Keep quiet, don't move, she thought and re-peated it as a mantra. Keep quiet, don't move.

Easier said than done, she thought, steeling herself to return to the first room. The room with Argyle in it. The room with Argyle's victim. She hesitated at the doorway, cocked her ear to the noise on the first floor again. It was quieter already. Some, if not all of them had moved out, likely exploring other buildings. Hunting. They'd have to stay away from the windows.

She heard another familiar sound. Cassidy was just about to strengthen her efforts to return to the room with Argyle when the low pitch tickled her ear. It wasn't some-thing she had yet heard in this world, and she'd become so accustomed to the pervading silence that entombed this version of New York that she couldn't place it at first. It was loud. Even at a distance it was loud. Like the roar of some wild animal echoing over the vast dead wasteland. But that wasn't it. Then it roared again.

Cassidy's eyes popped open wide and she turned towards the blackness that contained Argyle. "Is that a car?"

Though she couldn't see him do it, Cassidy knew that Argyle was nodding. "Beckett is moving."

"What the hell does that mean?"

"He has many homes in Argyle's city," said Argyle's disembodied voice. "Many homes, many hiding places." That last word he drew out with a long 's' sound.

Cassidy she ran up over the stairs. If there was a car running in this version of New York, she had to see it.

CHAPTER NINE

She took the stairs two at a time, her throbbing muscles an afterthought as Cassidy pushed her way up one floor after another. Her footsteps sounded like small explosions that boomed through the building, though she paid little heed to them. The only sound that she focused on was the roar of the engine as it got closer and closer.

Far too loud to be a Toyota Tercel, Cassidy thought, turning the corner on another set of stairs. Has a lot of rumble to it, maybe a truck or a suped up Mustang? Better yet, a Camaro.

Cassidy's mind rolled over the possibilities as she made her way up to another level still, but there was something else nagging at her. Something Argyle had said.

Cassidy came to the top of the stairs. There was a metal door to her right, a large number 8 stencilled on it next to a window that had what looked like chicken wire running through the panes. Not giving herself enough time to take a deep breath, she pulled open the door and ran into the room, her eyes searching for the nearest window, or exit. She had to see the car.

She busted through an office door and tossed a chair

to the floor to clear her path to a dust-ridden, dirty window. She was in luck. With a flick of the lock and a twist of the handle, Cassidy was out on a small metal balcony, a cool breeze blowing her hair across her eyes.

The rumble of the engine grew louder as it got closer, a roar that was interrupted by a harsh clanking noise. "Gear change," Cassidy muttered, and placed her hand over her eyes to stop the sun from interrupting her view. Plumes of black smoke appeared in the sky not far off, and another belch of gear changing as it pushed itself forward. Diesel, Cassidy thought, a truck.

It was more than a truck that turned a corner and pulled into view. A tractor trailer pulled into view; its roar not silenced by the turn into the main drag. The truck itself was a shining red, two chrome exhaust shafts climbed up behind the doors and continued to unfurl black plumes into the air. The sun struck the windshield and hid the driver behind its glare as the trailer behind it continued to pull itself into view.

Cassidy thought the sight of the truck, of such a familiar object, accompanied by its commonplace, if unwavering sound, would shake the unnerving emptiness that she felt in this dead world. She thought that it might make her feel more comfortable, even at ease. It didn't. The sight of the truck was like a stone sinking in her stomach. The earth-shaking noise made her flinch, and she suddenly had the urge to hide away from the smoke-spewing, mechanical beast that was about to thunder toward her.

Try as she might to pull away, to flee back through the window, something continued to draw her towards the truck. Was it something Argyle said?

"Beckett is moving," whispered in her mind. Cassidy turned to see if Argyle had crept up behind her, but the window was empty.

He has many homes… many homes, many hiding places.

Cassidy strained her eyes trying to see the driver, why were Argyle's words sticking with her?

The Heart! If Beckett was moving, he would be taking the Heart with him.

"True," Cassidy said and bit her lip, but there was something else. Something on the tip of her tongue.

Besides, what was she going to do, jump on the trailer and hitch a ride to his new hideout, ambush a small army of armed men, just because Gamgee saw some graffiti? Not a chance. It would make more sense to head home, tell Gamgee about what she found. Tell him about the dead world, the eerie facsimile of New York, about the make-shift feudal government, and about Fletcher's freedom fighters. Let Gamgee decide if it was worth it.

Fletcher.

Cassidy cursed herself. Fletcher was in that truck. He was on that trailer.

"Stupid, stupid, stupid," Cassidy said and paced the small balcony. Fletcher was an asshole of the first degree but leaving him to Beckett now was as good as leaving him alone in the first place. Besides, coming back here was about helping Fletcher, not the Digital Heart. Right?

He might be dead. Or Beckett might have left him behind, travel light and all that.

"Does he look like he's travelling light?" Cassidy waved a hand toward the eighteen-wheeler that rolled her way.

Good point.

"Thank you," Cassidy said and climbed over the railing in front of her.

Below her she could see a similar balcony to the one she'd just left. She eased herself down and swung into it, a loud clang resounding as she landed. There were shouts from below, but she didn't have time to worry about that. She repeated the process and moved to a lower balcony.

Let me figure this out, she thought and moved down to another level. *An average tractor trailer is about fourteen feet high. Each storey in a building is about ten feet high.*

Another level.

"So," she said out loud between gulping breaths, "second story will be about twenty feet high, right?" She stopped and looked for the truck. It had completed its laborious turn and was chugging straight for her. It was picking up speed.

"Or, would the balcony of the third floor be at twenty feet and the ceiling of the third floor be thirty feet?" She cursed. "What bloody storey am I on anyway?"

It didn't matter. The truck was picking up the speed that it had lost in the turn but getting faster and faster. If she was going to do this, she had to do it now.

She climbed over the railing. *The last railing I'll be climbing over*, she told herself. Making sure her heels were able to fit between the bars easily; she reached her arms back to hold the railing. The position had the strange benefit of stretching out some of the aches and pains that she had managed to push out of her mind for a moment or two. It felt good.

The truck blared its horn as it passed underneath her,

and the sound almost made her lose her grip. Cassidy chuckled and watched as the red truck moved from her sight and the large white trailer filled her view.

"Am I still too high up?" she managed before yelling a loud litany of curses and letting herself fall on the trailer. *This is going to hurt,* she managed to think before she slammed into the trailer and everything went fuzzy.

CHAPTER TEN

The trailer top was slick. Cassidy slapped at the surface and willed her palms to grip tight. She cursed when they failed to do so. Cassidy flailed and slid towards the edge. She kicked her boots out, the thick rubber soles tried to do their job but couldn't catch and wouldn't hold.

"Idiot," Cassidy growled. "You're an idiot."

With one more big effort she pushed herself up on her knees and lodged a boot along the slightly raised edge of the trailer to slow her momentum. She took advantage of her borrowed time and wiped her hands on her pants. She couldn't stretch across the width of the trailer to grab a hold of the other side while her boots lodged where it was for a foothold.

So, it's either my hands or my feet, Cassidy thought.

Cassidy pushed off the small edge and grabbed a hold of the side, her hands latched onto the small outcropping. Her body tried to roll to the side and her arms strained against the momentum to keep her in place. With another grunt she sprawled her legs out so that the sides of her boots connected with the trailer top. With more area coverage the rubber grips kept her from moving. With an ex-

tra effort she pulled herself up, her biceps tight and painful with her elbows tight to her ribs.

She was secure enough, her hips moving with the motion of the truck to keep her in place. Everything hurt but
she held on, her fingers numbing.

Turning her head towards the building she'd leapt
from Cassidy caught a glimpse of the bright white eyes of
Argyle staring from an open window. His bright red gash
of a mouth agape as he watched the truck go, a grimace of
pain or sadness painting it.

"I hope you enjoy the EMF buddy," Cassidy grunted
and focused on making sure she didn't fall off the speed-
ing truck.

***

"Shut up and move," a gruff voice came from somewhere below. Cassidy slid herself closer to the end of the
trailer.

The trailer had backed up to a derelict building about
three stories high. Whatever colour it had been painted in
the past was lost to the years and the only colour that at-
tracted any attention was the rust that was smeared across
the building's surface. The truck pulled up to a loading
area complete with a tattered awning that, despite being
completely shredded, managed to block Cassidy's view.
With a silent curse she manoeuvred herself around just to
get a glimpse of what was happening.

"Move it," the voice came again, followed by the sound
of a hard shove that sent someone scrambling. A flash of
grey appeared through the torn cloth of the awning; the
back of a grey hat, brown hair crawling from underneath

it. Another head passed under the hole a little too quickly to get a clear picture of anything but a blur.

Was that Fletcher's ill-fitting stocking cap? Cassidy didn't want to speculate on it. She had to believe he was alive and that she was able to help him.

A flash of a bald head followed the blur into the building. Cassidy pushed herself out of sight, the loud chunk sound of metal bending and popping back into shape rose from underneath her and she froze, a curse ready on the tip of her tongue.

The shuffling of feet stopped, a pregnant silence fell that caused Cassidy to hold her breath and hug tighter into the trailer's roof. A cough broke the silence, but the tension only increased. Cassidy could feel her heart beat against her chest and she had a momentary fear that the thudding might beat a tattoo on the top of the trailer and reveal her position.

A door closed and the tension disappeared. Cassidy poked her head over the edge of the trailer once more. There was no movement, no sense of anyone out there except her, and the brief elation disguised as relief that allowed her to breath again in long, deep sighs.

After another ten minutes of waiting, silent with her cheek resting on the cool trailer's surface, Cassidy climbed down to rest her feet on the solid ground.

"Still got my sea legs," she said, one hand on the trailer to steady her as she peered around the back. The large metal doors under that awning were shut and there was no apparent handle on their dented surface. The trailer door was left open, its plywood floors empty save for some garbage strewn about.

"They made quick work of it," she said studying the water stains and dirt encrusted boot prints. She tried to count the differing boot treads, but they crossed over each other too much, and she was never good at tracking live people. Give her a footprint preserved in a fossilized lakebed or volcanic ash and she'd follow them all the way to their end. Tracks of living people were just too unpredictable.

"There's only one thing for it," Cassidy said and moved up the three concrete steps to the doors. Her legs still wobbled, and she had to force herself to walk without a limp. Pain crackled up her legs to her hips, but it was manageable. For now.

The doors were steel, heavy and thick. A solitary deadbolt receptacle marred the face of the right-hand door and it looked new. Well, newer than the rest of the building anyway, Cassidy thought. Pockmarks of rust and corrosion were smattered about the otherwise shiny surface.

"It has to be locked," Cassidy whispered and tried to wedge her fingers under the lip of the door. It opened with a gentle pull; the setting sun cast an orange light into the shade of the building's interior.

Cassidy grabbed her shovel from her bag and moved into the building, her eyes on every corner.

The shade disappeared as Cassidy walked into the building. The light was artificial, a throbbing unnatural yellow that buzzed into desperate life. The fluorescents stung her eyes, and Cassidy put one hand over her brow to tone it down. She'd only been away from the electrical world for three days and already man-made light was giving her trouble. For someone like Fletcher, who hadn't experienced that sort of light in years, it must have been torture.

The door closed behind her with a subtle click. With her shovel cocked back and ready to strike, Cassidy moved further into the room. It was a storage bay, aging and decrepit boxes still hugged into the walls, their wares long since removed or stolen. A counter greeted her about halfway into the room, an old cash register stood a silent guard, its drawer left open like some ancient robot with its tongue torn from its own jaws. The cash was long gone.

Cheap tiled floors matched the tiles in the dropped ceiling above, and large, steel shelving units cut across the remainder of the room. Boxes and filth lined them, untouched and covered in a thick layer of dust. The light had stopped working over the empty shelves and Cassidy plunged into darkness towards a sliver of light that may have been the outline of a door.

The next room was plagued by offices, a haphazard few of the fluorescent lights above painted a trail through the open space. The office doors were ajar, ransacked within, their desks and chairs overturned, broken. Cassidy moved on, cautious of each shadowy entrance, hoping an arrow or crossbow bolt wouldn't come at her from a dark corner.

A shuffling sound brought her to a halt, the far-off echoes of a casual conversation carried to her from above. Cassidy shuffled into an office with little debris blocking its entrance directly to her right. Shovel still at the ready, she waited.

"Not sure why we had to move again," a voice said as its owner approached. "They didn't find anything, and it was only the girl."

"And the Rat, don't forget about him," said another voice, younger than the first. "That girl you're talking about claimed to be a garbagemancer and she gave Harrison a nasty bump on his bald head."

"She did at that," the first voice said, stifling a chuckle. "Still, hard to believe there's any more garbagemancers out there. And the Rat, well, he'd be as fine with a joint of meat and some trinkets as anything else."

The grey coats passed by Cassidy's hiding place, her back pushed against the wall while her head strained to maintain her view on them. She held her breath.

"Well, garbagemancer or not, she had a working piece of tech. If those, what does Beckett call them, the rebels? If the rebels have working tech, Beckett is going to want to know. He'll get it out of the other one. No problem."

Another laugh.

"Especially with Harrison in such a foul mood. Poor fella will wish he was dead before too long."

Laughter followed them out of the room.

It was another minute before Cassidy allowed herself to take another breath. The silence had resumed outside of the office, and she stepped into it willingly. Her heart pounded in her chest and her grip tightened on her shovel. It seemed to her that Fletcher and the Digital Heart would be in close vicinity to one another. With another deep breath, Cassidy girded herself to climb the stairs. It was a steep, narrow stairwell; the yellow painted walls were sloughing off chipped paint and was much too close to her shoulders. Her shovel's blade scraped along the wall for a split-second, sending a shriek of metal against concrete through the small area and sent paint chips floating to the floor. Yellow snow flakes dusted the ground.

Cassidy fought her instincts, pushed her way through the door at the top of the stairs and hurried away from the stairway. The icy fingers of yellow paint reached out to her, beckoned to her as the door swung shut behind her.

This level of the building had a more open floor plan, with the immediate area in front of her devoid of anything. The torn linoleum floor was empty, scuff marks and long-standing dents from furniture that had once littered it still stood as a reminder of life before everything went to ground. The room was divided by a wall, one door at its centre.

Cassidy moved forward and leaned on the wall next to the door. Playing a slow game, she placed her ear to the door.

CHAPTER ELEVEN

Nothing.

Whatever was on the other side of that door, she couldn't hear it.

Her hand glided over the brass doorknob, it rattled at her touch and she jumped back as if she'd laid a hand on a hot stove. She sighed.

"Come on Cassidy," she said and wiped the sweat from her palms, "no pain, no gain." With a grimace she pushed open the door.

"Crap," Cassidy stared into the eyes of Baldy, or Harrison, as he leaned over the bound form of Fletcher, his head drooped to his chest.

Harrison's eyes burned, his face clenched like a fist. Free of his grey coat, wearing only a white tank top spattered with blood, Cassidy could see his thickly corded arms mapped with scars and thick, black hair. Black leather gloves adorned his hands, which were filled with Fletcher's shirt, in mid-throttle.

"Howdy," Cassidy said with a small wave. "Am I interrupting something?"

Harrison dropped Fletcher and stood at his full height.

It was only then, as the bald man's head caught the light did Cassidy notice the large bump that protruded from Harrison's forehead, and the purple bruise bloomed around his eye.

Everything that came next happened in slow motion. Harrison adjusted his gloves, wiggled his fingers into place, a smug grin grew under his thick moustache. He bolted forward, his arms pumping with purpose, his legs a blur, his eyes on Cassidy.

Cassidy's instincts took over. She spun away from the charge with a gasp and gave herself some space and time to think. Harrison growled and spun on her, his feet skidded to a stop casting off dust in light clouds.

He charged again, his teeth clenched and the glint of saliva running down his chin. A curse on her tongue, Cassidy was ready for him. Legs braced, she took a deep breath and raised her shovel.

As he got closer Cassidy feinted with a swing aimed at his face. Harrison reacted, brought himself to a stop and covered his face with one hand, the other reaching out as if to grab the shovel.

A smile lit on Cassidy's face and she dropped her swing downward. The flat part of the shovel blade slammed into one of Harrison's knees, emphasized by a loud popping sound. The effect was immediate. Harrison cried out in surprise and agony as he dropped to the floor holding his leg and rolling around on his back.

Cassidy stood back, dropped her shovel to the ground. She could still feel the vibration of the impact in the palms of her hands.

"Finish it," Fletcher coughed from behind her. He

wasn't in good shape. The bridge of his nose sported a thick slash and blood (both dried and fresh) had cascaded down around either side of his nose and into his beard. One of his eyes was swollen shut, red and angry. The opposite cheek was purple with the outline of fingers bruised there. His mouth was the worst. His lips had been smashed into his teeth so often that they were twice their usual size, cracked, bleeding. A mixture of spit and blood dripped down his chin.

"What?" Cassidy said hurrying to untie Fletcher, ignoring the groans of pain that Harrison's screams had devolved into.

"Kill him," Fletcher fell forward out of his chair, landing on his hands and knees. He spat a glob of blood to the side.

Cassidy rushed to his side and helped him up. "He's down. He can't do anything right now. It's safe for us…"

"Not if he calls out for help, or if he gets to his…" Fletcher pushed Cassidy out of the way and launched himself toward the small table that was next to his chair. His fumbling hands struck the table and knocked it to the floor, instruments sliding further into the room. A gun slid with them. It was a Glock, dark as a black hole, that drew their eyes. The room went silent, as if it was holding a breath.

Fletcher's eyes locked with Cassidy's and they both scrambled forward to grab the gun. Fletcher growled, his face red, his expression livid. Cassidy, for her part, didn't know why they were fighting over the gun, not really. Her gut though, it screamed at her to grab it, that it was important for her to reach it before Fletcher or Harrison could.

Crawling over each other, they fought. An elbow thrown here, a fist looped to the midsection there, a shoe scraped over shin. Fletcher was more savage than Cassidy and he lashed out with tooth and nail. Cassidy was fresher, her injuries much more subdued than Fletcher's own, and her strength held. She was winning.

Her hand stretched out so that her fingertips grazed the butt of the gun, but Cassidy was stopped short. Fletcher had his hand wrapped around her belt and was pulling her back. She looked back at his ruined face and saw a stinging hatred in his one open eye. With her leg cocked, she jammed her foot into his stomach and pushed off.

Cassidy could see her hand's shadow over the gun; she had it.

"I'll take that," a calm, high pitched voice said. A thin hand scooped up the gun and pointed it down at Fletcher and Cassidy, "I think you're both here for me."

Fletcher, still sprawled on top of her, groaned and released her. Cassidy pushed away from him and looked up at the figure before her. Toothpick thin legs extended out of maroon slippers, faux fur tickling at his ankles. A too short bathrobe, maroon to match the slippers, clutched eagerly around his waist, the same faux fur poked out of the sleeves to grip to the man's skeletal elbows. Sticking out of the robe on a pencil thin neck, a globule of a head with sunken eyes and pointing jaw with a wisp of a goatee covering it. Long, golden brown hair that was piled high in a self-important man-bun.

"Beckett?" Cassidy's face twitched with a grin.

"At your service," Beckett said and did a little bow, his hair flopped forward with his head. The gun didn't waver in his hand.

"I suppose you're this one's partner then?" Beckett jabbed the barrel of the gun towards Fletcher. "The one that got away." He rolled his eyes and paced back and forth in front of them. He actively refrained from looking at Harrison, whose groans had resumed.

"I hope you know that you ruined a perfectly cushy and comfortable lair. This," Beckett waved his free hand around the room, "this... warehouse is a plan b. Plan c! Never had I expected to be imprisoned here, not when the hotel had everything that I needed. Follow me," he beckoned with the gun and backed into another room, his grey eyes never moving from Cassidy or Fletcher.

They followed him into what turned out to be little more than a kitchenette. Linoleum floor with some long-faded pattern and speckled with some ancient grey paint that had been painted over with the pale yellow that now adorned the walls. In one corner of the room was a small table covered in all sorts of kitchen accoutrements, the necessities of any workplace break room: coffee maker, toaster oven, microwave. Each appliance dirty under several years' worth of dust. An electric tea kettle was the only thing in the room clearly spotless. It sat on the counter of the kitchenette next to a single tub sink, its cord dangling toward the shabby flooring.

"Harrison," Beckett called, leaning on the counter, a smile creeping slowly over his bulbous lips. "Do you want tea, darling?" He switched the gun to his left hand, his eyes still focused on Cassidy and Fletcher as they stumbled to a halt just inside the door.

With a nod to himself, Beckett reached his free hand

out and touched the base of the electric kettle. A subtle twitch came over his face, and he took two long blinks, his eyes rolled and fell back onto his prisoners.

To Cassidy's surprise, the orange light on the base of the kettle flickered to life.

"Come now," Beckett said, a less subtle grin stretching across his mouth, "you've seen me drive a truck, and a little tea kettle is more shocking to you?" He chortled, and steam began to rise from the kettle's spout.

"Well, it's just that, uh," Cassidy could feel her cheeks flush, "I didn't really think about the truck. This is, well, different." She pointed to the neglected cord, its three pronged plug swaying in front of the counter.

"More of a visual, eh?" Beckett shot a quick look at the kettle, steam rising quickly from it now. "Be a dear, get me a cup from that cupboard," he indicated the cupboard furthest away from him, the gun waving her toward it.

"Thank you," Beckett said when Cassidy had a tea cup set on the counter in front of her. "Now, just in front of you, in the canister, pull out a tea bag and place it in the cup."

Cassidy gripped the canister in her hands and pulled it forward. It was an old-fashioned yellow with white highlights depicting a tea kettle, a dish, and a mug that smattered itself into some out of joint pattern. The lid was held shut by two latches on either side. She hesitated to open it.

"So," she said, playing with the first latch, "how did you, of all people, manage to become a garbagemancer?"

Beckett made a show of clicking back the hammer of his gun, "That isn't a very polite term, young lady."

Cassidy shot a glance over her shoulder at Fletcher. He was bent over, one arm was laced across his stomach, the other was keeping him steady and standing against the door frame. Fletcher raised an eyebrow and shrugged.

"I'm, uh, sorry," Cassidy said, "but how did you get your powers? I mean, why you and not everyone?"

Beckett removed his hand from the kettle's base and rolled his eyes. "Not very bright, is she?" Beckett said to Fletcher, a frown now diminishing his face.

"I heard it was because of the Digital Heart. Is that true? Do you have the Digital Heart?" Cassidy said and removed the first latch of the tea canister.

"You mean this old thing," Beckett reached into his robe and pulled out a long silver necklace. Fastened on the bottom was something that look like a jump drive, but without the casing or the USB mouth. It was a microchip. "I suppose it doesn't hurt to have something like this lying around. But, to be honest, I had a bit of a natural talent for it." He waved his hand towards the kettle again.

"What is the Digital Heart? It doesn't look like it can do much of anything," Cassidy said and opened the canister. Inside it was a dull, thin metal casting hazy reflections of the light that managed to find its way within. Several tea bags lay at the bottom, awaiting use amongst the remnants of its fallen brothers.

"It's not important," Beckett's voice became serious, his grey eyes hardened. "Let's just say that it gives me and the other Governors a gift. Now, put that god damned tea bag in the cup and bring it here."

Beckett jabbed the gun at her and Cassidy hurried to bring the cup over to him. That done, he shooed her back to stand next to Fletcher.

"I heard that it was the Heart that gave you your powers," Cassidy said and eyed Beckett's necklace. "I just can't figure out how that would work. The Heart is obviously a microchip of some sort, but what's the point of that if you can't read it? You need a computer to read a microchip, and to use a computer you need power."

Beckett frowned, "I have the power," and gestured with his free hand.

"Sure, you do now, but what about before? If you didn't have power how could you use a computer to get the power?" Cassidy could feel Fletcher's stare burn a hole in her back, and she wondered what his thoughts might be on the line of questions she just gave his resident garbagemancer.

"You certainly have a lot of time on your hands, coming up with stories and implying many things that you wouldn't understand and are just not true," Beckett said, his gun firmly trained on Cassidy. "Ah, Mr. Harrison, I see you've decided to join us. At last."

Baldy pushed his way past Cassidy and Fletcher, and limped his way into the kitchenette, resting his shirtless girth on the edge of the counter on the opposite side of the sink of Beckett. He crossed his arms and seemed to hesitate as to whether he should keep an eye on Cassidy and Fletcher, or pay attention to his boss.

Beckett solved that particular issue for him. Closing his eyes he held out the gun to Harrison, "Please take this and watch our guests while I pour myself some tea." Beckett's voice dripped with disdain bordering on disgust. He didn't hold the gun at a distance, pinched between his index finger and thumb like a dirty diaper, but Cassidy wouldn't have been surprised if he had. Harrison took the gun, an ugly sneer crept out from under his moustache as he pointed the business end at Cassidy and Fletcher.

"Thank you," Beckett said and poured his tea.

Then, with an ear-splitting bang, the world turned upside down.

CHAPTER TWELVE

The explosion shook the building and threw Cassidy to the floor. Judging by the thud she heard behind her, Fletcher had fallen as well.

Both Harrison and Beckett were thrown off guard and sprawled to the floor. Harrison still had his hand wrapped around the gun. Cassidy wasn't surprised; he wouldn't chance letting that go again.

The shaking stopped as quickly as it had started, the telltale signs of tinnitus buzzed in Cassidy's ears, and by the amount of ear cupping she had witnessed, the others were feeling it too.

"What the hell was that?" Beckett's voice carried to her as if through water; a dull sound that Cassidy could barely hear. Harrison looked at his boss, confusion painting his face as he stuck a finger in one of his ears and shook it around.

Cassidy took her chance. She didn't get herself back to her feet, but instead crouched like a cat and pushed herself from the ground in a leap that bridged the small gap of the kitchenette. She landed on top of Harrison, her two hands gripping his gun hand and pushing it to the floor.

A distant pop sounded as the gun went off, the bullet digging into the worn linoleum.

Harrison bucked underneath her and grabbed a handful of hair with his meaty fist to pull her off. Cassidy kept her weight on the arm with the gun, though she was now forced to look up, her head pulled back and pain lancing through her scalp as her hair ripped away. Finding her bearings wasn't easy with her head pinned back, but she managed to get to a good base, her knees underneath her, and she rammed one into what she hoped was Harrison's crotch. A low grunt escaped from Harrison and he released his hold on Cassidy's hair. She snapped her head forward and let the momentum carry it all the way down until her forehead impacted on Harrison's nose with a sickening crunch she couldn't hear but could certainly feel.

Cassidy felt Harrison release the gun. Her head throbbed and she felt woozy, but she made for the gun. She was slow and it was hard for her to focus. A dull ache grew behind her forehead and her vision blurred with tears.

Her hand grazed the handle of the gun before thin but strong fingers wrapped around her neck from behind. Cassidy reached for her throat, the gun forgotten. She could hear Beckett as a distant echo, though the heat of his breath was hot on her ear.

"What have you done, what have you done?" Beckett's voice was high and strained, his skeletal fingers dug deep into the flesh of Cassidy's neck. She dipped her chin and grabbed for Beckett's hands with her own. His grip was stronger than she imagined for someone with those pale, bony legs.

A red haze flickered at the edge of her vision, her breath came in shallow wheezes that weren't getting the work done. With as much strength as she could muster, Cassidy pushed herself backwards. She could feel the slim frame of Beckett hit the ground and now she was on top of him. His grip hadn't loosened.

With a final gasp, Cassidy gritted her teeth and drove her elbow hard into Beckett's groin. A shriek and an entire body flinch signalled the garbagemancer's loosened grip. Cassidy drove another elbow into his groin and, upon hearing a whine of pain and the harsh exhalation of breath, grabbed at the thin fingers that were now only fumbling at her neck.

She rolled away from Beckett; the man's hands had taken to grabbing at his crotch as he curled into the fetal position. Cassidy held her throat and took short, aching breaths.

A flash passed in the periphery of Cassidy's vision. Without thinking, she turned to face the newcomer; her hand slid over the grip of the gun.

"That's an interesting piece of tech," Argyle said, his mouth a familiar slash of red, his back stooped so that his fingertips grazed the worn linoleum flooring. He looked out at Cassidy through his Green Bay Packers helmet, a smile touching his eyes.

"Argyle?" It hurt Cassidy to talk, her throat hurt, and her voice was hoarse.

"This one's friends," Argyle inclined his head towards Fletcher, "asked me to bring them to Beckett."

"How did you know?" Cassidy said and tried to swallow. She moved towards Fletcher, but hooked the gun in the back of her pants as she went.

"It's my city." Argyle shrugged and moved toward the fallen Harrison and writhing Beckett.

Cassidy moved Fletcher to his back, cringing some from the dried blood that caked his face and the bluish welts that would surely blacken and swell before too long. The ringing in her ears cleared as she stroked Fletcher's hair and tried to coax him into wakefulness. The building was filled with the sounds of fighting; people cursed and screamed and yelped. The twang of arrows and bolts being loosed, the whoosh of a fire starting anew, a short laugh that turned to a harsh cough all flooded Cassidy's recovering ears and attacked her mind.

"Argyle," she said at length, "could you please get someone to help?"

The Rat nodded, his bright eyes tinged with worry as he looked upon her, and then he was gone.

In Argyle's wake, Beckett still clung to his groin with one hand and his whimpers had begun to fade. His other hand was handcuffed to the larger, and still unconscious, Harrison. It wouldn't keep them in place when they were both roused, but Beckett wouldn't be going anywhere while his henchman was out. Beckett knew this. Cassidy had no doubt that he would try to rouse Harrison as soon as his pain subsided. If Argyle wasn't back by then she'd be left alone with them once more. Cassidy put one hand on the pistol grip that poked out of the back of her pants.

"Cassidy?" Fletcher's hand fell on her wrist, his eyes fluttered to life.

"Yeah, I'm here," she smiled and moved his hand to her own.

"What happened?"

"I kicked ass, oh and the rest of your motley crew crashed the party," Cassidy said waving her hand in the air; a far off explosion boomed.

Fletcher tried a smile but settled for a grimace.

"You really weren't kidding about just needing to find this guy?"

Fletcher shook his head. "He's known this would be coming for a while. That's why he kept moving. Potshotted us, reduced our numbers. It could've gone on for a while. We're lucky you came along." He squeezed her hand.

Argyle sauntered back into the room, the small frame of Arturo followed carrying a crossbow nearly his size. An older woman followed after that, someone Cassidy recognized from Fletcher's home base, but whose name escaped her.

"Hey kid," Cassidy said as Arturo took a seat beside her. "Fighting the good fight?" She nodded towards his crossbow, now laid to the side. Arturo gave her a smile, but his focus was on Fletcher.

The old woman took over. From her backpack she produced two first aid kits. One was orange and was labelled as a roadside safety kit, the other was a small white box, the familiar red cross emblazoned on the cover. She removed supplies from each and began to poke and prod at Fletcher.

"I'll need you to give him some space," the woman said and cast a cold stare at Cassidy.

"Wait," Fletcher tightened his grip on Cassidy's hand. "Is it over? Is Beckett dead?"

Cassidy's throat clenched, her chest tightened. Arturo looked beyond them all towards the small counter space. She knew his eyes were running over the prone bodies of Beckett and Harrison. She knew that he was watching to see if their chests still rose and fell with breath.

"No, he's not dead. Neither is Harrison. They're both down and out. They're your prisoners now."

"Harrison..."

"They're worth more alive than dead. You could probably bargain with the other governors, buy yourselves some extra supplies, some more breathing room."

Fletcher patted her hand, nodded his head, "You're right. Of course, you're right. We'll talk more about this later. Please, let Magda get me wrapped up. We'll talk later."

With some effort Fletcher sat up, her hand still in his.

"Thank you, Cassidy. Thank you," Fletcher said and hugged her. He held her tight in his arms and she returned the favour. When they let go, he nodded to her with a smile and she stood and felt a smile of her own paint her face.

It was as she stood that Cassidy realized the gun wasn't hooked in the back of her pants anymore. She reached to feel around, hoping it may have slid further than she meant it to. Her head scanned the floor, afraid it may have fallen out. Then she heard the click.

CHAPTER THIRTEEN

Cassidy looked down the gun barrel. The image was crisp, the gun's black matte colour stood out in a clear and stark contrast to the hazy and unfocused background.

"Who are you, Cassidy?" Fletcher's steady voice rose just above a whisper. "Who are you and what do you want?"

The room around Cassidy was still, silent. It was as though everyone held their breath in anticipation of what was about to come. All eyes were on her, wondering, questioning. How would she answer?

It was the same question that Cassidy was asking herself, and she didn't know. The truth would most likely come across as far-fetched and paint her at best as delusional or worst as a lunatic. Otherwise, she could continue to lie and tell them she was a garbagemancer, but a really nice one. Either way, she didn't have time to explain herself. It was the third day; Gamgee would be closing the portal whether she made it back or not.

"I'm the one who saved your ass," Cassidy said around a growl, the aches and pains of the last few days crashing down on her. "I'm the one that helped you find Beckett in the first place, I'm the one that surfed a damn tractor trailer to find you, and I'm the one that beat the crap out of those two to make sure we're both free."

Cassidy turned to look at Argyle, his helmet now in his hands, "Hell, if I didn't find Argyle and get him involved then you wouldn't have your reinforcements here to blow all this up."

The gun wavered for a second, Fletcher's expression softened with a flash of surprise that left as quickly as it came.

"Why?" Fletcher countered, reaffirming his hold on the pistol.

"Do I need a reason?" Cassidy looked past the gun, stared directly into Fletcher's green eyes.

"I've seen what you can do. Back on the streets, in front of the hotel. You're like him," Fletcher jerked his head towards Beckett, "and people like him are power hungry, manipulative, and controlling. Tell me, why did you want the Digital Heart?"

"I'm not a garbagemancer, Fletcher. I... I just have working tech."

A low murmur carried through the room, whispers and exhaled breath. Cassidy looked around the room, more of Fletcher's revolutionaries had crowded in; surrounding them in a loose ring of bloody and sweaty bodies.

"You... you have what?"

"Ask Argyle. He has my EMF detector. It detects Electromagnetic fields, and was how I helped you find Beckett in the first place. I gave it to him to convince him to help me out." She paused to look at Argyle who was already nodding his head. "Isn't that right Argyle?"

The Rat took a shuffling step forward, his head bobbing an affirmative. "Yes, oh yes. Good tech," Argyle reached into his coat and pulled out the small, black box. Cassidy's heart sank.

Argyle held the EMF aloft, a crooked smile made out of his red slash of a mouth. The meter was broken, Cassidy could see it. The clear plastic covering was cracked, and the needle dangled, lifelessly within it. The faint sound of parts floating freely within the case floated to her ears.

"Show us," someone called from behind her and she cringed. *Dang*, Cassidy thought. *This isn't going to be good.*

Argyle made a quiet flourish with his hands and held the EMF in front of him, his face a mask of concentration that was soon marred by confusion and finally by frustration.

Slamming his open palm against the side of the device Argyle said, "It worked before. The little arrow would jump in place from left to right and back again." He gave it a furious shake, its loose innards rattling.

"So," the old medic said from her place kneeling next to Fletcher, "it worked when she gave it to you. Has it worked since?"

Argyle gave Cassidy a timid look, "Haven't used it."

"You can leave now, Rat." Fletcher's stare hardened once more, the gun in his hand steady and pointed directly at Cassidy. "Make sure he gets everything he was promised."

Argyle slipped out of the crowd; he gave Cassidy an apologetic look as he went. It wasn't obvious, but Cassidy thought she saw two burly men push their way through the crowd to follow him.

Once Argyle had left, Cassidy tried to make eye contact with Arturo, the kid. She gave him a wink, hoping to see even the barest smile hitch at the corners of his mouth, but he refused to look at her. He stayed close to Fletcher and watched the ground. Cassidy was alone.

"Not so hard to trick a simple-minded loner into thinking you have already working tech, I imagine," Fletcher's face twisted into a mocking grin. "And don't think I'm not grateful. You're right, you helped us out. More than any of us can really put into words." Fletcher looked around the room with an obvious nod of his head. The others there followed suit, all of them except Arturo and the medic.

"The issue isn't the what, but the why. So, let me ask you again: why did you help us?" More whispers cascaded through the crowd.

"It seemed like the right thing to do," Cassidy said, her shoulders slumped forward, her head down. "I just wanted to help you."

"And it had nothing to do with your own self-interests?"

"No."

"Not even for the Digital Heart?" Fletcher looked at her around the gun.

"Well… if I had known…"

"And why did you want the Heart so badly?"

"I… I can't…"

"Is it because you wanted to establish yourself as a garbagemancer?" Fletcher's voice was ramping up to a fever pitch. His voice was high and strained. Cassidy fought the urge to cover her ears.

"I'm not a garbagemancer," Cassidy felt her voice

quiver and hated the weakness in it; the acceptance of what was happening.

"Then why didn't you want to kill them?" Fletcher was in a rage, his voice echoed in the little room. Cassidy couldn't understand why the others didn't shield their ears and flinch away from Fletcher, from his anger.

"Listen to yourself," Cassidy said, her back straight and her fists clenched. "I didn't want to kill them because you don't just kill people for no reason! You don't kill people, especially when they are helpless." She could feel the heat on her face as her cheeks flushed red.

"That's very obtuse of you," Fletcher said. His voice had returned to its normal cadence so quickly that Cassidy had to look at him twice to make sure it was the same person. "Evil begets evil, Cassidy. If Beckett or his second in command live they'll attempt to take back their position – their power. Men like them, men who have become accustomed to power, can't live under someone else's rule. Worst of all, they have the abilities and influence to regain what they lost. They have allies." Again Fletcher looked around the room, his followers nodding in agreement. "No, these men and their allies need to be taught a lesson. They need to be taught that we are not afraid of them. That we will not be subject to their rule, to their whim."

A roar of approval rose over the crowd, and a satisfied smile curled Fletcher's lips. He kept his eyes on Cassidy for a moment, and she could feel the anger and the hate barely contained within. A thought rose in her mind, what happened to him?

Then he turned and fired two shots into Beckett and Harrison.

CHAPTER FOURTEEN

Cassidy managed to suppress the scream that bubbled up in her throat, but she couldn't control the flinch that came with each shot.

Guns were nothing new to her. In her line of work she had spent plenty of time navigating hostile governments that were covetous of their artifacts and their history. She'd dealt with drug cartels, terrorists, treasure hunters, and poachers. Cassidy had become good at negotiation, but that didn't mean it worked every time. She'd been fired at more than she cared to count, and she'd fired a gun – multiple guns. Cassidy didn't like being on either side of it.

The room echoed with the gunshots, and it drew those gathered closer. Cassidy shivered at their ghoulish interest in the wreckage Fletcher had just caused. She stood, transfixed on the aftermath but thankful the room crowded with onlookers that blocked her view. They pushed forward to get a better look, and to congratulate Fletcher.

A tug at the hem of her shirt woke Cassidy from her trance and she turned, thin fingers pried open her clenched hands. Her fist wrapped around something thin and sharp.

Argyle was stooped there, his brown eyes meeting hers briefly.

"Come," he said, his thin spider-like fingers grabbed Cassidy's wrist and pulled her out of the small kitchenette.

They moved through the old warehouse quickly, those revolutionaries that had remained outside the kitchenette now hurried passed them to see what had happened. None of them paid the odd pairing any heed.

"Fletcher has gone insane," Cassidy said when they had made it outside. Her hands were shaking, and she gnashed her teeth, what had she done? "How could I help him do this?"

Argyle sauntered around the back of Beckett's tractor trailer, a relic now like the rest of its brethren, his large eyes peering inside, scavenging. "It's not your fault," he said picking up a wayward nail he found in the truck bed and stuffing it in his oversized coat pocket. "He tricked you."

"Did he?" Cassidy turned on Argyle, her hands still in tight fists. "I was the one stupid enough to think his plans were selfless, to believe he wanted to better this world. You'd think I'd know better: all the things I've seen, all the places I've been."

"It happens," Argyle said and flicked away a cracked piece of plastic with a sneer. "When you make choices with your heart, it happens. Fletcher, he's a good talker. He knows how to say things that make him seem better. Beckett has some of that too. They pander to anyone willing to listen, twist them with their words. They make promises they can't keep and make sure their forked tongue is out of sight behind a smile. Argyle learned this; he learned this a long time ago. That's why he lives alone. Why he doesn't get involved. Why he helps only when he needs help."

"I can't do that. I can't live my life on the fence."

"With choices like this, what else do you have?" Argyle shrugged and bent his head to the floor of the truck bed, his eyes scouring it.

They both turned, noise erupted within the building. People were shouting, running.

"Maybe there's a third choice," Cassidy said and fumbled her hand within her satchel. "Argyle, can you take me to the old subway tunnels?"

"There are many ways to get to the subway," Argyle grunted.

"I need to get to the entrance close to a park. This section of park was one of Beckett's fake hideouts. Do you know it?" Cassidy said and clasped her hand on the Digital Heart.

Argyle nodded and turned his head sideways, his eyebrows raised.

Cassidy pulled out the artifact and studied it as it hung from her fingers. "Maybe there are other ways to end a war without favouring one side over the other."

A loud crash came from the building behind them, and more raised voices still too low to hear. But getting closer.

***

"Beckett used many underground hideouts," Argyle panted, his loping stride still surpassing Cassidy's own panicked run. "Only one was as you described it. A place long forgotten even before the Night the Lights Went Out."

The shouts of Fletcher's revolutionaries had died away, confined to Beckett's final hiding place as they fled. Cassidy thought she heard an agonized scream of rage as they pushed themselves out of sight of the squat warehouse.

"I hope you're right," she said, her legs aching as she pumped them to run through the formerly deserted streets of the strange New York.

They ran twenty blocks before Cassidy called a break and collapsed on the cracked asphalt and concrete. She leaned against a rough brick building and massaged her thighs, her fingers pushing hard into the muscles in hopes of waylaying the cramps she knew were coming. Argyle's shoulders heaved as he sucked in air, and though he leaned one hand on the same building, he remained on his feet. His eyes were vigilant of the space behind them.

"It's not much further, we need to hurry," he reached out a hand to help her up.

"Why are you helping me, Argyle?" Cassidy said and let herself be dragged upright. "I don't have any more tech to give you."

"No more tech needed," Argyle said and shook his long coat, the jangle of broken parts emanated from within. He smiled.

"Then, why?" Cassidy said as they started a slow walk. "It's bound to make your life more complicated."

Argyle shrugged, but his red slash of a mouth maintained its crooked grin.

They'd made it to the playground. The city was remarkably still and overpowered by an eerie silence. The
broken-down pick-up truck kept a silent vigil over the
abandoned lot, useless in its lack of menace. Cassidy let
out a sigh of relief – finally something that she recognized.
They were close.

In the vast cityscape from which Argyle had led her,
Cassidy could hear the faint rise of voices. Distant, but
they were getting closer.

"They can't know which way we went," Cassidy said
looking over her shoulder. No sign of them yet.

Argyle grunted and pointed above her. Cassidy stared,
the blue sky fading to a sickly orange. Something glinted
in the distance, a patch of orange light that wavered like
an eye that blinked to a strange rhythm.

"They had spotters?" Cassidy said and turned her focus back to running.

Argyle was silent save for his laboured breathing.

Of course they did, Cassidy thought, what else would
Fletcher have the children do for his rebellion? Arturo was
the only one she had seen at Beckett's, she had just assumed that the rest were at home, safe. That was before
she'd seen Fletcher kill two men, before she knew how
important the cause was to him, and what he would do
to attain his goals. Having children use pocket mirrors to
signal directions seemed like a negligible offence at this
point.

They ran. Air fled their lungs, burning in a desire to
rest. Argyle maintained a steady gallop, his stooped form
unwavering. Cassidy pushed herself to keep up, but her

body was on the verge of revolt. Her muscles screamed, pleading for rest and relief. As she pumped her legs, she could feel every muscle ripple and quiver, could feel them strain in protest. Cassidy was tired, overwhelmed, angry. And exhilarated. She welcomed the pounding of her heart, the fever pitch of her pulse. It was enough; she pushed herself onward.

It wasn't until something buzzed passed her in a blur of colour and left a stark gust of cool breeze in its wake that Cassidy realized they were riding bicycles. Another passed by her, its driver released a high-pitched ululation that might have been meant as a laugh. She looked over her shoulder and dozens of bikes were approaching, each driven by a revolutionary with a maniacal grin contained as if in rictus on their zealous faces. Baseball bats were held aloft as they zoomed towards Cassidy and Argyle. Where there weren't bats there were clubs made of everything from a table leg to a cane to a cracked off tree branch.

Cassidy lurched forward, thrown off balance by her quick turn, she fell forward as another bike passed her. It was a bike she recognized from her childhood - a BMX. Its simple handlebars on a slight angle forward, its seat set low so that the driver's knees came precariously close to their hands with each revolution of the pedals.

She rolled forward and got to her feet. They were all riding BMX bikes, customized to their liking, but there was no mistaking them. Cassidy could feel a giggle bubble up her throat, she was being chased by adults riding bicycles.

The air above her head was parted by a baseball bat

that sliced through as she was regaining her feet. Cassidy cursed, the remnants of the laugh left a bitter taste in her throat.

Up ahead, the two bicycles that had passed them were discarded, the drivers out of their seats and prepared to meet Argyle and Cassidy as they came. The bicycle that just swung at her was turning in a wide arc; coming around to make another pass.

"Kill the Rat," Fletcher's voice rose above the whizzing bicycle tires, "leave the girl for me."

Cassidy chanced another look over her shoulder, Fletcher was there, riding tandem with another on a customized banana seat with a long back bar. His beaten and bruised face was livid with excitement, Harrison's gun lifted above his head in exaltation.

"How many bullets do you have left in there?" Cassidy whispered as she ran toward the two waiting revolutionaries.

Argyle had gotten there before her, a snarl issuing from him as he leapt on the first of their welcome party. It was a big, broad man with one end of a chain wrapped around his forearm, swinging the other end lazily in large circles. His smirk turned to a grimace once the grim realization came over him that the Rat was not going to back down.

They rolled on the ground; the chain made useless at the close range. Still, the big man hadn't given up. He launched his lunchbox sized hands into Argyle's side and stomach. Argyle ignored the blows, his focus only on scratching and biting at the man, drawing blood wherever he could.

Distracted, Cassidy ran into the clutches of the other waiting revolutionary. He wasn't as large as the other man, but his thin limbs were strong and tight as if they were corded with carbon steel.

He grabbed her around the bicep and brought her around to face him, his strong fingers had dug deep into the soft inside of her arm and she winced in spite of herself. Her assailant smiled, and drew her into him. She was dangerously close to the man's shaggy brown beard when she heard a chuckle.

"Not so tough, eh girlie?"

He was taller than her, but not by much. He leaned closer, a snarl of a grin beneath his unkempt beard. With a grunt, Cassidy slammed her forehead into the man's nose. There was a loud crunch as she broke the cartilage and bone, and a spurt of blood shot from his nose; he released Cassidy. She knew that his nose was broken, that his eyes would start to water and blur, that blood would ooze, and he'd have a hard time breathing. He grabbed at his nose and freed Cassidy from his grip, cursing her.

Argyle ran past her, his face and hands streaked with blood, and she followed. The buzz of the circling bikes and the yelling assailants filled her ears as they ran. In the distance, she could see the tunnel entrance.

A red BMX passed her. The driver, a middle aged woman with swimming goggles over her eyes and a white streak that blew back with the rest of her long curly hair, was swinging a bat above her head. With a devilish smile, the woman howled and brought the bat down on Argyle's back, slapping across both of his shoulders with a sickening thud. Argyle stumbled forward, but kept his feet -- somehow.

Cassidy tried to push herself, tried to make her aching limbs go faster, to support Argyle and keep him on his feet. She tried to do that, but the bikes were faster.

Another bike passed, the medic who had tended to Fletcher's wounds at Beckett's hideout, a crowbar speckled with white paint held out to the side. The medic gave Cassidy a lazy wink as she sped forward and slammed the crowbar into Argyle's back. This time he fell.

Argyle landed on his hands and knees, his arms quivering against the strain to keep himself away from the ground. Cassidy knelt beside him, one arm thrown over his back and hands on his shoulders.

"Come on," she said and tried to guide him to his feet.

"No," Argyle growled, but he didn't shake off her hands as he stood.

The bikes began to circle.

"You go," Argyle said, his eyes following the bikes as they passed before him.

"That's stupid," Cassidy said, her eyes lingering on the tunnel entrance that couldn't have been more than thirty feet away. "We're so close."

Argyle nodded. "We'll never make it. You might," he said and pointed a finger at her.

"Don't be an idiot, we can both make it. Once we're in the tunnel they'll have to abandon their bikes. Single file. It will be easy."

"It's a good plan," Argyle stood straight, "you should use it."

The Rat sprang forward and grabbed a bike by its

frame, stopping it in its tracks. The driver, a small man with round glasses and a too thick moustache, was too surprised to act and fell off with a grunt when Argyle lifted the bike in the air.

"Go," Argyle yelled and threw the bike into the midst of those that still circled, knocking even more from their seats.

Cassidy didn't move. She watched Argyle as he repeated the same manoeuvre, dislodging more bikers as he did, but there were too many. For everyone he knocked over, there were two more waiting. They flanked him, and then swarmed. They forgot their bikes, but not their weapons, and went to work attacking Argyle.

When she finally unrooted herself, Cassidy made to follow Argyle into the fray, ignoring the time, the darkening sky, and the probability that Gamgee would block the portal and keep her in this reality forever.

"No," Argyle roared, his bulging eyes falling on her for a moment. He was holding his own, despite being outnumbered and unarmed. His lanky form slunk away from blows, but returned them with as much, if not more, gusto. Still, Cassidy knew it was only a matter of time. Argyle did too.

"Go," Argyle said again as he sidestepped an attack from a table leg. And he smiled. Not his nervous, twitching smile that he had given her when he first met her, or when he helped her escape just hours before, but a full, big, and pleased smile. A happy smile. "Go."

Cassidy ran.

CHAPTER FIFTEEN

The door swung open, its rusted hinges squealed in a unheeded protest, and Cassidy slipped into the dark tunnel beyond.

Argyle had kept them at bay, but Fletcher and his mob were on her heels and she was running out of time. In a moment of hesitation, Cassidy scoured the floor for something to jam up the door with, something to slide across the handle to delay its opening, but there was nothing but rat feces and dust. She cursed loudly. Not for the first time that day did she regret forgetting her shovel at Beckett's hideout.

The tunnel was gripped in shadows. A darkness that wouldn't have been fully pushed back even if the dead amber lights that spotted the curved ceiling had been working. Another curse was on her lips as she braved the darkness, her feet trying to follow the path she'd taken just a few days before; her memory would have to light the way.

It wasn't long before the echo of her running feet and hitched breath was joined by the metal scream of the door opening behind her. Cassidy could feel her heart hasten, her eyes grow wide, and her fists clench. She ran. She ran as fast as she could with the gibbering sound of an unruly gang flowing into the tunnel behind her.

The exit from the tunnel was open, a subtle glint of light helped Cassidy see the door frame as she leapt through it.

She was back in the subway tunnels, the tiled walls and iron tracks a welcome, familiar sight. Without slowing, she planted one hand on the precipice that stood guard over the tracks, pushed herself up and into a roll, before taking to her feet again. A grin slathered her face, "I can make it, I can make it," she said between harsh exhalations.

A crowbar smashed into the column she was running past, the subway tile exploded in a fine mist that caught one of Cassidy's eyes. She rubbed at it with her fist, large tears welling up to displace the irritant.

"We got her," a young man's voice crowed, from behind her an echo of breathless chuckles followed.

Cassidy waded through the subway, her balance offset while she dug at her eye. She had slowed, but it couldn't be helped. It was either that or fall onto the tracks or smash into a column. Judging by the growing roar, Fletcher's revolutionaries were close behind.

More objects were thrown at her, the former clubs now makeshift missiles launched with reckless abandon and bolstered by the original success of the crowbar. None since had been as successful and Cassidy hoped they littered the ground behind her, something to slow her pursuers down some.

She dodged past another column and flinched away

from a crossbow bolt that was dug into the tile. "Cross-bows. Great," Cassidy cursed and pushed on, pondering her worsening situation.

"Wait," she said aloud, "they didn't have crossbows." Cassidy tried to think back to the blur of events that brought her here. The image of Argyle's red slash of a mouth growing into a sincere and happy smile attempted to force its way to the forefront of her thoughts. Even so, she couldn't recall seeing any crossbows, or any bows for that matter.

Beckett's guards, she thought and chanced another smile. The grey coats who were acting as a decoy for their boss. The same guards that she ran afoul when she first slipped into this reality. The exact same shoot-first-ask-questions-later thugs that had managed to chase her away from the portal and into the arms of Fletcher and his cronies. The portal wasn't far now. She just had to hope she got there in enough time to vanish and not bring anyone with her.

The tracks sloped in a gradual curve and Cassidy started to recognize her path, even though she hadn't had much time to study anything on the way out. She caught sight of a particular piece of graffiti, a sprawl of letters as tall as she was. The neon colours were bright enough to make out even in the near dark of the subway tunnels. The Digital Heart. Cassidy clutched her satchel close to her and didn't see the figure appear from the shadows in front of her.

The man Cassidy bowled into had been equally un-aware of her and a loud yip escaped from him as they collided, his crossbow clattering to the floor.

"What the hell?" said another grey coat emerging behind the first, his crossbow firmly in his grip. Cassidy looked at each of them, they mimicked her. It was an unspoken stalemate, that Cassidy felt could have went on forever if the screams and howls of her pursuers didn't reach them.

"What the hell was that?" the first man said, picking up his crossbow.

"It was rebels, you idiots. Beckett sent me here to warn you they were coming. We're to hold them off until back-up arrives," Cassidy said and pushed the two grey coats towards the sound of the oncoming gang. She saw more than confusion on their faces, but ran off before they had a chance to question her on it. Besides, they'd have their hands full.

Cassidy had no illusions that the two grey coats would stop Fletcher and his cronies for long, but it might give her just enough time to get through the portal.

She peeled through the hesitant darkness and was sure that the portal couldn't be much farther when she heard the curses of the two grey coats, and the unmistakable sound of crossbows launching. Screams followed, tinged with pain, anger, and fear. The crossbows that the grey coats carried looked top of the line. Hunter modifications, for the man that didn't want a challenge when he wanted to kill something. Cassidy knew the crossbows were easy for a quick reload. As long as the grey coats had some extra bolts on hand they'd do the job. But for how long?

That was the gamble. Cassidy pushed herself onward. Her legs were so tired that they squealed for rest and continued to threaten mutiny, but she gritted her teeth and bullied them on. She distracted herself by trying to count the number of bolts fired, the sharp twang of the crossbow string as it let a pointy stick fly.

Cassidy managed to count to ten before the rage fuelled roar of her pursuers took over. The grey coats let loose five each. Not bad. She tried not to think about what happened to them next.

Finally, after ten more minutes of running with everything she had left, Cassidy tumbled into the cavern where she'd originally entered this world. The less elaborate tags spouting the Digital Heart crawled to the ceiling. The darkness that settled there was almost complete, and she was reminded of Gamgee's mistaken assumption that it was some sort of cave.

"Wait 'til he hears about this," Cassidy said aloud, bent over to catch her breath, hands on her knees.

"Who?"

The voice rolled behind her, a languid and perfectly calm voice for someone who had followed Cassidy across the better part of New York. She turned to face Fletcher, her hands curled into fists, her legs (still trembling) prepared to run or leap, kick or knee; she turned to make an end of it.

"Who is going to hear about this?" Fletcher was by himself, aside from the gun he held down at his side. His misused face was swollen and bruised, scratches and cuts outlined a roadmap of the beating he had received at the hands of Harrison, the torture he'd been through, and still he was calm, confident.

"Where's the rest of your posse?" Cassidy backed up, a shimmer of hope that the portal would swallow her whole and she'd walk right into Gamgee, his head cocked in the study of some sort of anomaly or insect that had caught his eye. She wasn't that lucky.

"Oh, they're taking care of a couple of loose ends," he motioned behind him, a smirk on his face.

"You didn't want them to accompany you, didn't want them to see you get your ass kicked again?"

Fletcher laughed, a false bark that made Cassidy cringe. "Oh, it won't come to that will it, Cassidy?" He raised the gun.

"Let's say it doesn't," Cassidy tried on a smile that didn't seem convincing, "you don't want an audience to your triumph?"

Fletcher shrugged, "Why don't you just surrender. Give it up. We could help each other, with your powers and my vision, we would be unstoppable."

"I don't have powers, you idiot."

"Then how do you explain this?" Fletcher took her beaten, broken, and certainly dead phone from his pocket. "I can't quite figure how to turn it on, I suppose I'd need to have powers for that. Just like the piece of tech you gave that Rat we left back there…"

"I don't have powers, I just have working tech," Cassidy said, fighting the urge to punch Fletcher in his stupid beard, to hell with the gun in his hands.

"Really, and where do you get that?" Fletcher moved closer, the gun jabbed forward to emphasize each word. "Is the 'he' you spoke of earlier responsible for this tech?" Fletcher's calm facade dropped, replaced by a sudden and ferocious hunger. Spit flew from his mouth as he moved forward, a hesitance or barely held urge to jump forward.

"It doesn't matter, you'll never see it." Cassidy continued to back up, could feel her skin crawl and prickle in gooseflesh.

"Oh, I'm sure we can make you see reason," Fletcher cocked the hammer of the gun and took aim.

"Bye, Fletcher." Cassidy smiled and fell backwards.

The change in her surroundings was subtle, but it was there and it was familiar. It was the noise that did it, the distant sounds of traffic, conversation, movement. It was loud and bright and familiar. Also familiar was the pair of scruffy, ill-used brown loafers that she had landed next to. Gamgee gave her a wide-eyed look, a pocket watch in his hands, and his mouth agape.

"Cassidy, I had almost–"

"Blow it," Cassidy said, getting to her feet. "Shut the gate. Shut it now."

Gamgee spared her a sympathetic look (was there worry in there too?) before he twitched two fingers and nodded toward the darkness.

The explosion wasn't loud, just a small pop that was no louder than a cap gun Cassidy had used when she was just a little girl. The effect – well, it did the trick. The ceiling directly over the portal collapsed in a wave of debris and dust that left a mound of rocks blocking off the rest of the tunnel.

The portal was closed.

CHAPTER SIXTEEN

The first thing Cassidy did, once Dr. Gamgee and his hired specialists (a mechanical engineer, a retired demolitions expert, and the relaxed security guard they'd seen on their initial trek into the subway) had led her out of the tunnels, was buy a suite at the Hilton. Gamgee didn't argue, and offered up his credit card in the lobby.

"How was the trip?" Gamgee had said to her as they waited for the room to be made ready. "You were gone much longer than we'd anticipated," Gamgee said around a deep frown.

"I don't want to talk about it," Cassidy said and dug into her satchel. "Not yet."

She handed him the Digital Heart.

"A… a microchip," Gamgee held it in his palm, unsure of what to do with it.

"The Digital Heart," Cassidy said with a ghost of a smile on her face, and held up a hand to dissuade any further conversation. "We can talk about it later."

Gamgee nodded his ascent, but adjusted his glasses as he looked closer and closer at the microchip he had pinched between thumb and forefinger.

***

After a long, hot shower she lowered herself into the crisp, white linen of the king size bed and slept. She stayed that way for nearly twenty-four hours, her aching body had demanded it and she had gleefully succumbed.

Cassidy woke in the dark, a man stood in the shadows at the end of her bed with a gun in his hand. She thrashed about in her blankets, fighting the tangled sheets that grabbed at her arms and legs, and pushed herself to the floor to put the bed between her and the gun. Her breath came in harsh gulps, her heart beat in a rapid staccato, and she cursed between her teeth. Cassidy was unsure of how long she stayed on the floor, but her eyes were fully adjusted to the gloom before she poked her head over the side of the bed.

Nothing.

***

Cassidy stared out at the orange sunrise from the balcony of her room. Her elbows rested on the low metal table and she cradled a small mug of coffee between her hands. Since she had woken to the phantom of a dream (or was it a memory?) she'd set herself up out in the cool early morning air to take in the city. She took in a deep breath and expressed a slow sigh. The bright lights of the tall buildings and the noise of cars calmed her. The unnerving silence of the Dead World still clung to her, but it was fading.

EPILOGUE

Tallis turned and fired a shot behind him at those who were trying to get through the mining bay doors he'd sealed shut. There was one Xik'en pilot with him -- the one he'd taken the weapon from -- who was cowering a few feet to his side.

"Prepare it!" Tallis yelled, the Vao stones in the Branch of Languages on the left side of his face shimmered as it translated him, the golden nanotech wires cradling his jaw.

The inside of the mining bay was a maze of activity, with automated equipment going in every direction. Mechanical arms grabbed the massive hunks of asteroid when the mining pods dropped them after coming inside. Tallis stepped past its synchronized beauty without taking note of it, making a bee line for the craft he'd come for: the mining pod. When the pilot didn't follow he pointed the weapon at him and gestured him along. He did.

Emergency lights flashed as equipment overheated and got overloaded with material with no one to remove it.

Sirens blared in various tones, and Tallis had to fight

the urge to cover his ears as a result.

Forcing his captive to move, Tallis got himself under the hull of the mining pod and placed a steady hand on the open canopy. It opened at his correctly applied weight with a pressurized hiss. He smiled, motioned for the Xik'en pilot to join him, and then motioned to the controls: "Tell me how to fly it."

The Vao stones shimmered again.

***

Tallis' mining pod breached the environmental seal at a tight angle, revving immediately to top speed. Xik'en guards followed, breaking through the barrier he'd erected just as he left the station's atmosphere.

Within minutes the seasoned Xik'en pilots were in their stations and in hot pursuit, following the glowing blue trail of plasma Tallis' engines left behind. They were far behind but catching up, and there were only asteroids between him and the rest of space. They poured on the speed and followed him, knowing he had nowhere to run.

"Keep the fuel pod behind us," the Captain said, setting his visor's targets onto Tallis' craft. "If we follow until he's out of fuel, we will be, too. We'll need it to get back."

Tallis heard the command from within his own com link, the Branch of Languages translating it for him. He smirked and continued to push the gas as hard as he could, weaving between asteroids.

They stayed behind him for thirty-five miles, until the station was a small speck in the void behind them and they were clear of this side of the belt. There was nothing ahead but open space.

Tallis' wristwatch bleeped. He was lucky the Xik'ens hadn't taken it, that they had deemed it to be inferior mammal technology. He nodded as if it were speaking to him, and smirked. He turned his pod at a forty-five degree angle, veered downward, and prayed. "Got to hit it just right," he whispered to himself. "Just the right angle." He squeezed the stress ball between his left palm and the control stick.

"What's he doing?" the Captain said, lulled from the boredom of the steady course they'd been on and turning to follow. "There's nothing out here. Does he think we'll just stop?"

All at once, Tallis' ship blinked from existence before their eyes.

The Captain gasped. His ships sped toward the spot where Tallis had vanished, but none of them were at the exact angle, and they flew right by. The Captain turned around, breathless, unable to fathom what had happened.

JD Ryot is the reclusive creator of the *Slipstreamers* series from Engen Books. JD is an avid fan of young adult literature and adventure serials. When asked if they had come to this world through a portal themselves, JD Ryot refused to answer. No record of their birth has ever been found... on this world.

Nicole Little is an award-winning short story and novella author living in St. John's, Newfoundland. In her spare time, Nicole has either a pen in her hand or her nose in a book. She is married with two daughters. *The Lotus Fountain* is her first novella.

Jennifer Shelby hunts for stories in the beetled undergrowth of New Brunswick's fairy-infested forests. She fishes for them in the dark space between the stars. These stories, and many others, are made available through her catch-and-release program. *Plague of the Dreamless* is her first novella.

Jon Dobbin is an award winning author living in the St. John's, Newfoundland metro region. He is a father of three, the husband to an amazing wife, an educator, and a tattoo and beard enthusiast. In 2019 he released his first novel, *The Starving*. In 2020 he released his second novel, *The Broken Spire*. *Cassidy Cane and the Quest for the Digital Heart* is his first novella aimed at a Young Adult audience.